DEADEYE

What Reviewers Say About Meredith Doench's Work

Crossed

"*Crossed* is an eyeblinkingly good first novel with unique and original takes on old subjects."—*The Art of the Lesbian Mystery Novel*

"A very well written serial murder investigation that is made different by the emotional state of Luce Hansen, and her personal story. The layered approach works really well and ensures the reader is often off-balance, just what you need in a murder mystery."—*The Lesbian Review*

"I highly recommend *Crossed*, which turned out to be a great freshman thriller from Doench. While there was not a lot of romance, prepare yourself for an emotional ride filled with disturbing scenes that show a lack of human decency; a ride that also makes multiple explorations into the human psyche."—*Queercentric*

Forsaken Trust

"What's not to love? This is a proper police procedural with lesbian characters that is not propped up by a romance. I'm ecstatic that this kind of book is being created, it shows how much the lesbian fiction market has grown in the last few years. This book gives lesbians (and others) a really good story that you would probably see on *Law & Order*, *CSI* or *Rizzoli and Isles* without the heteronormative characters or the need to 'ship' characters."—*The Lesbian Review*

"If you love crime fiction or television shows you will love this book, but do not go in expecting a romance. Readers of James Patterson, Sue Grafton and the like will enjoy this book."—*The Lesbian Talk Show Podcast*

Visit us at www.boldstrokesbooks.com

By the Author

Forsaken Trust

Crossed

Deadeye

DEADEYE

by
Meredith Doench

2019

THIS TRADE PAPERBACK ORIGINAL IS PUBLISHED BY
BOLD STROKES BOOKS, INC.
P.O. BOX 249
VALLEY FALLS, NY 12185

FIRST EDITION: JULY 2019

CREDITS
EDITOR: RUTH STERNGLANTZ
PRODUCTION DESIGN: SUSAN RAMUNDO
COVER DESIGN BY TAMMY SEIDICK

Acknowledgments

Many talented and kind people have helped to make this third book in the Luce Hansen series possible. I'm grateful for every encouraging word and reader.

The specifics of this book would not have been possible without the help of TJ Turner, who I refer to as "The FBI Guy." His detailed knowledge of weapons, bullet trajectory, bullet injuries, and experience with the work of special and federal agents made this story possible.

A huge thanks to my family. I cannot thank them enough for their encouragement and willingness to support my writing. I'm particularly grateful for my mom who listens to endless crime plot lines, most of which rarely make it into writing, and for watching endless true crime documentaries/series with me without too much complaint.

I'd also like to thank a few great friends who answer my crazed anxiety-filled texts and still show up to work alongside me the next day: Patrick Thomas, Jennifer Holt Sammons, Lindsey Light, Erin Zak, and Liz Mackay.

I cannot thank Jennifer Holt Sammons enough for slogging through the early drafts of this novel that were filled with a million gaping holes.

A tremendous thanks to my cousin, Sarah Ruppert Maynard, for her sharp eye and editing skills that made all the difference with the late stages of the book.

I'm very grateful for those whom I've come to know as my writing tribe, some of which I write with regularly and others I've only interacted with on social media. Your written work, tweets, and posts inspire me to be a better writer: Erin Zak, Laura McHugh, Kristen LePionka, Katrina Kittle, Jessica Strawser, Sharon Short, TJ Turner, Jennifer Holt Sammons, Jessica L. Webb, Jamie Lyn Smith, Jeannie Levig, Cheryl Head, Stefani Deoul, Maggie Smith, Andrew Welsh-Huggins, Kris Bryant, and Dena Blake.

I'm grateful to the Bold Strokes Books family. A special shout-out to Radclyffe, Sandy, and Ruth Sternglantz for all the tireless work they do to help writers like me.

A special thanks to the University of Dayton English department for its support and encouragement.

A big thank you to Boston Stoker Coffee Co. and the Washington-Centerville libraries for the long hours you've allowed me to occupy your tables. I couldn't have written this book without my offices away from home.

Finally, I am forever grateful to the fans of Luce Hansen who have sent me messages, posted, and tweeted about the novels. Your enthusiasm for the books has kept me going on my worst of writing days. All of your reviews on Goodreads and Amazon have helped to keep the series alive. Thanks so much for all of your support.

PROLOGUE

Simmons County, Ohio
Thanksgiving Day

The Holden brothers' three-mile run came to a full stop near the old one-room schoolhouse on County Road 571. There, alongside the two-lane road, stood a deer with her two fawns. The trio leaned their graceful necks forward to chew on the long brown grasses and season-dead wildflowers at the pavement's edge. There was a distinct chill in the air, more than usual for late November, and the gray clouds lay low. Despite the cold, Logan Holden's Ohio State University hoodie was soaked with sweat and the heavy humidity.

Logan couldn't remember when he'd last been so close to a fawn without it racing off into the forest. Reaching into his empty pocket, he was reminded that he'd left the phone on the kitchen table. His mother had shooed him and John, his brother, from the kitchen while she rushed about tending to what she looked forward to most every year: cooking a Thanksgiving meal. She liked to remind her family that timing was key to a hot and perfect holiday dinner, and that timing did not involve her boys hanging around the kitchen. *This dinner isn't going to cook itself, and that run isn't going to run itself,* his mother had said as they made their way out the door. In their haste, Logan had forgotten his phone. But John, who hardly ever parted with his, now let his earbuds hang around his sweaty neck by their white wires. A backbeat spilled from those tiny speakers as he held up the phone and pressed *record.*

A mist rose from the blacktop, curling between Logan's ankles and smoking around the deer's spindly legs. Soon the chilly fog would thicken and cover the Ohio farmland. Slowly, Logan moved closer. The mother deer looked up, her dewy brown eyes meeting his. For a frozen moment, they examined one another—he with his feet planted firmly on the misty road, and she with the stray ends of grass hanging from her lips. Then, suddenly, she leapt into the high grasses and darted into the surrounding woods leaving behind her fawns who had already lost their white spots. They watched their mother go with alarm but soon resumed chewing away at the winter-yellow grasses.

John's phone gave a shrill bark with the message of a failed text. Cell towers were scattered few and far between among the country hills and deep forest; devices burned up their batteries with the constant search for a clear signal. One fawn stood alert at the noise and then bolted in the same direction its mother had gone only moments before. The remaining fawn froze, staring at Logan and John.

"Why doesn't she follow them?" Logan asked.

John shrugged. "Too trusting, I guess. What's that saying—a tame deer is a dead deer?"

Logan moved closer until he stood only inches from the fawn, her big brown eyes watching him as she tried to balance her weight on stick-thin legs. Ever so slowly, he reached out his gloved hand to her.

The relentless drone of an older engine wound its way along the two-lane road. The smoky fog made it nearly impossible to see the vehicle until it was almost upon them. As the muffler rumbled closer, Logan saw faint headlights over his shoulder.

"Go!" Logan shouted at the fawn, waving his arms. He turned to his brother. "If it's a hunter, he'll tag this area."

Overenthusiastic hunters were known to enter the game areas a few days early in order to track places with a high density of deer population. Then, on opening day of gun season, these hunters returned to make their easy kills.

John shoved the phone into his pocket and then raced toward the fawn. "Get out of here. *Go*, you fool!"

The vehicle crested the hill behind them, and the fawn finally darted into the wood. The muffler, rumbling like a speedboat, rolled to a near stop beside the brothers as if the driver might recognize one of them. John nodded at the window and gave a tentative wave. Then, without warning, the driver hit the gas and the rumbling truck soon disappeared over the next hill.

"Who was that?"

"Not sure." John shrugged. "Lost hunter, I guess." He play-punched Logan's arm. "Dinner is waiting on us, and this run isn't getting any shorter." John plugged his ears once again, and with the blast of music, he took off, leaving Logan standing on the side of the road.

Ten minutes later, Logan finally settled into a long stride. He had just found the rhythmic movements of his body and breath when the rumble of the same vehicle's engine cut through the fog, this time headed directly toward them. It drove down the center of the unmarked road, edging closer and closer toward the brothers. The driver came upon John first, a good twenty yards in front of Logan, slowing…slowing…until the truck finally stopped beside John.

John gave a friendly wave at the dark shadow of the driver in the cab of the truck and stepped closer to the open window. Logan heard his brother say, "Need some help?"

A sharp, quick *crack* filled the air, scattering a flock of crows from a nearby tree. Logan watched as his brother's body simply dropped to the ground. John tumbled over the berm of the road and fell hard on his back, crushing a thicket of brown shrubs that bloomed wild in the summer. Everything around him fell into slow motion as if Logan were trapped inside a movie. He watched as the casing tumbled to the ground near his brother, and a spot of bright red spread along the blacktop.

Panic stole Logan's breath. A strange sensation filled him, as though his physical body separated from his mind and he floated above the entire scene. But this was no dream: the blood thumped louder and louder inside his ears until he could hear nothing else. Logan tried to run to his brother's side, but Logan's body remained frozen, as if struck still by the beam of the truck's headlights and the sound of its rumbling engine. Although Logan couldn't see through the tinted windshield, he *felt* the driver's eyes narrow in on him. His hackles rose and a quick chill scattered up his spine. The image of

John's spreading pool of blood brought Logan back into his reality—he needed to get help. He reached again for his phone that wasn't there.

And then the truck rolled forward.

Logan didn't hesitate—he tore into the wooded area not far from the road, taking the same route the deer had only minutes before. Logan churned one leg over the other, willing his strides wider and wider, and didn't dare look back to see if the driver had the rifle leveled at him. A bullet shot past his ear before Logan made a hard right, a curve in his path meant to throw off the shooter. Seconds later, a shot sank into his left shoulder and felt as though it might have taken his entire left arm off with it.

Logan face-planted into the cool wet ground. The earth, not yet completely hardened by the winter months, held him. The edges of his sight blackened, and Logan bit his lip until he tasted blood. Relief washed through him when he saw that his arm and hand were still attached to his body. He did his best not to move even though every muscle in his body spasmed and the warmth of his own blood spread across his belly and thigh. The hole in his body felt so small, but he remembered what his father always said about gunshot wounds— *stay conscious or you slip into death.* Logan had to stay awake—it didn't matter that his body was screaming with exhaustion. But he also needed to play dead. Logan understood the shooter needed to see both him and his brother down for good.

The truck thundered in its place for a few more excruciating minutes until the driver pushed open the squeaky door. Logan lifted his head ever so slightly to get a peek through the underbrush. A few yards away, Logan caught a glimpse of the shooter dressed in full camouflage with an enormous rifle hanging from his right hand. A black skullcap covered the shooter's hair and ears. He kicked John's ribcage with a heavy black boot once, waited for a response that didn't come, and then kicked John again. Logan watched as the shooter knelt down next to his brother but couldn't make out exactly what was happening.

When the shooter stood and walked toward Logan, he shoved his face into the earth until his breath became shallow and strained.

Wetness seeped through his running shorts and along his thighs. Prayers had been a constant in his family, and he started a continual loop of Biblical passages in his mind as he braced himself for the next shot into his body. It wasn't a bullet that hit him, but a heavy boot to his ribs. Logan cried out in pain, and a stream of blood ran from his open mouth. The shooter knelt down beside Logan; he knew *the killer* knew he was still alive. Fading in and out of consciousness, Logan felt his upper body rise from the ground and the pressure as his hoodie was yanked over his head. Bare chested, he slumped back to the cold ground as the shooter slowly walked away.

The rumble of the truck's engine felt like it stayed in one place forever. Logan remained as still as possible until the old vehicle finally lurched forward, rolling away from the brothers on the side of the road.

Eventually, the length of silence became the certainty Logan was looking for. His breath hitched, and each inhalation sounded like a phlegmy whistle. He pushed through the agonizing pain until he balanced upon his knees. He tried not to hold his breath as he inched toward his brother, a stretch of space that seemed to take hours to close. Once he finally dropped at John's side, he felt the unusual stiffness of his brother's arm. Tears spilled from Logan's eyes as he searched the area for John's phone. He found it at his brother's side, just out of reach, the screen shattered. The phone, though, was still recording—John hadn't turned it off after he recorded the deer. The server icon spun helplessly for any kind of a connection, and Logan knew he didn't have much time. He spoke directly into the camera because someone needed to know the truth.

"Mom?" Logan coughed on his words, blood splattering the small phone screen. "Love you. I couldn't stop h—"

Logan collapsed beside John's body, and the brothers' dark blood congealed together.

CHAPTER ONE

Near Charleston, South Carolina
Thanksgiving Day

The South Carolina sun blazed down, a welcome change from Ohio's dreary and wet November. A wooded trail opened up, and I ran a few feet behind Bennett as the high tree boughs encased us in shade. Spanish moss draped from the branches giving everything around us the look of another world. The temperature hovered near eighty, a summery-warm temperature my body wasn't ready for, and I was drenched in sweat. I wiped away the rivulets from my brow and thought for probably the hundredth time about how much better I liked swimming than running. In the water, at least, you don't have to deal with your own sweat.

Bennett turned, and her lean body, runner built, effortlessly floated along the trail. "You slowing down there, Special Agent?" She ran backward to face me, her grin full of play.

"Show-off."

"Nothing shows athletic prowess like a six-mile run," she ribbed me. Bennett tossed out a laugh, and I savored the way her laughter moved her whole body with its genuine happiness. Her laugh, so rich and deep, was one of my favorite sounds in the whole world.

"We'll go for an easy jog, she said." I mimicked Bennett. "No pressure, she said." I groaned. "Last time I listen to you about running."

"Aw, darlin'." Bennett faked concern. "Is the southern heat getting to you?"

"I'm hanging in there, Doctor, which is more than can be said for you in the swimming pool."

Bennett gave me a wink, turned back toward the trail, and took off. I watched her long legs move with a gait and form as graceful and quick as a gazelle.

We'd taken the week of Thanksgiving off work to be together, to kayak through the Francis Marion National Forest and explore the town of Charleston. That was the plan, anyway. Instead, the two of us had hardly left the resort except to kayak the waterways or run the trails. And then there was our room—small and cozy and perfect for us to catch up on all the nights we'd spent apart for our jobs. Without the constant tension of our work hovering over us, Bennett seemed happier than I'd seen her in some time. Although we hadn't seen a wink of Charleston except in the ride from the airport, the national forest area was shaping up to be one of my favorite places I'd ever visited.

Even on vacation, though, we couldn't get away from our workouts—let alone our pact for clean living. It had been Bennett's idea, this agreement that left me hiding empty crumpled Cheetos bags and sticky honey bun wrappers underneath my truck's seat. Everything that I considered to be tasty, including alcohol, had been sworn off in this new life of clean living. While Bennett regularly railed on me for my sugar and carb intake whenever she got the chance, her real worry was about when I might take that first drink and break my four-month run with sobriety.

Bennett and I were training for a half marathon in early January. Running wasn't really my thing, particularly long distance, although I'd done my fair share of it while training for the Bureau's required physicals. When Bennett first asked me to run with her at Walt Disney World, I wasn't sold on the idea, but when she added that I could dress up as my favorite Disney character, I couldn't say no.

"I'm assuming you'll race as anything Star Wars," she'd teased me. "Han Solo in black boots and a row of bullets across your chest?"

"Is there really any question?" I asked, thinking of all the times I'd imitated Han Solo when we'd had our Star Wars marathon nights. "I'm assuming you will go as the one and only Princess Leia?"

Bennett shook her head at me and played coy. "You'll have to run with me to find out."

It had been a guessing game of which Disney character she planned to be ever since. The mystery of it kept me running, although I wasn't always sure the payoff would be worth it.

"Snow White. Belle. Wait, I know—The Beast!"

Bennett rolled her eyes at me. "Some runners are there for the sport, you know. Not everyone dresses up."

"What's the fun in that?" I teased her. "Why put yourself through the run?"

Water had always been my true love. Give me a pool, lake, or ocean, and I'd swim for miles. Nothing soothed me more than the submersion into water and the silence that came with it. Distance swimming, however, wasn't a favorite of Bennett's, who claimed her arms felt like wet noodles after only half a mile. Jogging along the wooded trail, though, my *legs* felt like noodles. As we neared the five-mile marker, I cursed this woman who ran a few yards in front of me as if her feet weren't even touching the trail.

"One more mile, Special Agent!" Bennett hollered to me over her shoulder.

My sweaty body celebrated the news. Only one mile—I could finish.

I met Dr. Harper Bennett, forensic pathologist extraordinaire, while I assisted with a serial murder case in Wallace Lake, Ohio. More specifically, I saw Bennett for the first time as we stood together over two dead bodies that were lodged against land bars in the middle of Ohio's Powell River. I loved that we first met surrounded by water. As a person who believed in signs and gut feelings and karma, I took the presence of water as a promise—or at the very least, a smack to the back of the head to wake me up and pay attention to the beautiful being there with me.

Bennett, though, liked to remind me that it wasn't all burbling river water and the sweet singing of nature that surrounded us that day, but two very dead bodies. "And the ripe stench of decomp, Hansen. Let's not forget that." She would throw me a wink. "So, I ask you, what kind of a sign is that?"

"A message from the universe," I said. "I heard it, in the water around us."

Bennett rolled her eyes, a practice she'd become quite good at in our relationship. Unlike me, Bennett gave little credence to signs and karma and any sort of messages from beyond. Her job required her to think logically and avoid jumping to conclusions. Evidence, in Bennett's world of steel gurneys and autopsies, ruled. While she understood my beliefs about gut reactions and instinct, Bennett saw things very differently. Water, she liked to say, had the power to give life and take it away; the toss of that coin could shift any day.

The Wallace Lake case had been difficult—four women found murdered along the Powell River, all sharing a matching wrist tattoo. The tattoo wasn't the only thing the women shared; they had all been drug addicts at some point in their adult lives, which led the early investigators to believe the deaths were tied to the opioid crisis raging wild in Wallace Lake County. From its start, I'd been in a bad place. I drank too much, ate too little, and drowned in a murky depression that nearly sank the rat hole of an apartment I'd been renting in Columbus. In the wake of a bad breakup, I felt lost. There was also the frustration I felt with my placement at the Ohio Bureau of Criminal Investigation. I'd thought my work in my first serial case at Willow's Ridge would have put me in line for a shot at the FBI—I was wrong.

Bennett had her own share of frustration and baggage. She'd been overworked and underpaid for years, her services stretched thin in the tri-county area that needed at least two of her to get the job done, maybe three. Bennett was simply exhausted and had been dealing with her own heartache—a woman, she said, who gutted her whole.

After the Wallace Lake case ended, though, things brightened for both of us. I'd been promoted to the codirector spot at the Ohio Bureau of Criminal Investigation to work alongside my mentor and good friend Colby Sanders. Bennett had been hired on as a forensic pathologist. She was able to leave her county work behind, and offered her an office in one location. It also gave her some much needed free time to pursue the activities she loved like running, writing poetry, and kayaking. Over the past few months, the trauma of my past slowly faded, and I'd fallen for Bennett—something I swore I'd never again do after Rowan. For once, though, it wasn't only me who had a past to contend with; I found myself navigating the new terrain of a relationship where each of us lived our own lives, sometimes together and sometimes apart.

Colby Sanders, however, hadn't been a fan of the decision to hire Bennett. The Bureau had strict rules about romantic partners working together. I argued that Bennett and I technically wouldn't be working together, given that she managed everything medical in the morgue and I would be out in the field. Even I understood the laughability of that argument—as a forensic pathologist, Bennett would need to be in the field in order to determine the time and cause of death. She'd be an important member of the team no matter how I played with the words.

"Bennett's one of the most competent and gifted pathologists the BCI has worked with," Sanders admitted when I pressed him. "She's a real asset to our team. I just worry about the two of you working together—the strain it will put on your relationship."

I understood his cautious subtext: Sanders worried about what would happen if Bennett and I broke up. He wasn't only worried about the possible disruption to the team and the dynamics of the office. He also worried about the emotional damage I might suffer if fallout ensued. I appreciated Sanders and the way he looked after me. My father had unexpectedly passed a few years back, and I'd been left without much of a family to call my own.

"Relax," I told him. "I've got a good feeling about this."

Sanders shook his head in a way that said he didn't believe me, but would negotiate. "That famous gut of yours," he half teased.

We finally settled on an agreement: Bennett and I would stagger our time, shifting schedules so that we rarely worked together in the field. So, for the past months, Bennett and I had been at crime scenes and different stages of investigations without one another. At work, we were those proverbial ships passing in the night; her office was in the basement and mine on the second floor. When our schedules allowed for it, we met for meals and shared an occasional day off for hiking and floating on the Powell River. We continued to live separately in the small community of Spring Rock. I bought a small bungalow and gutted it, rebuilding it from the floor up during my time off work. I loved my new home that stood so close to the river I could hear it burble and churn after a hard rain like it was a living breathing thing.

"The first sign of trouble," Sanders warned me, "Bennett's gone. Understood?"

I'd been so excited, I almost hugged Sanders, something he never would have forgiven or forgotten.

Bennett waited for me at the six-mile marker at our resort with her hands on her strong hips and a look that said *Could you be any slower?* I'd never been so happy to slap the side of an ancient oak tree with its branches dripping in Spanish moss. Bennett stood in a sweat-drenched tank top with damp dark curls about her face. God, how could she run six miles in humidity as thick as mud and still look so good?

"Glad to see you made it. I was worried I might have to call the EMTs for you."

I shrugged and used the edge of my T-shirt to wipe the sweat from around my brow. "Who needs EMTs when I have a doctor running with me?" I leaned in for a quick kiss, our sweaty limbs intertwining.

"Your times are getting better," she told me as we headed back to the room. "In another few months, you might be able to keep pace with me."

I threw my head back, laughed, and felt the frazzled ends of my braid against my low back. "It sure would be fun," I told Bennett, "to beat you across that finish line one of these days."

❖

The sun sat low on the South Carolina horizon. I leaned back in my seat, let the paddle rest across my lap, and welcomed that familiar bump of Bennett's kayak against mine. The ocean had been too difficult to manage in the kayaks out beyond the break of the waves. The resort directed us to a small inlet where the water shimmered with the evening calm and views of the sunset burned an array of oranges, yellows, and purples. Bennett and I settled into a silence as the movement of the water gently rocked us. This, I thought, was the true measure of trust with another person—how long that comfortable silence could hold between the two of you.

"Sure beats the office, doesn't it?" Bennett turned to me, the sunset reflected in the lenses of her sunglasses. She wore a full-body suit because she couldn't stand to be in water below seventy degrees, as if she might suddenly be submerged while kayaking. A film of sweat lined her upper lip.

"Not to mention the unforgiving weather in Ohio this time of year," I added. "Let's stay another week."

Bennett laughed. "Amen to that."

A large two-tiered boat idled through the inlet, the upper balcony full of visitors out for an evening cruise. Some shouted and waved, and I arced my paddle through the air. Thanksgiving was one of the resort's busiest times of the year—the 400-room hotel had been full all week with people doing everything but eating a traditional turkey and dressing meal with their family.

When the sun finally sank to only a burning orange sliver, Bennett interrupted our silence once again. "I've been meaning to ask you something."

"Uh-oh."

Bennett laughed. "No, it's nothing. I just wanted to check in with you. With us."

I held my breath. Despite the fact there was no indication that Bennett wanted to end our relationship, my mind always went there first—a negative thinking loop that rarely left my mind quiet.

"Are you happy, Hansen?"

If Bennett could have seen beneath my oversized sunglasses, she would have noticed the furrow in my brow and the tension lines beginning to crease around my eyes. I tried not to let my paranoid thinking take over, but still, my mind churned with questions. Had I done something wrong? Where was this coming from?

"I am happy, Bennett," I said cautiously, "but the bigger question here might be, *are you?*"

Bennett nodded. "It's been about a year since we met."

So much in my life had quieted over the last twelve months. Work hummed along, a little too fast-paced at times, but it kept my mind busy and my sense of justice in play. Bennett and I had settled into a rhythm in Spring Rock, a rhythm I'd gladly fallen into. I didn't want anything to change.

Along the shoreline, a seagull screamed and cawed for its mates. "Almost a year," I joked, "and we still call each other by our last names."

Bennett grinned. "We aren't exactly the conventional lesbian couple, are we?"

"If by conventional you mean U-Haul trailers and month-long camping trips filled with crowded ride festivals, then no. But it's okay—we do our own thing."

Bennett nodded. "Sometimes I wonder if our unconventional way is the right way."

"Bennett, where is this coming from?"

"It's nothing." She waved her hand as if she could swat the conversation away. "Really."

"It's obviously something or we wouldn't be having this conversation." I nudged the edge of her kayak with my paddle. "Come on. Tell me what's up."

Bennett shrugged as if the entire conversation didn't matter. "I saw Harvey a few weeks ago." She avoided my eyes. "I didn't want to tell you."

My back bristled with the mention of Detective Alison Harvey— the woman who, at one point, stood between Bennett and me. Harvey was one of Bennett's past lovers who also worked the Wallace Lake case and had been my mistake after a night of too much drinking and not enough clear thinking.

"And? What did Harvey say?"

"She's surprised we're still taking things so slow."

Even though Harvey had only been a rebound relationship for Bennett, it still made my jealousy boil. I wondered if more happened in the surprise meeting between Harvey and Bennett. Harvey wouldn't commit to a long-term relationship, which had made her the perfect rebound for Bennett and a one-night stand for me, but I sensed Bennett still thought of Harvey. Would she tell me? Did Bennett *want* to fall back into the way things had been between them? There was also the question of what Harvey wanted; she'd proven she wasn't the type to settle down, but that didn't mean she wouldn't play around and create chaos in other people's relationships.

"It's not like we're twenty anymore, Bennett. We both have our pasts to contend with. I'd rather take things slow and do what's right for us," I said. "Besides, what does Harvey know? It's not like she's the romance know-it-all. God, if we had Alice's *L Word* chart for the Midwest, Harvey would be the central hub for all heartland lesbians."

Bennett chuckled—she was a huge *L Word* fan and could quote whole passages, particularly from Shane McCutcheon, the grand player of the series. Bennett's fascination with the character gave me all the more pause given her recent encounter with Harvey who in some ways resembled Shane.

"Why were you talking to her about us?" I didn't mean for it to come out as defensive as it did.

"It was nothing, okay? Nothing. We do work together sometimes, you know."

"Our relationship isn't work, Bennett."

Bennett shook her head. "This is why I don't tell you things. Right here! It always starts an argument about *your* work."

I groaned and leaned back into my kayak. If Detective Harvey had been out on the water with us, I would have punched her big smug nose. "I'm just trying to figure out what you want, Ben."

"I want a relationship that's stable. I need someone I can count on. I need to know that you are safe at work and will return home at the end of your day. I want to grow old with you, Hansen."

"There is nothing that says we can't do exactly that," I said. "There are no rules, you know."

The sun was nearly below the horizon, and somewhere outside the mouth of the inlet, the cruiser's horn blasted and cheers erupted from its passengers. Bennett sat silent a moment, her hands fisted over the oar that rested across the kayak.

Lack of commitment, I knew, was a serious issue with Bennett, who claimed she could find a wayward woman anywhere. Ten years before I met Bennett, she had been in a long-term relationship with a woman she planned to marry. Bennett caught her partner cheating, and it caused the end of the relationship. Bennett retained ownership of the house the two of them bought and still lived in that home.

"There is only one thing I am certain of, Hansen," Bennett said. "I will not be that woman who stands by her partner's grave after she has been murdered by some senseless idiot while on the job. I will not be that sobbing widow they hand the folded flag to, the one who nearly faints while the blank shots fire from the gun salute."

"Come on, Ben. That's not going to happen." I reached across our kayaks for her hand.

"You cannot promise that."

"No," I said. "But I also can't promise I won't die of a heart attack in two years or a car wreck or cancer, either." I squeezed her hand. "Love is a gamble, but we are worth it."

Bennett didn't answer, but she squeezed my hand back and wound her fingers through mine.

The sun had completely dipped below the horizon, and the running board lights of boats flipped on around us. Just as we began to paddle toward shore, my air-raid siren ringtone screamed out. I'd assigned that vicious sound to all work-related calls.

For a few seconds, both of us froze. Then Bennett threw her head back and groaned. "You brought your cell phone on the water? What about our rule!"

I hated the rule, and little did Bennett know, I regularly defied it. Floating time, according to Bennett, was unplugging time—no phones, no music, no texting or email checking. *The world can wait,* she always told me, *at least until we come in from the water.*

"It's not a safe rule, Bennett," I said, reaching for the phone. "What if something happened?"

"You're a special agent, and I'm a doctor. Who else could we possibly need in an emergency?"

The phone's siren screamed again in my hand. I didn't want the argument that had been brewing between us to suddenly land.

But this mattered, and I couldn't let it go. It mattered a lot because of Marci Tucker. I'd struggled long and hard with the effects of PTSD since I found my first love murdered. I'd only missed her murder by minutes when I found her body, still warm, bludgeoned inside a cave where we regularly met. It was the moment on which everything in my life hinged, the moment that defined me.

I gestured to the trees and water surrounding us. "I know the terrible kind of mayhem that can go down in nature without access to phones. Death won't wait for a 9-1-1 call."

Bennett looked away from me as the story of my past washed over us. We didn't talk much about Marci, yet she was frequently around us, lingering in some of my words and actions like a ghost I couldn't shake. It had taken years for me to come to terms with the fact that the murder might not have happened if I had been on time to meet Marci, if I hadn't gotten caught in a traffic jam on the highway, if I had taken a different route to the caverns.

If, if, if. This tiny word endlessly needled me, particularly when it came to the death of Marci Tucker.

I reached up, my fingertips landing on the cool pendant with Marci's Celtic cross that I still wore around my neck. It was one of the ways she was always with me.

"Hansen here."

"It's Sanders."

For a few seconds, neither of us spoke. Then he added, "Gobble, gobble."

I laughed at Colby Sanders's sad attempt at a joke and suddenly missed him. His voice was one I never wanted to hear on vacation, but if I had to, at least he always made me smile. "What's up, Sanders?"

"I hope you're having a good Thanksgiving down there," he started, "but we have a situation. A prison break at Hartford Correctional."

My mind turned over everything I knew about the Ohio prison: high security, older prison, with some disturbing reports of officer violence toward inmates. Then it hit me. "No, Sanders. Please tell me this has nothing to do with Deadeye."

His silence on the other end of the line told me it did.

I looked over at Bennett who mouthed and gestured *What?* to me. "He's a high risk inmate. How could this even happen?"

"A transport situation and help from the outside. David Johnson, aka Deadeye, slit both wrists pretty good. No medics on campus today due to the holiday, so he was rushed to the local hospital. Turns out his latest fiancée is a nurse at the hospital and helped plan it all."

I pressed the heel of one hand against my forehead, the place where a headache teased me. Holidays, I knew, tended to be a time on prison campuses when officials let their guard down, when fewer eyes focused on the inmates. Clearly I wasn't the only one who knew that secret. "How long has he been gone?"

"The last documented sighting was over four hours ago. Search teams are out, but nothing yet." I heard the *flick* of a lighter, and I imagined him igniting the end of his cigarette. "This is big, Hansen. We need to catch him before the media gets ahold of this one. We need to get out to that prison as soon as possible."

Sanders went on about the flight details out of Charleston, and I thought about Deadeye. I knew his case well. The serial predator had been hunting humans long before I joined the BCI and was finally apprehended in Southeast Ohio after murdering at least six victims, hunter style, in the rural hunting areas of Simmons County. Deadeye was better than a good shot—generally the victims were taken with a single bullet through the head. And he always removed and took with him the victim's bloodstained shirt, his trophy of death. Deadeye loose and on the streets was more than dangerous—he was explosive.

"Hansen? You with me?"

"Yeah." I blinked myself back to focus. "I'll see you in a few hours."

I hung up and looked out over the glass-calm water. The evening breeze felt good against my face.

"Hansen?" Bennett maneuvered her kayak even closer to mine. "What's going on?"

"Deadeye," I said without looking at her.

Her eyes widened at his name. "What do you mean?"

"He's on the lam."

I handed her my paddle and then rolled away from her, the weight of my body spinning the kayak upside down. Cool, salty water enveloped me. I slipped out of the kayak underwater and let my body sink into the cool darkness. My T-shirt floated toward my chin and I let the heaviness of the ocean water hold and rock me at its will. Finally, when my lungs began to burn for fresh oxygen, I scissored my legs and reached up, letting my fingertips break the surface of the water.

Bennett held on to the end of my kayak with the edge of a paddle and looked down at me. "Have you lost your mind?" she asked. "The water is freezing."

I shrugged; trying to convince her to join me in the water would be next to impossible. Instead, I reached up to guide my own kayak.

Bennett kept pace with me while I swam in to shore. I explained what little I knew about the escape and that my flight would leave in about five hours' time.

"I should go with you," she said, her voice filled with disappointment.

"No, Ben. Stay if you want to. We have the room until Sunday, and your flight is already booked."

"You're okay with that?"

I shrugged. "I'd rather be here with you, and this sucks, but it's your vacation week, too. If you want to stay, stay. Get in a few more floats and runs and sunsets—more inspiration for your poetry."

I gave her a quick smile before dipping lower into the evening-dark water. I tasted the salt on my lips and frog-legged a little faster. When Bennett mumbled something I couldn't quite make out, I let my head slip beneath the water's skin and kicked toward shore.

Once we reached the landing area, I gave my kayak a strong push and then swam back out into the depths of the water. Bennett stood on the shore watching me with her hands on her hips. Her mouth moved, but I couldn't make out her words as I sank beneath the surface. My body ached for the feel of water against my skin, the pressure and silence of its weight that helped me to do my very best thinking. My feet eventually found the sandy bottom, and I butterflied my arms as I raced to the water's surface. It wasn't just the swim that had my heart rate up, but that all-too-familiar pull of a strong case. My work always had a way of digging its hooks into me, of gripping tight my mind, body, and soul in a way that made my breath quicker, my heartbeat stronger. Nothing, absolutely nothing else had ever made me feel more alive than the hunt for a killer and the need for justice.

I hoped Bennett would wait on me before heading back to the hotel, but I already knew she wouldn't. By the time I would come in from the dark water to shower, she would have already organized my things for the flight and headed into bed.

CHAPTER TWO

Hartford Correctional Institution
Friday, 4:30 a.m.
Day 1 of the investigation

The county sheriff and prison officials held Debbie Turner, RN, in an isolated conference room at Hartford Correctional Institution. Ironic, really, given that she had just assisted her fiancé's escape from that very place. The sheriff reasoned that the setting would persuade her to talk. Such an explanation fell short with me—clearly they'd decided to use the nurse as some sort of bait for Deadeye. The sheriff was not only sending Deadeye a blatant message, but also all his prison colleagues: *We have your woman. It's you or her—decide wisely.* It was only a matter of time before one of Deadeye's brothers on the inside got word to him on the outside. As Sanders and I made our way through the first security gate and emptied our pockets into plastic bins for the detectors, though, I knew such a ploy would never work. In order for Deadeye to respond, he would have to care about Debbie Turner. Deadeye was a classic sociopath—he didn't care about anyone except himself.

Hartford was one of the largest prisons in Ohio and had once been the administration site of the state's death penalty. When that distinction had moved on to a newer and shinier prison, some of Ohio's most dangerous criminals were left behind inside its walls. The large campus spread over twenty-five acres along a rural route that was mainly used by farmers and prison employees. Fields surrounded the prison grounds, and for many years the inmates worked the land that was at one time filled with cattle and tall stalks of corn. Since the state deemed that kind of work too physical for inmates, the fields grew wild. There was no question that escaping from the campus would leave someone with very limited options without some kind of transportation out of the vastness of rural Ohio. Deadeye, as usual, had planned well.

Once we cleared security, Robert Spen, Hartford's warden, met and walked us through Deadeye's movements the day before. Still on mandatory lockdown, the prison halls were virtually empty except for the guards who monitored the facility. Nervous and speaking much too fast, Spen tried to explain the escape. As we walked, his eyes never left the tiled floor. Spen was wiry thin, and he struck me as a man who lived in a constant agitated state. The recent happenings had only heightened it. He knew his team had screwed up, and it was obvious he worried what an escape of such a high profile inmate would do to his career.

Spen led us to the isolation cell where Deadeye had cut his wrists. "Our best guess," Spen said, "is the new fiancée somehow slipped him the blade before he ended up in the tank."

"Did they have a recent visit?" Sanders asked.

"Five days ago," Spen said. "We've gone over the visitation room footage, and we can't detect that anything was exchanged between them. We do know that the nurse fills in on our campus when our regulars call in. She last worked here eleven days ago. It's possible she slipped him the blade then. We just don't know."

Sanders jammed his fisted hands deep in his pockets. "Are you telling me no one caught that the nurse who is employed here was also on David Johnson's approved and active visitation list?"

Spen hung his head and ran his fingers over his buzz cut. "Look, our campus is packed, and we're down three guards—"

"Save it," Sanders grumbled.

The holding cell had been recently cleaned and stank of a lethal combination of bleach and disinfectant. I stepped in and walked the tight perimeter of the room.

"Tell me about what brought him here. The fight."

"Right, the fight." Spen, happy for the distraction from Sanders, followed me in and hitched his fists against his waist just over his utility belt. "It happened with one of the newer guards, Trent Simon. From all accounts, the guard picked a fight with Deadeye. He insisted on searching Deadeye's cell based on reports of possible contraband. Simon tossed everything—he took some items from the cell even though he reportedly found no contraband. Deadeye reacted by breaking Simon's nose and jaw while pummeling his head. Simon is in a coma from multiple head injuries."

"Has that cell been cleaned up?"

Spen nodded. "His cellie took on that task, apparently."

I flipped over the thin plastic mattress in the isolation cell and examined the cement ledge that served as a bed for any scrawled messages.

"Deadeye was housed here just under twenty-four hours after the assault on Simon. The medical call went out at 2:25 p.m. yesterday."

"Deadeye alerted staff of his own condition?" I asked.

"Yes. The report states he was fighting consciousness when he called for help."

I scanned the cell one more time. Everything had been set up, and the only surprise in the whole scheme was most likely to the guard who ended up in a coma with a broken jaw and nose. Trent Simon was a lucky guy—most didn't escape Deadeye with their life.

I turned to Warden Spen who finally had the nerve to look me in the eye. "Take us to Debbie Turner, please. I'd like to hear what the nurse has to say for herself."

Colby Sanders sat beside me. His weathered hands, which had lost their summer tan from the golf course and the shooting range, wrapped around a steaming Styrofoam cup of coffee. As he considered Debbie Turner across the table from us, I considered him. Sanders's hair had grown so silver in places it was nearly white, and his face pulled with exhaustion. He'd been working hard to close multiple cases for the Bureau before the end of the year. By the looks of Sanders slumped in the metal chair, he was the one in need of a vacation in a southern beachside resort.

The prison-issued metal table had seen better days. Secured to the floor, its dull top was dinged in multiple places and warped with years of use. Sanders leaned in, spreading his elbows wide across the table—one of his trusted tactics in interviews to make his body appear bigger. "This song and dance is wearing thin," he barked.

Across from us, Debbie smiled. "I've told you all I can. My man is exactly where he is supposed to be."

Sanders sighed. We'd been at it an hour, and both of us had had enough of her cryptic answers. "And where is that, exactly?"

Debbie giggled as her thin blond hair fell limp around her long drawn face.

Sanders rolled his eyes at me, and I couldn't help but chuckle at the absurdity of the nurse. I hadn't slept in hours and interviewing this woman was like trying to extract a story from a three-year-old. She was hiding something, though; both Sanders and I sensed it, and we didn't intend to let her go until she told us something we could go on.

I took a turn with her. "He used you. You get that, right? You've been a pawn in Deadeye's plan, Debbie. Nothing more."

"You're wrong. And his name is David. David Johnson loves me," she said. She leaned back in her chair and folded her slim hands in her lap. "He loves me more than anyone ever has or could."

I flipped back in my notes. According to prison records, Debbie had only been corresponding with Deadeye for about a year. Their prison romance began when she filled in for a nurse and David Johnson came to the clinic for a common prison ailment—scabies. The red fiery rash covered his hands and climbed up his arms. It crawled over his back and down into his groin. He'd waited much too long to get the parasite treated, and he'd scratched himself bloody. Debbie assisted the doctor that day, providing Deadeye with a medicated wash and oral medication. Records showed that she later made written contact with him, and a series of letters followed between them. They handwrote the letters at first, snail-mailing back and forth until they burned out on the writing. The expensive prison phone system then became their chosen method of communication. Officers on site were sifting through the routine recordings of every conversation between the two.

"I can see the allure," I told Debbie, trying hard not to choke on my words. "David is handsome. But I bet it's something so much more that pulls you to him. His thoughtfulness, right? He actually listened to you. He paid attention to you."

Debbie gave us another grin. "It's not just that he paid attention to me. He *thought* about me. A lot."

I nodded for her to go on.

"Sometimes at night I would twist up in my blanket and think of him thinking of me. I tried to imagine what he noticed about me. Was it my smile? My conversation with him earlier that day on the phone? Or was it my hands?" She held up her hands for us to examine them, her fingers tapping against one another. "My healing hands—that's what David liked to call them."

"Because of the scabies," I nudged her.

"That, but he also talked about my hands like they had magic. Like they could cure anything if I touched a person. A little like Jesus, I guess."

"Seriously? You fell for Deadeye because he compared you to Jesus?" Sanders butted in. I shot him a look that said *hush up*.

"It was more than that," Debbie argued. "No one had ever thought of me before, longed for me like that. No one ever thought I was beautiful. And David…he saw me, you know? I mean, not many men really *see* me."

I imagined what was going through Sanders mind—*What in the hell is she talking about? Everyone can see her unless they're blind.*

On some level, I understood what Debbie meant. There were multiple ways to see a person, and I was willing to bet that most men overlooked Debbie or just plain saw right through her. In her early forties, she reminded me of a washed-out photograph, the vibrancy muted, the edges ratty and worn.

"It's not easy to find people like that," I said.

Debbie smiled big, almost prideful, and I noticed her chipped front tooth, a dark triangle in her smile. She was so pleased with herself that the plan had worked, that she had done everything *right*, and that Deadeye was out and in the world once again. She couldn't wait to be rewarded for her loyal work.

"We're holding your car as evidence," Sanders said. "There are BOLOs out in the tristate area and soon we'll go nationwide. He won't last long out there, Debbie."

"Surveillance footage from the hospital shows you left the car tucked in a underground parking garage. What did you leave inside the car for him?" I asked. "Besides the key?" Debbie rubbed her belly and ignored my question. "Have you told the world? That David is out? How much cash was in the car, Debbie? What kind of weapon?"

"The world needs to know that David is free," Debbie insisted.

"He's not free," Sanders corrected her. "He never will be. Things will be much harder for him every minute that he is gone. If you love him, help us. And we will help you. We might be able to work something out so that you're able to visit him."

We'd thrown out this carrot multiple times, the chance to meet face-to-face with Deadeye, but Debbie wasn't going for it. Over the course of the interview, we'd learned virtually nothing more than Debbie Turner was undoubtedly and wholeheartedly smitten with David Johnson, AKA Deadeye.

As Sanders prodded Debbie for more information, I watched her hands. There was something about the way she rubbed her belly, the knowing way she looked at us.

I interrupted Sanders. "How far along are you, Debbie?"

For a moment, no one moved or spoke. Sanders broke the moment when he jumped up and yelled, "Dear Lord, don't tell me. Don't you dare tell me it's his."

Debbie let out a crazed cackle-giggle. She was more than pleased with herself that I'd finally figured it out. "It's David's," she confirmed. "A boy."

"No," Sanders argued.

"Yes," Debbie squealed. "A real miracle child."

Sanders turned to me. "I don't even want to know how."

There were many crazy stories in law enforcement about the ways in which inmates impregnated their partners despite Ohio's ban on conjugal visits. We'd heard just about everything, from visitors swallowing small balloons full of sperm to kitchen workers sneaking out sperm on a delivery or a waste removal truck.

We didn't have to guess with Debbie. For the first time in the interview, she offered us information. "We timed it. You know, sperm only live so long outside the warmth of a human body. Those latex clinic gloves and a battery-operated slow cooker are great for just about anything."

I was skeptical at best—perfect timing or not, it was a far-fetched story. I questioned Debbie's mental health once again. Was she as delusional as she sounded? "What about the person you paid to bring it out? Who was it?"

She only smiled, but I had a strong guess—the same guard who helped Deadeye into a solitary holding tank. Trent Simon who was now in a coma. The cash could be hard for guards and prison employees to turn down, especially when it was as simple as bringing sperm to someone inside a medical glove

"How well do you know Trent Simon?"

Debbie only laughed, but she'd shut down in her glee over the baby. It was clear we'd get no more from her. She wanted us to know about the baby and about their clever plan to get Daddy out of prison. In all honesty, though, I doubted Debbie Turner could really tell us much more. Deadeye wouldn't have told her much, realizing that she might break under our questioning. Most likely he promised to contact her after he'd been out of prison for a few days.

Debbie Turner had already been arrested for aiding and abetting a prisoner's escape, and we could now add to that arrest hustling contraband from prison. Not that it would add much time to her sentence if she was convicted, but it was the principle of it—the disgusting lengths she would go to for Deadeye.

As Sanders and I walked out of the prison, I ordered a DNA test to be certain of the baby's father and checked my phone for any updates on the search. Nothing. It was like Deadeye slipped out of his hospital room and simply vanished.

"We have a few hours until the press conference at BCI head-quarters. What do you say we grab some shut-eye back at the office?"

"Sounds good to me." Since Sanders picked me up at the airport, I didn't have much choice. At least at the office, I could either check out a vehicle or hitch a ride home at some point to get my truck.

The morning sun crested the horizon, and Sanders drove over the backcountry roads in silence. Both of us worried about the escape and what it meant—nothing good could come from David Johnson's escape. He hadn't been able to control his urges to kill before prison, and he certainly wouldn't be able to control them now. It was only a matter of time until Deadeye claimed another victim.

CHAPTER THREE

OBCI Headquarters
Friday, 8:30 a.m.

Colby Sanders wore a suit well, and he stood on the steps of the BCI building in a handsome navy tailor-cut. The red tie against the crisp white of his button-down had been the idea of our media specialist. "A hint at American pride, but not a slap upside the head," she'd told him.

I hated public speaking in any capacity and was happy to let Sanders take this one. I kept two changes of work clothes in my office, and thankfully the pale blue button-down was clean. I stood with the collection of cameras on the steps and watched the crowd for anyone who looked out of place or someone trying much too hard to be *in* place—there was an ultra-fine line between those two extremes.

Sanders didn't have much to report about Deadeye's whereabouts, and that sort of vague information—saying just enough but not much at all—had a tendency to calm the public. We only had Debbie's car as evidence of his movements, the vehicle he drove to the Ohio–Kentucky border and ditched in an abandoned gas station parking lot. There were two options for Deadeye in that gas station parking lot—either someone was there to meet him, a person designated to pick up the next leg of the transport, or he'd taken a vehicle, one that was waiting for him in the lot. No vehicles had been reported stolen from the surrounding area in the last forty-eight hours. Everything indicated that Deadeye had been a master planner in his escape and had more than just Debbie's help on the outside. We had Debbie under close observation, but I was certain Deadeye was done with her. She had served her purpose and served it well—she'd gotten him out of prison and on his way. More importantly, if he was truly the father of the baby, she carried his seed, giving him a legacy to live on. Deadeye didn't need Debbie for anything else.

A large display had been set up behind Sanders, and photographs of David Johnson flashed on the screen along with the tip line number that had been established for the case. In the cameras' bright lights, Sanders looked pale, almost ashen, as if he was on the edge of the stomach flu.

"The Midwest is on high alert," Sanders said. "We are confident that David Johnson will be apprehended soon. If you see him, call 9-1-1. Do not try to approach Johnson on your own."

When the conference opened up for questions, reporters called out inquiries about vigilantes and the possibility of Deadeye killing again.

My phone dinged with a text from Mike Snyder, another agent I worked closely with at BCI. *2 dead in Simmons County less than 24 hours ago. Shirts taken.*

I groaned. Even though we had worked hard to keep Deadeye's bloody souvenirs from the press, it spread like wildfire once the detail had come out in court. Since it was public information, we wouldn't be able to use that evidence in order to determine whether the killer was really Deadeye or some other deranged copycat.

Other identifying markers of Deadeye? I texted back.

Rifle used, one shot in chest. Second victim shot in back. Rural area, opening of hunting season.

Simmons County. Southeast Ohio near the West Virginia border. I recognized this area; it had been Deadeye's hunting grounds. However, neither victim had been shot in the head, and taking on two people at once was not part of Deadeye's MO. An unnecessary risk, and one that alarmed me—it said that the killer was raising the stakes.

I texted, *Date and place of first known Deadeye victim?*

After a few minutes, Snyder shot back, *November 26, 1992. Simmons County.*

I checked the calendar on my phone. November 23.

Sanders answered his last question from the press as I put the latest information all together. November 26 had been Thanksgiving Day in 1992. Yesterday had been the anniversary of the first known Deadeye murder—whoever committed the double murder was going by the Thanksgiving holiday, not the day's calendar number.

Agent Snyder drove me home and I had enough time to dump out my bag of vacation gear and reload it with work clothes, badge, weapons, and my laptop. I'd flown home from South Carolina in a Cleveland Cavaliers sweatshirt, well-worn jeans, and flip-flops. I left those along with my vacation clothes in a heap on my bedroom floor and put on my lucky Frye boots. My father, the best detective I'd ever known, swore by Frye boots and their ability to help catch criminals. My dad was nothing if not superstitious, and I loved him for it. He'd given me a pair of Fryes when I graduated from the academy—it was the last gift he'd given me before he passed away.

I took a minute to smooth my dark hair in its long messy braid and thought about the last time Bennett had been in my house, a few days before the trip. In a rare moment of a hunger attack, she'd raided my kitchen cabinets for protein bars.

"Come on, Hansen," she called out to me. "What do you eat, anyway? There is no food in this house."

"We are *clean eating*, remember?" I teased, careful not to mention the numerous empty fast-food bags that littered the floor of my truck.

Bennett was the cook between the two of us, and it always impressed me that her meals didn't come from a box or some kind of powdered mix. She took her vegetables seriously, and her fruit intake even more so. In the summer months, Bennett had a small garden, and she talked about one day expanding it to grow enough to donate to our local food bank. When Bennett's rummaging turned up very little in my cupboards, she'd settled on a small packet of crackers.

My stomach rumbled when I thought about those crackers, and I found one last very stale sleeve in the box. I gave up on my hair and threw on a black leather coat to chase off the chill in the morning air. I was out the door, holding the sleeve of crackers between my teeth while I locked up. A worn tennis ball and a ripped rubber Frisbee waited for Gus beside the back door. Seeing his most loved toys made me miss the dog even more than I already did. At least Gus always had fun with our friend who kept him, and for the time being, it was the best place for my dog.

Simmons County was about ninety miles from my home in Spring Rock. As my truck rolled toward it, I couldn't help but to go over the conversation I'd had with Sanders again and again before I left the office.

I'd found him after the press conference, mopping the sweat from his forehead with a tissue. He spoke before I could tell him about the victims. "I just heard. I need you in Simmons County ASAP. The local sheriff called a full department meeting for noon."

I nodded. "You feeling okay, boss?"

"I'll be fine, but I'm going to need you to set up and lead the task force on this one."

I tried to hide my surprise. Since becoming the codirector of BCI, I'd mostly led small cases that closed within two weeks, cases that involved serial rape or theft. I'd yet to lead my own serial murder case, particularly one that had garnered national attention.

"Your feet are already wet, Hansen. It's time to dive in."

I knew that it wasn't feasible for Sanders to lead all our big cases, and that was precisely why BCI had taken me on as a codirector. I just didn't imagine I'd be leading a major task force so soon.

"I'll meet you in Simmons County within a few days."

I stopped in my tracks. "A few days? It's Deadeye, Sanders."

"Deadeye or not, you can handle things until I get there. I only have three more cases to close out—it won't be long."

I wondered about what sort of backlog of paperwork would keep Sanders away from such a big case. Pressure from the state could be brutal, I knew that. They wanted every case wrapped up and every action of the agents involved accounted for. But couldn't that be put on hold for a jailbreak of a serial predator? Or until we got the new task force up and running? Sanders had always been one to welcome a challenge, particularly in high profile cases—what could be more of a challenge than the break of Deadeye and the recent murders in Simmons County?

"Come to think of it," I said aloud in the truck, "Sanders hasn't made much sense in the last few weeks."

Sanders had been having a rough time with his daughter, Riley, in the past few months. While he never said much about his family, I knew she'd dropped out of college and moved home to live with Sanders's ex-wife. There had been some concern about a boyfriend at school, something Sanders said couldn't be worked out. I'd assumed it was a nasty breakup and Riley needed extra support. Now, though, it seemed his daughter's situation could be worse than Sanders initially let on. It was the only thing I could come up with that would keep Sanders away from a case as big as David Johnson's.

While the countryside rolled past, the midmorning sun warmed away the night's frost. I listened to the truck's tires roll over the pavement and worried about whatever might be going on with my friend, Sanders.

CHAPTER FOUR

Simmons County Sheriff's Office
Friday, noon

Sheriff Carl Daniel of Simmons County was a dead ringer for Santa Claus complete with the white woolly mustache, caterpillar-thick eyebrows, and jolly belly. He greeted me at the station door with a toothy grin and his full cheeks flushed with what I guessed to be stress from housing one of the biggest cases in Ohio's history.

"We've set up a war room," Daniel said as he led me through security and toward the task force area.

"War room, huh? Let's hope we don't need it too long, and we can close this case with Deadeye before it goes any further."

"I hear you," Sheriff Daniel said. "Our county is exhausted from being the center of his rifle scope all these years. We had a bit of reprieve with him in prison, but now the community's fear has returned."

I followed Daniel and thought about the fact that David Johnson had never explained why Simmons County was the locus of his murders. Investigators hadn't uncovered any close friends or family in the area or job duties that would bring Deadeye to the small rural town. The popular theory was that because Deadeye lived not far from Cleveland, the drive to Simmons was a straight shot down the interstate. On a good traffic day, he could have made it in less than three hours—not too far to travel for the most popular hunting area in the state of Ohio, and the perfect place for a serial murderer hunting humans to fly under the radar. As a serial killer, Deadeye was a bit of a rarity in that he didn't kill on his home turf.

The war room was really an oversized conference room that featured multiple tables pushed together in the center for a shared desk space. Two-sided dry-erase boards had been wheeled into the room, and a large county map almost covered one board in its entirety. Nothing fancy, but certainly functional, and the makeshift office would serve as my new home until we could take Deadeye back into custody or he killed himself—whichever came first. In rural communities like Simmons County, the sheriff's office functioned as the hub for everything—reporting, a working crime lab, and the coroner's office.

It was Black Friday, and most of the officers and detectives in the room appeared to be on a turkey hangover. Even though I hadn't had any turkey for Thanksgiving, I felt the same. I hadn't slept much since Sanders's call, and at least half of my brain was still on vacation mode. Badges of all levels filtered into the room, most milling about the steaming coffee and cookies on a side table. I reached for the tallest cup I could find and poured it full of dark, steaming coffee.

The purpose of the sheriff's department meeting was to introduce the task force and clear up any rumors that had surfaced about the case. Strategies would be evaluated and various teams in the department would be sent out to search for any evidence that Deadeye was or had been in the area. Then, the task force would settle in, and it would be up to me to assign each five-person team with individualized assignments.

"As if I need anything else to eat this week," Sheriff Daniel joked with a cookie in both hands. "Rowdy group," he added for my benefit, setting down his cookies and then using his oversized belt buckle to yank up his dark jeans.

As I stood beside him, I felt the sudden sting of Sanders's absence. I wanted the security of him at my side, and I longed for the respect his mere presence brought with it. It wasn't easy to walk into a room of professionals who had already been working hard on a case. Most weren't too happy to see *anyone* ride in from the BCI and take over. My position, though, was compounded by my gender; there weren't many women who'd held director positions at the state level, not to mention that the law enforcement world was still very much a boys' club. No matter what I did, I'd never be able to cross that gender barrier many of my colleagues had set up for me, consciously or unconsciously. My age didn't help matters either—I was older than I looked, but many perceived me to be too young to carry the reins. Add *queer woman* to that mix and you had one heck of an intimidating mountain to climb. Sanders had everything I didn't—loads of testosterone and the gray hairs to boot.

Sheriff Daniel gave a quick whistle, his fingers mussing up his thick mustache. "Pop a squat after you reload on caffeine. We've got the case of our lives to solve and just the person to lead us." Daniel paused long enough for the room to quiet down. "Welcome to Simmons County, Special Agent Luce Hansen. We are looking forward to working with you."

The crowd of officers, detectives, and staff turned their gazes to me. There weren't enough chairs in the room for everyone, and a few leaned against the side walls. It was an intimidating number of people in such a cramped space.

"Hello, everyone," I said over their half-hearted applause. "Thanks for the welcome. Let's get to it, shall we?"

I hoped my voice held strong, particularly when I noticed the slight tremor in my hand. "David Johnson—Deadeye—was tried and convicted for six serial murders in the Simmons area. As of yesterday, we may be adding two more to that death count. We need to consider that this is not Johnson's work, but that of a copycat. Which just so happens to coincide with Johnson's jailbreak."

Chuckles erupted around the room.

"Unlikely, yes," I agreed, "but we cannot rule anything out before the investigation. Our first order of business is to find David Johnson and apprehend him. The search areas have expanded. Be sure to get your team's assignment on the way out. Second order of business," I said, "is to determine why Johnson chose to make the break and kill on *this* particular Thanksgiving. It is the four year anniversary of the first kill, but that doesn't explain why he didn't break out to kill last Thanksgiving or the year before that."

We all knew that anniversaries held tremendous weight in the world of the serial killer. These monsters loved to plan dates and times and locations the way wedding planners delighted in arranging celebrations. The date, though, it was key—I felt it in my bones.

"Special thanks to Dr. Mike Duncan and the detectives who compiled the victimology books for our case." I nodded to the county coroner who had been doing autopsies for the state for about forty years. "Dr. Duncan."

Duncan looked like he'd been pulled off the golf course for the meeting with his bright yellow polo shirt and khakis. He stood and reached for the tall stack of bound books beside him. "Here is everything we have on the Deadeye case," Duncan said, distributing the pile around the room. "Guard these books with your life—no leaks, people."

I took one and flipped through its pages, internally cursing the very existence of such books. It was a matter of preference and style, really; I'd been taught by my father to use a murder board. He believed the only way to fully build one was to occupy significant space where every piece of evidence could be featured. My father argued that the visual field of such a construction couldn't be simulated on computers or paper because the murder board was a living thing—a model that breathed and moved in and out of the team's mind. My dad always said a murder board did its best work when you were away from it, and your unconscious mind could noodle around with the images. I'd found my best connections happened when I wasn't at work at all, but swimming laps in the pool.

Some would argue that active murder boards displayed in stations left too many chances for the vital information of a case to be leaked to the press. Too many grieving family members had been paraded past a murder board that featured gruesome images of their loved ones, or revealed them to be suspects in the crime. So, the discreet victimology book was born: a bound collection that could be copied and carried anywhere. More importantly, it could be hidden at a moment's notice. Once the case closed, these handy little books were easily filed away. They contained every possible photographic angle of the victim and the crime scene, background information and

IDs, as well as autopsy findings and photos—everything nice and neat inside one coiled bind. As if serial murder, at least on an investigator's end, could ever be so neat and organized.

"We have no obvious motive for the double murder and very little evidence from the scene. No eyewitnesses have come forward." I paused for emphasis. "We must keep in mind the variations from Deadeye's MO. David Johnson is known for his single, deadly shots to the head. Time is of the essence. If we are dealing with Deadeye, and that is an *if*, we know from his previous timeline that he will kill again within a few days. Whoever the killer is, Deadeye took full advantage of that Thanksgiving weekend, and this killer will do it again."

I didn't tell the group what they already knew—everything in this case was stacked against us. The victims had not been robbed, sexually assaulted, or mutilated. We were faced with the fact that this killer might be targeting individuals based on opportunity—time and location. This created the potential for any person in the rural county and beyond to be the next possible victim.

"Everything is complicated, exactly as it was four years ago, by the opening of gun-hunting deer season in the area. With the influx of hunters, we've got the potential for a lot of chaos. Our goal, after bringing in Johnson, is to keep this community calm but alert."

Simmons County was a popular hunting spot in Southeast Ohio, and the sport brought many to the sparsely populated region. Bow-hunting season had been in effect since the end of September, but we were only two days away from the opening of gun-hunting season. It had been reported that Simmons County had a record number of deer this year, and the state had recently upped the county's allotment so that each hunter could take home three deer. Simmons County expected more than the usual number of hunters to arrive within the next twenty-four hours.

An officer called out from the room, "How will the poachers be handled this year?"

The room grumbled with the problem of poachers. The issue of these rule-breakers grew worse every season. Each year the recreational hunters took the sport of hunting deer too far, camouflaging themselves and using all sorts of high-tech weaponry—as if the deer posed any sort of threat. Every season, they dealt with amateur hunters who shot at anything that moved and who did not stay within the designated hunting territories. The season, though, was big business for Simmons County, a boost to their dwindling economy they desperately needed.

"Same as always," Sheriff Daniel answered. "Bring in anybody without a permit or with an unlicensed firearm."

I agreed. "No leniency, folks. If the slightest thing feels off to you, ask questions. And then ask some more questions. It's very probable that Deadeye, or his copycat, is running around out there disguised as a deer hunter. After Johnson's first kill four years ago, investigators suspected that he spent that week hunting in the area and celebrating with other rowdy hunters in local bars. We know Deadeye likes his patterns and rituals. So we start there. We end with cuffs or a coffin."

"And he loves his bloody shirts, apparently," someone called out. The room erupted in uncomfortable laughter.

I couldn't deny that Deadeye's chosen souvenir item was odd. His choice to take the victim's bloody shirt or jacket mystified many. However, I saw the clothing as a marker, something he could hang up on his wall the same way someone might hang their blown-apart cardboard sheet from target practice for all to see. Bragging rights.

"We have the tip line up and running." I steered everyone back on track. "Local radio and television channels will continue to report the warnings about David Johnson. West Virginia is on high alert. At this time, though, we have no evidence that any of our suspect's murders have taken place across the border. Therefore, we are keeping the task force in Ohio."

Another officer called out, "will the task force findings and actions be made public?"

I shook my head. "Not at this time. We need to get a handle on the case and our feet firmly planted before we deal with the mass media."

I became distinctly aware of the look that passed between the locals in the room. Finally, someone spoke up to help me out. "What about the father?" an officer said.

Beside me, Sheriff Daniel cleared his throat.

"I don't follow," I said.

"Of the two brothers that were killed yesterday?"

When I didn't respond, Sheriff Daniel picked up and unfolded a newspaper from a nearby table. He passed it to me. "This morning's *Simmons Tribune,* front page and center, a letter to the killer written by the deceased brothers' father."

I read the local newspaper's screaming headline: *To the person or persons who shot my dear sons.*

I wanted to scream, *Son of a bitch!* Instead, I took a deep breath.

"I'm sorry." Daniel's face reddened until it almost glowed against his stark white mustache. "I didn't have time to get a copy to you."

"We'll deal with the father and the press later," I said, folding the newspaper and tossing it aside. "Right now, we have an active investigation to get off the ground which is already hours behind."

CHAPTER FIVE

Friday, 4:00 p.m.

For the sake of my profile's accuracy, I had to physically put myself into the scene. While it was routine for investigators to do crime scene walk-throughs and re-enactments, I took things a step further. I needed to be alone, to be free of the questions and banter that usually came with multiple officers in a crime scene area all at once. I needed to see what the victim saw, hear what the victim heard, stand where the victim stood, and even fall where the victim eventually fell. I couldn't do that with others asking me questions or trying to bounce around possible murder scenarios.

It had taken some time to get the task force out in the field and provide each of the five task force members with a different assignment. We also had to stay in close connection with the officers canvassing the homes and businesses within a sixty-mile radius of the crime scene.

The area's spotty coverage meant I had to follow a hand-drawn map from Sheriff Daniel to the location where the brothers had been killed. My truck wound its way along the narrow country roads. Not more than thirty miles from the West Virginia border, I guessed there had to be more than a few abandoned barns, cabins, and farms where someone could hide away in the Ohio countryside. Once I left the Simmons town limits, the homes were large, old, and weathered—expensive places to keep up and full of family histories. Horse barns and cattle spotted the hills and fields that rolled out around these homes. As I drove farther, the terrain became rougher, rolling farmland broken up by the intermittent vast forest. Camping grounds and the occasional abandoned house or trailer provided near-hidden locations where one could hide out for days, possibly even weeks with enough access to food and water.

Finally, the orange cones that blocked County Road 571 came into view. Beyond the cones sat a patrol car parked horizontally across the road. Once the officer saw my truck, his blue lights flipped on. I pulled up to the cones and got out, reaching for the thermos of fresh coffee Sheriff Daniel sent with me for the officer on duty. The officer's job was to keep out the public and the press until we were completely finished documenting the crime scene. Local detectives and forensics had already been through the area combing it for any clues and photographing every angle of the area. They were only waiting on my walk-through before they reopened the road.

The young officer rolled down his window when I approached, my badge held out in plain sight. He nodded, his dark hair cropped so close I could see the white of his scalp.

"Welcome, Agent Hansen. Sheriff radioed that you were headed this way. Let me know if I can help."

"Thanks." I handed him the thermos of coffee. "A little something to keep you going out in the field, huh?"

"Just what I needed." He took the thermos, and I heard the soft voices of an NPR show from his car radio. "Not a thing going on out here, and that makes it hard to stay awake."

"I bet." I tapped the roof of his patrol car twice. "I won't be long, and then you can head in. Wait for my signal to release the scene."

I felt the officer's eyes follow me as I turned and made my way into the area where two brothers had been murdered.

❖

I stepped off the berm where forensics marked the spot of the killer's parked vehicle, the place where he left the engine rumbling. Investigators worked a single tire track left on the side of the road, the remnants of the white plaster still visible where the tire impression had been poured and then removed. Despite the killer's focus on a perfect location for murder, he'd left a mark. I generally put my faith in human error, and the loose plaster indicated just one of the killer's major mistakes. Deadeye was a seasoned predator. This wasn't his first, second, or even third kill, so I wondered what would have pulled his attention from his actions for those mere seconds when he let the tire spill off the blacktop—had something taken him by surprise? Or maybe Deadeye hadn't been here at all.

The chalked outline of where John Holden had been shot at point-blank range lay only a few feet away. John hadn't stood a chance against the shooter; I imagined how unprepared and terrified he must have been at the moment he realized the weapon was leveled at him. Yet, in that terror, John revealed more information for our investigation than all of the other victims put together by leaving a partial recording of the murders.

John's phone recording during the murders had the power to be a game-changer in our search for Deadeye, and forensic electronics specialists were combing it for any audio and visual clues they could enhance. They also sent a copy to my phone so I could play it at the scene. It had been very hard to keep knowledge of the recording from leaking beyond the task force, but in order for the recording to help us, and to honor the risk John took—and Logan, whether he knew it or not—we desperately needed the existence of this information to stay hidden from the killer.

In the world of these murders, our killer had the distinct ability to disappear. He drew little to no attention and had to have melded into the community as someone who belonged. Our killer took pleasure in the fact that his actions put a harrowing fear into his victims. His ability to terrify others gave him power. But I had to remind myself that the killer didn't live in this world alone—he had to be part of another world, a world where he wasn't so invisible and where he held very little power.

Standing beside the body-shaped outline of John Holden, I cued up the file on my phone and hit the play button. The brothers had been recording a trio of deer when the suspect's truck emerged. If this killer was Deadeye, he'd already ditched the nurse's car and found a late model truck to get him to Simmons. John must have forgotten to end the recording because there were a few minutes of him jogging, and the landscape slipping past the lens. When the murderer approached, the camera caught the make of the truck and some of its defining features. We didn't have any images of the suspect, but we did have the gift of clear audio. I listened as John asked the driver if he needed help. The response was jumbled followed by an enormous speaker-muffling blast, which knocked John and the phone to the ground.

The forensics report highlighted the location where Logan fled in an effort to find any sort of safety. My own boots brushed through the dead grass beside the road. The farther I went, the ground tangled with thick patches of undergrowth. In the summer, raspberry and honeysuckle grew rampant, but now the damp ground held the bramble of underbrush and downed branches. The fog had left the ground relatively wet and it generally held the placement of footsteps. I followed the path of the previous investigators to the location where Logan's blood had been found. I stood still in that exact location as my senses took in the space all around me. The recording rolled on, video of the sky that featured only the distinct sound of a truck door opening and the sound of footsteps near the camera. The picture on the phone jumbled and skidded across the landscape. I imagined it had been dislodged while Deadeye took John's shirt. Then, the distinct thud of John's dead body falling back to the ground. What followed were several minutes with no recognizable sound during the time when Logan was hunted and terrorized. I stood on Logan's path listening to the muffled sounds of the recording and dreading what I knew would eventually come—another shot followed by the unnerving silence of a target down. Minutes later, the truck door opened and then closed, the engine's sound steady for some time before it slowly dissipated down the country road.

Most of the underbrush had been removed where Logan had lain, most likely because it was covered with blood and could eventually be used for evidence in an upcoming trial. I turned to look back to the road, at most fifteen yards away. Forensics had already combed the area—they were only waiting on me to release the scene—so I felt comfortable dropping to my knees in the area where I expected Logan had fallen. I positioned myself faceup, plank-like, feeling the moisture of the earth seep through the fabric of my pants. I looked above at the thicket of woven tree branches and listened to the sounds of what must have been a squirrel or some other small rodent scrabbling up a thick tree trunk. The sun tried to burn off the clouds in the early afternoon sky, and from this position, I couldn't see much of the road. If Logan had been on his back, he would have had to rely on his hearing and not much else to determine the killer's whereabouts.

Logan's death intrigued me most because he was not like any of the other known victims of Deadeye. As far as we knew, there hadn't been a double murder before, and Logan wasn't killed with a shot to the head. Another issue was that Logan didn't die instantly. I struggled to make sense of those differences. I wondered if Deadeye had reached that stage many serial killers do when they grow so comfortable with their process, they believe they are godlike and immune to capture. Deadeye had earned his nickname in the law enforcement community because of his precision shots to his victims' head—either directly between the eyes or into the temple. Logan's death deviated from that pattern; it was a different kill. Comfortable or not in his process, why would Deadeye have taken the unnecessary risk that someone might see him stopped along the road? He must have considered the possibility of a poacher or a farmer in the area who might have come running toward the gunfire.

I flipped onto my stomach so my head faced away from the road. This position felt safer—it was probably easier to hide the rise and fall of breath or reflexive blinking. Ultimately, though, it didn't matter how well Logan played dead. He would have been alive but struggling when Deadeye approached him, sat him up, and took his shirt. Deadeye knew the wound would be deadly, no doubt, but he'd never left a live victim at a crime scene. I wondered if it was merely an issue of his process—did he only allow himself one shot per victim? Or could it simply have been an issue of preserving precious ammunition? I thought about cases where I'd heard of killers attempting to preserve supplies. The survivalist or prepper movement was known for such measures but had no ties to murdering innocent victims. Still, there were active members in the rural area of Simmons County, and I hoped the sheriff had them on his radar if for no other reason than they might have heard something about the murders. People who followed the movement's advice to prepare for the end of the world generally avoided police at all costs. The more I thought about it, I vaguely remembered hearing that a major leader of the group had moved to the area in the last few years—Coleman Frank. He had a large internet following where he preached doomsday scenarios and offered advice on how to build impregnable bunkers.

As I rested on the ground, I wondered if any words had passed between Logan and the killer. I wondered if Logan cried out in pain as the killer yanked off his shirt, if Logan had begged for his life, or asked about his brother. For some reason, the killer chose the unnecessary risk of leaving Logan alive.

I lifted my head just a little, a miniature version of that cobra pose that Rowan swore by for chronic back pain. I imagined Logan's struggle, his lack of strength. Yet in that pose he would have been able to see his surroundings better. To my right, I saw a place where the ground cover had been disturbed. The only reason Logan would have risked moving had been his certainty that the gunman had gone. Logan definitely wouldn't have wasted his strength moving *away* from his brother and into the dense forest.

The recording had been playing on my phone, and it came to the part where Logan had found his way back to his brother's side. I listened to Logan's labored breaths, his groans of pain, and ultimately John's phone dropping as Logan tried to hold it in his shaking hands.

"Mom," Logan whispered into the microphone. "I love you," he cried. The lens showed his mouth seeping blood, his skin so pale and sweaty. "Couldn't stop…" The recording stopped at that point forensics determined because the charge had run out. The phone had been found clenched in Logan's fisted and bloodied hand.

I stood up and weaved my way through the thick spread of trees. Someone had moved quickly through them, leaving the fresh snap of a small branch, the pressured outline of a foot still partially visible in the undergrowth. I followed the disturbed land deeper into the forest, the trees a hunting blind.

Instinctively, I understood I was not tracking a copycat or any kind of an imposter of Deadeye, but the very man himself. He'd come back to Simmons County for reasons unknown to commit a double murder on the anniversary of his first-known kill. I could sense him, feel him—Deadeye wasn't far away. At the same time, everything felt so different than Deadeye's other murders. I wasn't sure what to attribute the changes to.

Deadeye's prison garb had been found stashed under the driver's seat of Debbie's car, and I imagined that she left him a full camouflage outfit and a fistful of cash. In other words, he most likely looked like every other hunter arriving in Simmons County for the week. He'd changed vehicles and most likely had again since the murders. I imagined him pulling into a gas station in town, filling his mug with steaming coffee, and picking up the morning paper: *To the person or persons who shot my sons.*

I took in a deep breath, the country air cool against my skin. With a sudden grip of my heart, I missed my father. No one had the ability to talk through a crime scene scenario like him. After his death, his ghostly image had appeared to me when I needed him most. It had frustrated me that it was only in regard to my work—what had once been his work—until I came to the understanding that my father was still an investigator, even in death. The loss of his life and physical body couldn't take that away.

But recently, my father's presence had slowly dissipated from my life. I hadn't seen him in months, and I wanted my father at my side. I wanted to hear him ask a barrage of questions about the crime scene and reenact the murder with him. Since that wasn't possible, I did the only thing I could think of: I closed my eyes and imagined what he might say.

Lucy-girl, he would say to me with hands planted squarely on his hips above his service utility belt, *think about the tracks and their movement. Where are they headed?*

"Both directions," I said aloud. "Toward Logan's body and away."

And there are the tracks near the other body. Are they the same?

My eyes shot open. The tracks and edges of footprints were similar, but I couldn't swear they were the same. I walked back to the place where Logan's body had been and examined the area around it. It was hard to tell, particularly given that so many investigators had been working the area around the body. Still, the physical space and movements within it *felt* different.

My imagined father reminded me of the three motives most associated with murder: sex, money, and revenge. *It doesn't fit, Lucy-girl. Move outside that box. What else would motivate someone to kill?*

"Why would Deadeye walk farther into the woods?" I asked myself. "Time was a-ticking. Why would he leave Logan alive and *not* head back to the safety of the truck?" There was only one answer: someone else had been there, someone who had unknowingly walked upon the scene through the woods or someone who purposely watched the entire murder.

The tracks show the person turned back. Why would that person leave? I imagined my dad asking me. *This person would have seen Deadeye drive away. Why wouldn't this person come back to help Logan? Or, at the very least, call for help?*

I was left with one answer. In order to walk away from a grisly double murder, no matter how terrified that person might have been, and *not* report it, they had to be involved. Judging from the gunshots, the person in the forest watching had to be Deadeye, which meant the killer had to be some kind of participant in Deadeye's murders. There were a multitude of scenarios for the role this other person might have played, but I had to assume the two stayed together until I found hard physical evidence that they didn't.

Just like that, the serial predator case of Southeastern Ohio doubled itself. Deadeye, it seemed, had a deadly partner who met him outside the prison walls. I needed to alert the team that we weren't necessarily tracking one killer anymore, but two.

CHAPTER SIX

Simmons County
Friday, 7:30 p.m.

The Holden family lived on Holden Lane, a rural strip of a road named after their family generations ago. The home sat nestled into the side of a hill surrounded by expansive cattle pastures that bordered the public hunting areas. Holden Farms was one of the biggest independently run family farms in the region with over 150 acres of land. The farm had been in the Holden family for generations and had made their name as a butchery selling fresh beef, venison, and chicken. Over the years, the employee rolls had grown from only immediate family members to about ten others who worked the land and the cattle. John Holden, the current owner, had been running the farming business for the last twenty years, since his father's death and his own career in the military ended.

Sheriff Daniel informed me on the ride out to the Holdens' that they, like so many others in the region, had lost money on a bad fracking deal. Since then, the farm had taken on more investors. "Investors may bring money," Daniel had said, "but they also bring with them demands and all sorts of wild ideas about how things ought to go."

Now Sheriff Daniel stood beside me on John and Joyce Holden's front step, adjusting his uniform shirt and pants one more time—a constant habit with him, I'd noticed. Inside the large home, a dog barked.

"This is the worst part, I think. Dealing with grieving families. I can't even imagine—two sons in one afternoon." The sheriff shook his head in disbelief.

Because he knew the family from the community and church, I worried that Daniel might fumble the interview. I'd seen it before, an agent or officer fumble an interview with a victim's family due to compassion overload. No matter how many times we told ourselves to separate our work from our personal lives, it was easier said than done in such situations. It was clear he thought investigating the Holdens was a waste of time, but he agreed we needed to stop them from working so openly with the press. They attended the same church in town, and Daniel had clamored on about the respect the Holdens held in the small community.

"It doesn't have to be terrible," I reminded him. "Our questions can sometimes help take the family's mind off the tragedy, if only for a little while. Sometimes they really need to help us for their own sanity."

"I'm just worried about these folks, is all."

Before Sheriff Daniel could ring the bell, a shadow moved across the window next to the front door. The door opened a crack as the person shooed the barking dog away.

"Mrs. Holden? Could we trouble you and your husband with a few questions?" Daniel made our introductions and the woman considered me through puffy, red eyes.

"It's really not a good time."

"It won't take long," I said.

She stepped back from the open door. She corralled the yapping dog into a nearby bathroom, and I followed Daniel through an expansive hallway into the kitchen. While we waited, I marveled at the space—modern updates had been made to the kitchen, but there were remnants of the original stone walls and plank wood used in the initial construction of the house.

"Amazing stonework," I said, running my fingertips over the cool uneven stone of a fireplace. A shaved log served as a mantel complete with framed family photographs of kids at different ages. The counters were lined with covered dishes and baked goods, signs of tremendous community support for the grieving family that most likely couldn't even think of eating.

"That old fireplace sucks out all our heat," Mr. Holden said, entering the kitchen. "Story is, all the rocks and stones were handpicked. Whatever kind of cement they used back then was impenetrable—I don't think the thing will ever come down."

"Special Agent Luce Hansen." I held out my hand to him. "You have a beautiful home. I'm quite interested—I've been doing some renovating of my own this past year."

"Renovations are never fun, but my family left us a place with some very good bones." He offered us seats around the dining table after greeting Daniel with a brief hug. "The original house was built in 1903," Mr. Holden said. "It wasn't much bigger than the kitchen and two small rooms. The house has been added to over the years, but we've worked hard to keep some of the original structure."

Although Holden's face was flushed and exhaustion showed in his eyes, the responses were clear and alert for someone who'd suffered such a sudden double loss in the last twenty-four hours.

Mrs. Holden brought us steaming mugs of coffee and sat down across from me. Her eyes teared up when she saw the paper I'd brought with me. "I shouldn't have let the boys run. I should have kept them here with me."

I leaned in closer to her. "You couldn't have known about David Johnson's escape. Trust me, I know all about those should-haves and shouldn't-haves. Don't give them power—you did what you thought was best. Your boys know that."

Sheriff Daniel handed Joyce Holden a tissue while she cried. Her husband sat beside her but made no move to comfort her. I wondered if he blamed her for the deaths, if this had been the topic of too many painful conversations between the two in the last twenty-four hours.

"I've read your letter in the paper a few times, and I have some questions for you. First, did you both write it? Whose idea was it to write a letter to the killer?"

Joyce looked at John as if she needed direction, as if she wasn't sure how to answer the question.

"I wrote it," John finally said.

"And it was your idea to print it?"

"I guess it was more the reporter's idea. I wanted to speak to the killer, and writing a letter was the only idea I came up with at the time."

Earlier, as she requested, I sent Bennett a copy of the paper and she reviewed the case files online through the BCI portal. Bennett's curiosity always got the best of her, as mine always did, and we'd tossed back and forth some ideas about the letter. One of Bennett's theories caught my interest and I'd saved her text: *I wonder if the father is in recovery or long-term therapy. Addiction recovery and mental health love to use the letter-writing technique. Indication of possible stressors in family. Line of inquiry?*

John Holden's confidence irritated me. He'd put the remainder of his family in danger and didn't have the sense to know he was playing with fire. Yet by his very presence and use of language, I knew the man wasn't an idiot. Had the letter been a spur-of-the-moment thing brought on by the pressure of the reporter?

I unfolded the *Simmons Tribune* and placed it on the table between us. The headline screamed along with a photo of the two brothers together in their early teens on a vacation at a beach. Their freckled noses wrinkled at the camera lens. *So much life taken away*, the caption announced. Everything about the newspaper spread seeped a manipulative construction of pathos.

I picked up the paper and began to read: *"It would be much easier for you if I wrote words of hate. But I am a man of peace and even though my heart feels like it could explode, I know I must offer you forgiveness. This is the word of the Lord, and I want to know if you have considered your own death. Have you thought at all about how you will answer to the Lord on Judgment Day? My conscience is clean, but yours, yours is blood soaked and hate filled."*

John Holden Sr. stared down at the table where his wife had taken his hand in hers. No one spoke for a moment.

"The letter asks the killer to come forward," Daniel said softly. "I think what we are questioning here is your safety."

Daniel might have put on his kid gloves, but I hadn't. I picked up reading where I left off: *"You know who you are and soon everyone*

else will know what you've done. Stop terrorizing this community—
you will soon face the fires and angry fury of hell. Nothing stays
hidden for long."

I folded the paper and set it on the table, settling my gaze on Mr.
Holden. "Inciting words, don't you think?"

Holden shook his head and refused to meet my eyes. "I thought
it would help. The papers wanted a statement. They wanted to know
what we had to say as a family about the crimes."

"I'm sure Sheriff Daniel warned you to stay away from the
press."

Holden gave me an ever-so-slight shake of his head. "I hoped the
killer would see it."

"I'm sure he has," I said. "This killer, though, he's ruthless. He
thrives on the emotional response he provokes. The letter was probably
the highlight of his year, particularly since you ended it with the threat
that his family and generations to come will share in his guilt."

The threat was reminiscent of a biblical quote, one I vaguely
recognized from my ex-gay-ministry days—the threat of punishment
that would last for generations and generations.

I leaned back and crossed my arms over my chest. "Interesting
tactic in order to get someone to confess."

Sheriff Daniel interjected, "I'd like to know if either of you
received any sort of communication regarding the letter? Anything
at all." He shot me a look that said *cool it*. By changing the line of
questioning he'd helped Holden and relieved some of the stress I'd
been applying.

Daniel had been certain the Holdens had nothing to do with
the murders of their sons from the start, but I couldn't be so certain.
Something about the entire scenario didn't sit right with me. Logan's
last moments on this earth were the words he sputtered into his
brother's phone. And those words only addressed his mother—not
his father.

Mrs. Holden spoke up. "We have had more messages than we
can handle. The outpouring of love has been overwhelming, to say
the least." She wiped a tear from her cheek. "Nothing negative or
hateful."

"Our pastor calls them love bombs," Holden said, giving Daniel a knowing nod, ignoring me. "You've heard his sermon on love bombing before, Sheriff? Bombarding those in pain with messages of strength and courage." He pointed to the kitchen counters. "Love bombs also come in the form of food."

"And social media messages," I added.

Members of the task force had been monitoring the Holdens' social media accounts, and nothing had caught their concern yet. Both the brothers' social media accounts had already been scoured for any clues, but their sites read a lot like a graveside service since the shootings occurred. Childhood friends posted old pictures and messages of farewell.

"I'm not sure what your relationship is with the local press," I started. "We want to be clear that publishing messages directed to the killer without our input can have deadly consequences. It's like hitting an angry bear with a stick. Just don't do it."

"If he's read it, maybe he will turn himself in," Holden said. "You think that this killer, Deadeye, could still be in the area?"

"If your sons were murdered by Deadeye, he won't turn himself in," I said.

I listened as Daniel gave the Holdens vague details about Deadeye's past behaviors and what our efforts had been to stop him. Holden ground his teeth while he listened, his jaw set tight and off-center. Anger, pure and simple. But, I wondered, why he wasn't asking a version of the question most survivors ask, *Why my boys? Why us?*

Stressors in the family.

Daniel seemed to be wrapping up the meeting, but I pushed on. "I know you've been asked so many times, but do you have any ideas who Logan spoke of in the recording? Is it possible he knew his killer?"

Tears filled Mrs. Holden's eyes. "I've gone over it a million times. If he knew the killer, though, I think he would have told us the name."

"How was your relationship with your sons, Mr. Holden?" I asked.

A defensive glare shone in his eyes. "Meaning?"

I shrugged. "Meaning did you all get along? Were there any issues between the boys and you that we need to know about?"

The Holdens answered with a simultaneous *no*. "We are a family," Joyce Holden said. "All families have problems, but our love is strong."

"It might help us to know what sorts of problems you've had as a family." I pushed for more.

Holden glared at me. "I assure you, we only wanted to guilt the killer into a confession with the letter to the paper."

When I asked about family issues again, John Holden stood. "It's late. My wife needs her rest."

As usual, I'd outstayed my welcome. I followed John to the door, while Sheriff Daniel offered more condolences and assurances that we would catch the killer soon.

On my way out, I offered my hand to Holden who took it. "The problem with your theory is that in order to feel guilt," I said, "one must feel remorse. Deadeye doesn't feel either one—it's one of the things that makes him so dangerous."

On the way to Daniel's vehicle, I scanned the vast property around us. There were so many places to hide, so many ways to simply vanish into the lush landscape.

As if he could read my mind, Daniel said, "Don't worry. We'll find him. No one knows this land better than my team."

I nodded in agreement as we drove away from the Holden property. As we traveled along the country roads, Daniel avoided any conversation about the Holdens. Instead, we talked about how rare stranger killings, or random shootings, are. Most killers know their victims, and this difference made Deadeye's acts very unsettling. He certainly wasn't the first to think of committing his serial murders in a remote area—there had been others who killed in national forests, killing hikers on desolate trails. With very few witnesses in these remote areas, serial killers fare a better chance of continuing their murders undetected. These crimes were different because there was a higher level of hubris involved, a risk-taking that told me he believed his actions were sanctioned, as if God ordered the killings.

At their core, though, serial killers were hunters. Hunters of humans. They perfected the act of watching others and hiding in plain sight. I liked to think of them as the camouflaged among us, the ones who purposely created an appearance that didn't stand out in any way. They were our neighbors, our fellow church members, our PTA members. They were the ones we didn't look at twice, and they prided themselves on the ability to fit in, to fool others. And from this place of camouflage they waited...and they watched.

When serial killers attacked, they did so the way a hunter took down a deer—complete surprise. The moment the victim relaxed, the second they settled into the conversation...*boom*. The attack happened so fast it felt like a dream—a nightmare you couldn't escape from. But for the serial killer, this was the moment of sheer pleasure, the release to all the pent-up frustration that rushed out so fast it was like a high.

What the serial killer rarely took into account is that the investigator was also a finely tuned hunter. She also hunted humans, but in a different sort of way. She read the tracks, followed the footsteps, rooted out their hiding places. She prided herself on the ability to mesh into a crowd as well, the same skill the killer used to hide in plain sight. But we had something on our side, a specialized tool that most serial killers seemed to not have access to—intuition.

Somewhere near midnight, I flipped off the bathroom light after my shower and climbed under the covers. My phone's screen glowed with Bennett's image.

"I can smell the chlorine on you all the way down here," she teased. "How is the hotel pool?"

"Nothing like the resort." I groaned. "It's about eight strokes from one end to the other."

"Lots of flip turns." Bennett yawned. "You know, you're the only woman I'd stay up until midnight to FaceTime."

I grinned and blew the screen a kiss. "Thank you."

Bennett listened with interest as I detailed some of the day's highlights for her. Bennett, like everyone else remotely involved with law enforcement, was greatly interested in Deadeye. She'd also been a secondary forensic pathologist on two of the past victims with Dr. Michael Duncan, the Simmons County coroner.

"He's a scourge," she said. "A total narcissist. Misogyny is Duncan's middle name."

"Wow, Ben, tell me what you really think."

Bennett rarely spoke ill of a colleague, but I'd noticed she didn't always play well with other coroners. I chalked it up to some kind of professional rivalry, given Bennett's penchant for competition and love of winning.

"He always has to be right, even when he isn't. You're forewarned."

"I'll keep that in mind for tomorrow's postmortem evaluation."

I studied her in my screen. It always amazed me how Bennett could do virtually nothing but shower and shake out her wet hair and look so stunning. Without her glasses, the green of her eyes shone through. Ultimately, I understood that Bennett wanted more than anything to be a part of the case. She'd spent the day kayaking and reading, two activities she loved. But she was itching to get back to work and anxious to help out with the Deadeye case. Duncan didn't want our help, and from what I'd witnessed so far, he had it covered, which only added fuel to Bennett's irritation.

After we disconnected, I lay in the dark and wondered if sleep would come at all. My trick of a long swim at night to physically wear my body out usually worked, but not tonight.

My brain churned until my thoughts landed on a comparison: Deadeye and the sniper who thrived on terrorism. There were differences between the two, of course. Snipers generally killed from a distance, not point-blank. However, both made the act of murder impersonal, which also made their method of killing terrifying— everything was indiscriminate and based on perfect timing. Anyone at virtually any time could become their victim. These types of killers took away all the elements that many other killers found irresistibly arousing: the pleading for mercy, the promises to never tell a soul, the tears full of fear and hopelessness, the gasping of breath, the way the body fought to cling to life until the lifeless roll of the eyes skimmed over to tell the killer that no one was home in that body any longer. So many serial killers savored these last moments with a body, living for the second they fully took control of the situation and told the victim to just let go. The killer often relived the way piss ran down the victim's leg or the way the whites of the eyes cracked red with strangulation. While these acts completely turned my stomach, enjoying such a close-up view of a fierce death required not only sickness, but also some twisted kind of bravery. To watch without turning away, to listen to the cries for life without flinching, and to follow through with the evil one had begun—in my mind, at least, this took guts.

A sniper, though, or a killer like Deadeye, was exactly the opposite—a coward. He simply fired, took his trophy, and then hid from the murder's aftermath in the safety of society. Many serial killers saw the cleanup of a body as part of the act, something they worked hard to perfect and manage on their own. It took a level of commitment and self-discipline. Guys like Deadeye left their messes for everyone else to clean up and thrilled themselves with the blatant brutality of the crimes. They could explode at any time, their behavior difficult to anticipate. And our work on the task force put us directly within angry crosshairs. Everyone in the field was at risk.

Even me.

CHAPTER SEVEN

Simmons County
Saturday, 9:00 a.m.
Day 2 of the investigation

Sometimes the best news an investigator can get in an active serial case is news of a survivor. When word came that we might have two survivors of Deadeye near Lake Erie in Longston, Ohio, my hopes brightened. With any luck, the survivors saw the killer's face and possibly recognized him. These were the fears that haunted a serial killer and kept him up at night imagining possible arrest scenarios. They knew as well as I did that most serial killers are caught because someone survives them. Someone lives to tell. Jeffrey Dahmer and Ted Bundy were both apprehended because a victim lived and was able to guide the police to the killer's location.

Longston was the northeastern equivalent of Simmons County—rural, conservative, and a mecca for hunters and campers. They had a small police station, but the sheriff's office handled most of the crime in the area. I pulled in next to Sheriff Daniel who was waiting for me. I'd missed him at the station, so we'd both driven ourselves.

"This could be a real long shot," Sheriff Daniel told me, adjusting his leather coat over his broad shoulders. "They don't sound convinced of a connection, particularly since it occurred when Deadeye was incarcerated."

I caught up with Daniel's long strides toward the building.

"It's worth checking out," I said. "The partner could have been active while Deadeye was locked up."

David Johnson's home was near Mansfield, about an hour's drive from Longston. The local police had a close watch on his family's residence and anyone else he had communicated with while in prison. There had been no reported sightings of him in that area since the prison break, fueling my theory that Deadeye was still in the Simmons County area.

The Longston County sheriff, Randall Borton, met us at the building's entrance. He wore his official uniform and kept his hand near the Glock prominently displayed on his hip. With his military buzz cut and a height of at least six and a half feet, Borton was an intimidating figure.

Inside the office, Borton briefly introduced Detective Rachel Donovan who was already seated at the table, the investigator who had made the possible connection to Deadeye and prompted our contact.

"Any leads on David Johnson yet? I've got all my people on high alert in case he ventures in this direction," Borton said.

"We're banging away at it," I said with a smile. Borton was clearly fishing for information and wanted control of the meeting. It was his house, so I was willing to give him that control, but we couldn't share everything we knew just yet.

"To be clear," Borton said, "I've only just learned of this possible connection or we would have contacted you earlier."

Exactly one year earlier, two teen girls, sisters, had been hiking along the lake's perimeter. David Johnson had been tucked away in prison at the time of the shooting, but the bullets fired at the teens had been traced back to Johnson's weapon. Ballistics matched the weapon to the one used in all of Deadeye's known cases. Borton had been more than careful to cover his own ass with his claims of having only seen the reports since Deadeye's prison break. He shot Detective Rachel Donovan a stern look, a clear message not to override his statement.

I considered Donovan while her superior spoke of the great detective work in his department. However, he refused to give her the credit. She sat motionless, her hands carefully folded in her lap. Her navy suit jacket was crisp and professional, most likely brand new for this meeting. Her dark hair was parted directly in the center and pulled back into a bun at the base of her neck.

"I'm interested in hearing from Detective Donovan," I said, cutting off the sheriff's lecture on the lack of evidence found at the sisters' scene.

Borton stopped midsentence, irritated at the interruption.

Donovan's dark eyes flickered up to meet mine, something I wanted before I asked any questions.

"You are the one who worked the scene and the victims," I said. "Tell me why you are convinced these cases are connected to Deadeye."

"The killer told the girls they were both lucky to keep their shirts, that he needed to work on his shot. He said he was in a race to catch up, but the girls didn't understand what he meant." Donovan spoke directly to me, her voice surprisingly clear and confident given the circumstances.

At the time of this attack, David Johnson had already been tried and convicted. His methods of killing had been debated and discussed at length in the media. Everyone was talking about the serial killer who stole the very shirts off his victims' backs.

"It could have been a copycat," I said.

"That's what I believed it was until the ballistics report came back. I recognized the AR rifle from the Deadeye case and it turned out to be a match."

"How did these sisters survive the shots?"

Donovan reached for the file on the table and slid two photos toward me. "When the man approached the girls on the hiking path, he told them he was lost. Both girls saw the rifle, and when he continued to ask questions about his location, they ran off the path and into the thick forest. He fired and missed one. He fired again and hit the second sister in the shoulder."

I examined the photograph of the shoulder wound, a very similar image to the one I'd recently seen on Logan Holden. Her shoulder had been shot at a higher angle than Logan's and tore through the body.

"It was a beautiful fall day, and for some reason, the killer didn't count on other hikers in the area. They heard the report of the rifle and came running. The girls believe this is why he did not kill them. He needed to get away from the scene."

I set the photo down on the table between us. "And you?" I asked. "What do you believe?"

Donovan leaned back in her chair, crossed her arms over her chest. "I believe whoever shot at these girls is Deadeye's hunting partner. I also think they have some sort of competition going on between the two of them."

I nearly laughed out loud when I exchanged a look with Sheriff Daniel. I was so grateful to have someone else at least considering the possibility of a partner as a second shooter.

"The phantom partner, if there is one, had to have been working alone," Borton pointed out.

"Yes, but these shootings took place during the opening of gun hunting season," Donovan said. "The shooter told the girls he needed to catch up."

"What do you think that means?" I asked her.

"I believe this is the competition or game between them—who can kill the most. Proof is the bloody shirts. Who's to say this partner wasn't taking advantage of Deadeye's incarceration to secure a few of his own kills? To raise his own numbers?"

I nodded. This detective was smart, and her instincts were sharp. I wanted to know more about her theory. "The girls' survival was quite a risk for this partner," I said. "Why not kill them both when the girls huddled up together in the woods? Or why not go after them at a later date?"

"I'm not sure," Donovan said, "but I think it has something to do with the rules."

"Rules?" Borton asked.

"Yes," I said. "They've set up some kind of a game hunting humans."

Every competition has its own rules, even a deadly game imagined by Deadeye and his hunting partner. If I could understand these so-called rules, these limits they'd set to their killing, then maybe I'd be able to use their own rules to catch Deadeye and his partner at their own game.

Jessica and Kara Silas, along with their father, led us through the mouth of the forested path along Lake Erie. It took some convincing of the girls' parents that their daughters' recollections were vital to our current investigation, but ultimately the father agreed only if he could join us. His desire to see the shooter caught and punished won out over the possible emotional reactions the girls might have to revisiting the place where they'd been hunted down. Daniel, Donovan, and I decided to leave Donovan's boss behind—we really only needed Detective Donovan. She'd been the one to crack the case, and I was most interested in her sharp observations of the crime scene.

"Do you want us to take you to the exact spot?" Kara looked back at me, and then at her sister, the one who had been shot. Jessica held her left shoulder higher than the other while her arm didn't move from its place at her side. The father explained that Jessica had lost most of the movement and strength in her shoulder. Given the extensive damage, it was remarkable she could use the shoulder at all.

The sisters, now aged seventeen and thirteen, had been clear on very few details of the attacker. They both agreed the shooter was a man dressed in all black, Caucasian with a gray stubble of a beard, and was at least the age of their father if not older.

"It would be most helpful to see the spot," I told Kara. "I know this is hard, and I'm sorry."

Kara nodded and turned back toward the path. She took hold of her younger sister's hand.

I was convinced that the two sisters didn't realize how much they had really seen. Trauma had the ability to shut down the brain and allow the body to enter survival mode. My own PTSD had blocked me from my memories of the serial killer who had taken my Marci from me. I always believed I hadn't seen the killer; I believed that he had been very close and watched me as I found Marci. And then he followed when I ran to get help. Throughout the years, my dreams had given me clues, but it wasn't until Marci's case was reopened in Willow's Ridge and I went back to the crime scene that my full memory returned. The killer, I learned, had been so close to me that day he could almost reach out and touch me. I'd blocked out the chase that ensued between us, him following me through the forested quarry where I barely escaped with my life. It took years to simmer and the return to that haunted land before I could face the truth. I imagined that might have been the case for the Silas sisters as well.

The girls eventually stopped where the path opened up along the water, a place where we found ourselves sandwiched between thick woods on one side and a significant drop-off to the lake's edge below. A beautiful spot that was highly secluded. A hikers' paradise.

"He came up behind us around here," Kara said. "I always thought he must have been jogging because we never saw or heard him until he was right on us."

I stepped closer to the girls. "Think back the best you can. Was he sweating?"

Both girls considered me a moment, and then looked to each other. "No."

The man hadn't been running, at least not for very long. "What kind of shoes was he wearing?"

Kara looked down at her own feet. "Boots. Like yours."

I kicked a foot forward. "Black ones? Above the ankle?"

She nodded. Military-style combat boots and dressed completely in black. He definitely wasn't jogging. He'd been hiding in the forest along the path waiting for his prey to come along. And then he jumped out behind them.

"He said that he'd gotten turned around on all the paths back here and couldn't find his way out." Jessica finally spoke.

"Did you believe him?" I asked.

Jessica shook her head. "There is really only one path through these woods. It's the one we are on, and it goes for twenty miles. There are places to get off the path, but it's definitely not hard to know where you are."

I nodded and let the girls sit with my silence a moment—I wanted to give them space to think. The similarities of this case to the two brothers recently shot were startling. Just like these sisters, the brothers believed the person was lost and in need of directions. In both cases, the young people were shot in isolated locations with little visibility. And then there was the connection of the shoulder wound on two of them. Whoever shot the girls shot the Holden brothers.

It was Jessica who filled the silence. "He asked us to show him the way out so he could get back to his car." Jessica gnawed at her thumbnail. She'd been gravely injured that day, and I was willing to bet she'd been dreaming of the crime since it happened. "He said he had a dog in the car and it would be really sick with the hot sun. If the dog died, he said his wife would not forgive him. And then he turned around and we saw the long black rifle strapped to his back."

"You knew it was a rifle?"

Kara nodded. "It looked like my dad's. In his Army pictures from Afghanistan."

She recognized the AR-15 as the military version, M4. There was very little difference between the weapons.

"What happened next?" I asked.

"Kara told me to run, and she took off. I was scared and confused, so I was moving really slow. I couldn't figure out what to do. I wanted to help the man because of the dog, but I knew something might be wrong. I'd just started running when he fired at Kara and missed. Then he hit me in the back."

"With a bullet," I clarified. "Where did you fall?"

She led me off-path and into the thicket of underbrush. I waited for her to catch her bearings while the memories resurfaced. Jessica eventually pointed to a large tree.

"How do you know you fell here?" I asked when we both made our way to the spot.

"The tree," Jessica said, running her open palm over its trunk. "The bark was so rough. And I remember this hump on the side."

A tree tumor. It certainly made the tree distinctive. She'd fallen forward with the shot and into the tree's trunk.

"Sheriff Daniel, stay at the spot where he approached them," I said. "Detective Donovan, go with Kara to the spot where she was when the shots fired."

I waited with Jessica, both of us listening to the sounds of her sister's voice.

Jessica took advantage of our few minutes alone together. "You are going to catch him, right?"

"Yeah," I said. "And when we do, you can tell him all about the pain he's caused you. About all the things he tried to take from you but didn't."

She nodded. "I really want to do that."

"Good, because he really needs to hear it." I looked back toward the path. Daniel was nearly hidden by the foliage, and this was winter. In the bloom of fall, he would have been impossible to see. "Do you remember anything from when you were on the ground? Any sounds?"

"Kara. She was screaming and begging for help. Other people were trying to help us. They were looking for us."

"How do you know? Did you hear them?"

Jessica's shrug told me she couldn't be sure. "Maybe Kara told me that."

"Right about here!" Donovan waved.

I considered the distance between all of us, and thought of something. "Kara, when the shots fired and you realized Jessica was down, you ran back for her, correct?"

She agreed, and I wondered why the shooter didn't take the opportunity to shoot Kara as she came back for her sister. It had been one of my biggest questions all along. The shooter must have known she'd come back to help her hurt sibling, and if this was a competition for kills, why not take them both out with what could have been an easy shot?

"Jessica, I need you to really think back. Did the shooter curse when he realized you weren't dead? Did he say *anything*?"

Tears filled the young teen's eyes, and I knew we needed to stop or we risked pushing her too far. And then Jessica's sister called out, "I remember!" I heard Kara making her way down to us before I saw her. "He said that we didn't count, so we got to keep our shirts."

With Kara's words, everything shifted into place for me. In this sick hunting game, he couldn't count these two as kills or take the trophy because neither had been killed on the first shot. The goal was one clean shot to death, and the victims' shirts/jackets became not only the proof of that but also the trophy. Images flashed in my mind of some kind of hunting cabin or a hidden bunker. Bloody and holey clothing was tacked up on the walls. The taken clothing wasn't so much about the blood or gunpowder on them. It was all about pride—and bragging rights.

CHAPTER EIGHT

Longston County
Saturday, 3:00 p.m.

Detective Rachel Donovan sat across the booth from Sheriff Daniel and me. Her dark hair was sleek and straight without a single strand misplaced from the bun tight against the nape of her neck. She'd perched a pair of aviator sunglasses on top of her head even though the coming winter had already darkened the afternoon skies.

We'd stopped to eat after finishing up with the sisters' statements and combing through the files. I was starving and ready to eat everything on the menu, something I strongly reconsidered as I looked over at Donovan. Somewhere in her midthirties, this detective took her weight lifting seriously. I could see the push and pull of her defined muscles underneath her button-up shirt. Daniel, apparently, noticed it, too.

"You work with a trainer?" he asked. I listened as the two talked repetitions, weights, and lifting styles while I avoided the beer in front of me.

When I'd been in the bathroom, Daniel had ordered for me. He smiled at me when I returned and said, "You strike me as a beer drinker, Hansen." It was a kind gesture, a move that said he saw me as a member of his team. The offer of alcohol hit me at a low point, though; I was dealing with two of the red flags in the twelve-step program's Hungry Angry Lonely Tired watch list. I was hungry and tired from our hike in the forest and in need of a good swim. Nothing sounded better to me at that moment than a drink much harder than a beer, and then about ten more. The problem was, alcohol, for me, was like a switch in my brain. Once it had been flipped, I couldn't seem to unflip it.

Bennett had been on me to attend twelve-step meetings in our area. We had one at work for members of BCI who struggled with sobriety, so it wasn't difficult to find a meeting at a convenient time. I blamed Bennett for trying to control me when she brought the issue up. I blamed her when she didn't bring the issue up. The truth was I blamed just about everyone but myself. I could have used the extra support, but I wasn't about to sit in a roomful of men and women I worked with and spill my guts. If I wouldn't share my feelings and stress with a partner, how in the world would I ever be able to share with a group of people?

"That's why you should go to a meeting where everyone is a stranger to you," Bennett had told me. "Then you don't have to worry about what anyone thinks or says about you outside the meeting." She'd called me a stubborn goat for refusing to take her advice, or anyone else's for that matter.

Stubborn goat. I reached for the beer and held the chilled bottle in my palm. And then I took a long pull from the bottle. The cold bubbly liquid filled my mouth and tasted so good, I closed my eyes to savor it.

"Hansen?" Donovan said. "You asked to see the additions to the original files. I have them here." She pulled a thick folder from her bag and slid it across the booth. "I can't thank you two enough for taking the time with this case. I know the sheriff didn't give you much hope."

I flipped open the folder and scanned over the crime scene and victim photos and continued on to the notes. "When you do this work long enough," I told her, "you can smell when a detective has thoroughly done their work and when they haven't. Your sheriff didn't pass my sniff test."

Donovan laughed for the first time since we'd met her. The seriousness of her demeanor faded a bit, and I understood that her quietness could have been insecurity, particularly around a bullheaded boss like Sheriff Borton. I knew firsthand what it meant to have male colleagues outright dismiss your work for no other reason than your gender.

"You've got a good eye, Donovan," I said. "You caught something and pushed on it so that nothing slipped through the cracks. We need to be thanking you. I hope you will continue working with our team. If you need to be here, we could video-conference the task force meetings."

Donovan hesitated, and her stone-serious face returned. "I'd... yes, but what about...?"

"Borton? I'll clear it with him," I said. I sensed Detective Rachel Donovan wanted out of the sheriff's office, and I was willing to offer her an escape route. I was interested to see whether or not she'd take it in the days to come. "What records do you have of any interviews conducted at the scene?"

While we waited for our food, Donovan flipped through the files and talked us through the small collection of eyewitness accounts. There were only three people in the direct area of the shooting, one of whom called 911 when he heard the shots fired. No one claimed to see anyone running from the scene or anyone carrying a rifle.

"How fast were the girls taken from the scene? In all the chaos, it might have been easy for the killer to pretend to be a witness."

Donovan agreed. "I thought of that, too," she said. "But the sisters did not select any of our witnesses' photos in a six-pack."

All three men had given local addresses. "Did you follow up?" I asked. "Track these men down at their homes or workplaces?"

"They are real addresses and the records check out," she said. "That's about as far as I got before I was assigned another case. Basically, we found a whole lot of nothing. It's as if these girls were shot by a ghost."

A ghost. I understood exactly what Donovan meant by that reference—it was as if Deadeye and his partner committed a vanishing act after the murders. They had such an uncanny ability to meld into the landscape and somehow keep any possible suspicion at bay.

"I'm guessing you don't get too many shootings in Longston County," I said. "You're a green detective to be assigned an attempted murder. Were there other reasons for your interest in the case?"

"It struck me as a possible connection to Deadeye because of the way it went down," Donovan said. "I'd also just started working in Longston, so this was the first case I caught."

I finally understood why this detective had gone to such lengths to get the sisters' case to us. Her *first*—no one forgets her first—and to have it go unsolved…well, that's some very bad luck for a first-time detective. The older detectives always hope a murder goes smooth for the rookies, that the frayed ends are quickly tied up, and that all the questions are answered. It gives the detective confidence in their abilities, and maybe even more importantly, confidence in the justice system. This unsolved case must have eaten at Donovan, nagged at the corners of her mind, and called out to her in her sleep. For Donovan, this was the case that never let her go. Since I'd started working at BCI, I learned we all had at least one of those. My one case had been the murder of Marci Tucker. Even now, with the killers deceased, it still nagged at me.

Donovan leaned back against the booth and settled her dark gaze on me. "It irritated me that so many people in the community said this was only a hunting accident. People in town thought the shooter was hunting with an illegal weapon, so he ran when he realized he'd hurt the girl. They claimed *he* was scared. As if the girls didn't matter. And it took responsibility off the shooter for his actions. It didn't sit well with me, I guess."

"It's the double-edged sword of being a hunting community," Daniel said. "It's the income for the town, but it brings with it danger."

"Not all hunters are irresponsible, gun-toting fools," Donovan added, flashing her license.

Daniel laughed, clearly delighted with the knowledge that Donovan was a hunter. Once again, I listened as they swapped stories and strategies about an activity I had little knowledge of and couldn't really participate in the conversation.

"What do you hunt?" I asked.

Donovan grinned. "Anything I can eat. One day I hope to truly live off the land. For now, I only take what I need and nothing more."

Both Daniel and I were truly impressed. I listened to them as they talked about different rifles and guns and favorite hunting areas in Ohio. After a few minutes, Donovan turned to me. "Have you ever been hunting?"

"Twice. My dad and his partner tried to take me deer hunting one year. It was a disaster." I laughed. "He couldn't get me to fire on any living thing no matter how hard he tried."

"What did you use, a rifle?" She waited for my nod. "He should have started you off with a bow. Bow hunting is more humane and easier for kids learning the sport."

Daniel gave an amazed whistle. "Bow hunting is hard work," he said. "You're like that girl in the movies—what's her name? My kids drug me to the theater…"

"Katniss Everdeen," I said.

Donovan grinned. "I've definitely heard that one before."

I finished my beer before the food arrived and wanted nothing more than to signal the server for another. But I needed to stop now before I couldn't; I needed my mind clear for the drive back to Simmons County.

"How about you go on the night hunt with Donovan and me."

"I'm assuming a night hunt is exactly what it sounds like?" I asked.

Daniel grinned. "Sure is. We have an unofficial one every season."

"Why unofficial?"

"Regulations don't allow for night hunting," Donovan explained. "They say it's dangerous, but there is nothing more fun than putting on those night goggles and tearing through the woods with a bunch of hunters during gun season."

"Hmmm, sounds like a really safe game," I deadpanned.

Daniel laughed. "You haven't lived until you've tried it. This year's big event is tomorrow night, so you're in luck. As the sheriff of Simmons County, I can legally issue you a hunting license."

I directed Donovan back to the case and asked her to do a reevaluation into the three eyewitnesses' addresses and check into places of employment. I also suggested she show up on-site without warning—I wanted to see how these witnesses would react to her in their own space, particularly given that just about everyone in Ohio had heard about the latest murders and Deadeye's prison break. Donovan's arrival and the resurgence of questions could possibly stoke a guilty conscience.

My phone vibrated against my hip, but I ignored it. I'd get to my messages later.

As Daniel and Donovan continued their conversation about the eyewitnesses, I thought about the first hunt I'd ever really been on. I'd gone with my dad and his longtime work partner, Detective Roy Tyson. We didn't have to go far from home—I was from Chesterton and the land was as rural and hunter friendly as it was in Simmons County. The three of us set off one frosty morning at daybreak, Tyson and my dad with ammunition and gun bags, and me with my pockets secretly filled with carrots. I'd heard that deer liked carrot and apple slices best, and that they would follow a trail of these treats if you left one for them. I had no interest in leading any animal to its death; I just wanted to get close enough to watch the deer. Maybe even touch them.

I'd been shooting with my dad since I was big enough to hold a rifle. We had target shooting out behind our house with overripe pumpkins and bales of hay with targets tacked to them. When I could hit the mark two out of three shots, it was time for me to take those skills toward a moving target—something that was alive. But there was a problem, at least in the eyes of my hunter father—I didn't want to kill anything with a heartbeat, particularly something as defenseless as a deer.

"You might have to kill one day to protect yourself," my dad told me. "It might come down to you or the enemy. And I want it to be him, Lucy-girl. You need to know how to shoot."

As we loaded up for that day of hunting, I knew as well as any hunter that I wouldn't be put in any danger because of a deer. So I banked on the hope that we wouldn't come across any, and I wouldn't have to fire at all. I enjoyed being in the forest with my dad and Tyson, listening as the two of them talked about their current cases and workload. Their voices, I hoped, would chase away any live creatures. A haphazard line of carrot bits trailed behind us until the sun was high in the sky and my pockets were empty. I'd hoped to feed the deer but didn't realize that my carrot treats could bait them by bringing them into danger. We'd been out for what felt like hours and had seen nothing more than squirrels and a possible red fox, which Tyson argued was really a possum. As we doubled back for the long walk back to the truck, we came across a younger deer and her mother not more than twenty feet away.

My dad grabbed my coat, yanking me behind a tree. With the wave of his hands and excited gestures, I understood—he wanted me to shoot one or both of the deer. I took my time getting lined up, the long rifle secure against my shoulder. The deer, to my dismay, didn't use that time to scamper off into the woods. As I lined up my scope, I saw what the deer were doing—I'd dropped about ten round medallions of carrot in that one location. They ate the carrots happily, oblivious to their current danger.

"Come on," Tyson nudged me. "Take the shot."

I had the mother in my line of fire. I watched her chomp the carrot I'd laid out for her. And then I jerked the rifle up and shot into the branches of the trees. I thought I'd saved the deer, but I hadn't been watching Tyson. He fired when I did, his shell taking down the younger deer. As my dad's work partner and best friend, Tyson had spent many hours with me at our home. I loved him, but at that moment, I hated him with a fury that raged inside me. I stood and watched as he cheered over the dead animal with tears burning in my eyes.

In a few days' time, Tyson had the meat off the carcass and invited my dad and me over for one of his favorite meals—fried deer strips and mashed potatoes. I picked at the meat, its toughness lodging in my throat. Tyson said the deer was so small there was no reason to keep the head, and my stomach turned. The young deer's death, I knew, was on me. I'd been the one who left the trail of carrot slices.

"Child," Tyson chided me from across the table, "eat up! We don't want anything to go to waste."

I mumbled under my breath, "The deer's death was a waste."

My father shot me a warning look, but Tyson only laughed. "Lucy, we saved that deer from a painful death by a truck on the highway. Or the gut-wrenching slow death of starvation." He took another bite and watched me as he chewed the meat. "Girls," he said and rolled his eyes at my dad as if it was a joke, as if my gender was the joke.

It took a very long time for me to regain the respect I'd lost for Tyson that day. My father had been right—I did learn a lot by hunting with them. I learned that sanctified hunting had the power to bring out ruthless behavior in otherwise nonruthless people. And I learned, female or not, I never wanted to be one of those ruthless people.

My phone buzzed again, and I checked the screen. Both calls had come from a Columbus area code. I excused myself and listened to my voicemail.

Lucinda Hansen, a woman's voice said. *I've been asked to contact you regarding Colby Sanders.*

That sharp pebble dropped inside my gut once again.

This is a care team leader at the Ohio State Hospital in Columbus. You are on Mr. Sanders's call list along with Dr. Harper Bennett. Please return my call as soon as possible.

The breath caught inside my throat. Something was wrong with Colby Sanders. My stomach hollowed with the thought of Bennett— she must have known. Why else would she have been on Sanders's call list? My gut clenched with the thought that Bennett didn't just know something was going on with Sanders. She'd chosen to keep that information from me.

CHAPTER NINE

Columbus, Ohio
Saturday, 6:20 p.m.

I moved to Spring Rock to be closer to Bennett, and my life changed. I fell into the rhythm of the river that flowed not far from my house, a constant, steady stream that helped me to settle into my new space. Happy to be rid of the college-student neighbors, I reveled in the sheer quiet of the evenings and the ability to park my truck just about anywhere I wanted. I'd been in my new home almost two months when Bennett presented her idea of a pact for clean living.

The pact, as Bennett called it, was my nightmare—no processed foods, no sugar, no red meat. And the real kicker: no alcohol. Bennett overreacted to anyone who didn't follow her ideals of health, so it didn't surprise me when she said she believed my drinking was a problem. Even though she never used the word *alcoholic*, she pushed me to go to twelve-step meetings. At this point, I was already smitten with Bennett and wanted to live inside her curls that smelled like summer. I couldn't forget the trip we'd taken together after the Wallace Lake case ended, a weeklong vacation kayaking through the Florida Keys. Truthfully, I would have agreed to about anything if only Bennett and I could go back to that bliss-filled week in South Florida once again.

I'd managed to maneuver out of too many harsh agreements until Bennett stopped by one night on her way home from a late shift, surprising me more than halfway through a bottle of wine. I'd been saving it for a special occasion, and the occasion did indeed feel special—I'd spent the day hammering in a new hardwood floor to the kitchen and bedroom of my bungalow. That evening I sat in a lawn chair watching the colors of the sunset fade while I tossed the tennis ball across the yard for the dog.

By the time I neared the end of the bottle, darkness descended and Gus had given up the tennis ball for a bone. He spread out on the cool night grass close enough where he could keep an eye on the back door and me. He'd quickly become that great furry friend always at my side since I'd welcomed him into my home. I adopted Gus from Albert Finley, one of the key players in the crimes at Wallace Lake. Albert was sentenced to hard time for his actions, and he'd begged Bennett to find a good home for his best friend. Bennett brought the dog to me, and I couldn't let him go. I held great respect for Albert; in the end, he'd been the one who held the key to solving the case, and he'd chosen me as his confidant. That took guts and a whole boatload of trust. I visited Albert in prison to assure him I'd care for Gus until he got out, and Albert just shook his head and blinked back the tears that filled his eyes.

"Gus"—Albert choked up on his words—"is such a lucky dog to have you."

I wasn't convinced. Every morning and evening when I made the walk along the river's edge with Gus, I knew that I was the one who got lucky.

When Bennett joined Gus and me in the backyard that night, I lifted my feet off the only other lawn chair and motioned for her to join us. The dog nuzzled his wet nose against her hand and she buried her fingers deep into his fur, giving his skin a good rub. Bennett was still in her scrubs, something she didn't normally wear outside the office, a clue that she'd had a long and tiring shift. The patio lights shone off the rims of her glasses while hiding the rest of her face in shadow.

As she detailed the day's long cases, I offered her the remainder of the bottle.

Bennett shook her head. "I thought you weren't going to drink anymore," she said, watching me empty the bottle into my glass.

I groaned. I didn't want to have this conversation—again. I only wanted to turn off all the outside lights and spread out on the cool lawn with Bennett and Gus while we searched the cloudless sky for different constellations. I wanted to forget about our jobs and all our responsibilities, if only for the night.

Bennett reached for my hand. "I'm sorry," she said, winding her warm fingers with mine. "I just don't want you to fall back into that place."

That place. I knew what she was talking about—the dank, dark hole of depression that had nearly consumed me before the Wallace Lake case. It was true that I'd spent too many weeks in the wake of a bad breakup wallowing in alcohol and my crappy apartment. That hole, just like so many of the others I'd fallen into in my life, felt very far away. Most days, I hardly remembered them.

"I want you to be happy," she said. "I want *us* to be happy."

I bristled. I didn't like the insinuation that our entire relationship rested on my actions alone. Beside me, Gus rolled over and let his paws wave in the air, begging for a belly rub, giving me the perfect reason to drop her hand.

"Let's not do this tonight. Please."

"I thought you wanted to do this clean living plan with me. I thought you wanted to get stronger."

"I do."

"But you won't make any promises. You won't go to meetings."

"Come on, Ben. I don't need any meetings."

Alcoholism was a hot-button issue because of Bennett's father. His drinking and gambling addiction ruled most of Bennett's young life as he drank and gambled away the family's money. She told me that her childhood house felt like it was made of glass—one wrong step and it could all shatter. And it often did. Once Bennett went to college, she'd severed ties with her father and rarely saw her mother. Bennett didn't talk much about her childhood, but I understood the smell of whiskey and bourbon haunted her and that hidden bottles of any kind had the power to send her into a blinding rage. The bottom line for both of us was the traumas of our past carried significant weight, a weight we couldn't quite figure out how to maneuver around.

"If you won't go to meetings," Bennett said, "please go visit Eli. He can help."

Dr. Eli Weaver. I'd spoken to Bennett about him before, but I figured she'd gotten the majority of that information from Sanders. Eli was a professor of Religious Studies who specialized in ex-gay ministries. He'd been a valuable resource for the Willow's Ridge case, and because of our shared history with ex-gay ministries, he'd also become a friend. Dr. Eli ran a support group for people who'd been traumatized by ex-gay ministries, something he regularly invited me to attend. I hadn't taken him up on his offer.

I wanted to tell Bennett that I would agree to whatever she wanted, that I'd stop eating meat and sugar and chocolate if it made her happy. I wanted to tell her I'd focus more on my workouts, that I'd build strength and endurance in this new clean body, and that a drop of liquor wouldn't pass my lips. All of that seemed so much easier than telling Bennett the truth: a small, soft animal lived inside me who wanted exactly what it wanted. I didn't tell Bennett that this animal sometimes couldn't be satiated, or that in my heart of hearts I knew exactly what it was hanging around for—my eventual self-destruction. The mere thought of that conversation completely overwhelmed me to the point of near paralysis. Rather than go to that blinding and aching truth, I chose the easier path—I agreed to Bennett's terms. And then I gulped down the rest of the wine in the bottle.

I thought about that night in my yard with Bennett as I pushed through the hospital doors and took the elevator to the surgery recovery rooms. I thought about how much Sanders had kept from me in the last few months, and I thought about how you could never really know another person.

The hospital room was empty and cold—no flowers or cards to wish Colby Sanders a speedy return to good health. Until recently, Sanders had had very little contact with his two grown children. Lately he'd been in touch with his youngest, but I was willing to bet neither child nor any other member of his family had been notified about Sanders's health. No one had been told anything about his surgery except, apparently, Bennett.

Before I left the sheriff's office for the hospital, I called Bennett in South Carolina and demanded some answers.

"Don't be angry with either of us," Bennett started. "He needed my medical advice, and I promised him I wouldn't tell you about the cancer."

"Why *not* tell me?" I couldn't for the life of me fathom why either would make the decision that I shouldn't know about my mentor and good friend's health crisis.

"We didn't want to upset you."

I unpacked that response over and over again along the hundred-mile drive from Simmons to the Columbus OSU hospital. The message I heard underneath Bennett's words: *You are too weak to handle this. I'm afraid of what you might do to yourself with this information.*

Truth be told, I was afraid of where I might go with it as well. That fear didn't stop me from rushing to Sanders's side, though.

I pushed through the closed curtain and stepped inside the small room. Careful not to wake Sanders, I sank into an armchair near his bed. It took me a few moments before I could fully look at Sanders—before I could really *see* him. Instead I looked out of the room's large window while blinking back my tears. The window overlooked the roof of another portion of the mammoth hospital, and beyond that, the shining lights of the Ohio State football stadium.

When I finally looked closely at Sanders, the man before me was almost unrecognizable. The hospital bed and gown engulfed him and made him look so small. His iron-gray hair that was normally so neatly combed to the side stood up in haphazard clumps. Silvery beard stubble, probably a few days old, made him look even older. Tubing ran from a port underneath the gown and across his collarbone connecting to the machine beside his bed. The port's very presence raised questions: How much chemotherapy would he need? Were they able to get everything in surgery or had the cancer spread? Tears ran from my eyes, and I had to turn away. It was difficult to see a man I'd always known as strong and powerful appear so exposed—so incredibly fragile.

Almost four years ago, on my very first day as a special agent with BCI, I set off the security buzzer on my way into the main building. I was nervous, sweating profusely, and horrified to find that my new boss stood by watching carefully as the guard ran the security wand around my body. I blushed when the guard finally found the culprit—the zipper on my new dress pants. I hated the pleated slacks and jacket that made me feel like a kid playing the part of a grown up. When the guard finally cleared me, I made my way over to Sanders. Despite his average height, he was a larger-than-life figure; his reputation demanded respect. I wanted the floor to crack open and swallow me whole.

"I have great hopes for you," Sanders said, walking me to the elevator.

"I'll do my best, sir."

The elevator doors closed behind us, and for a few seconds, we were alone.

After an uncomfortable silence, he said, "It was all you, Hansen."

"I'm sorry?"

"I wanted you to know," he said, avoiding my gaze by watching the changing floor numbers, "you got this job on your own merits, your own skills and talents. Your father was a good man and an even greater detective, but your hire had nothing to do with him."

The elevator jolted as it arrived on the third floor, and I wondered if Sanders heard the sound of my breath releasing, like I had been holding it for days and was finally able to let it go. He'd finally answered the hard questions that had been knocking around in my brain since I'd received the interview call for BCI. *Is this all because Sanders knows my father? Is this all because he feels sorry for me, or is it some sort of penance to my dad?*

The elevator buzzed, and right before Sanders stepped out of the opening doors, he said, "Welcome aboard. We're lucky to have you."

I followed Director Sanders out of that elevator. My shoulders finally dropped from their chronic tensed position near my ears, and I stood taller than I had only moments before in that oversized pantsuit.

I'd seen Sanders only a few weeks prior to that elevator meeting at my father's funeral. My father had been the police chief for many years in our small town, a department of only seven, but his work brought him into contact with officers and detectives from all over the state. Colby Sanders was different in that he had gone through the academy with my father. After, they chose different routes. My father returned to his hometown while Sanders moved through the ranks of the FBI. My dad always said that it didn't matter if he hadn't seen Sanders for a few years or not, the minute they met up again, it always felt like old times. Maybe it was my father's feelings about Sanders, or it could have been the jitters of my first day and my need to cling to something hopeful—anything. Whatever it was, I chose to believe Sanders in the elevator that day. I chose to believe that my familial ties didn't matter, despite the unspoken rule that law enforcement liked to stick with its own. When I walked into my very own office for the first time, I couldn't have been more loyal to Director Colby Sanders.

The hospital's overhead speaker spouted a slew of nursing calls, and the squabbling noise brought me back to the artificial bright lights of the hospital room. Sanders opened his eyes, slowly peeling one eyelid open at a time to reveal the slate blue irises. Throughout the years of Sanders's investigative work, many described his eyes as cold and detached. Some even said it was the icy eye color that gave him an edge in the interrogation room. But I saw those same eyes in a much different way. Welcoming. Kind. Generous.

"Dammit, Hansen." Sanders tried to hoist himself up in the bed with his elbows, then grumbled with the pain as he thought better of it. "How did you find out about all this, anyway?"

"Ah! You've underestimated me, Sanders."

"I should know better." His voice was hoarse and dry from the anesthesia. "That gut of yours is sometimes *too* spot-on."

"We can't blame my intuitiveness this time. You had me listed on your medical contact list—the nurse called."

Sanders rolled his eyes—he'd forgotten to update his contact list before the surgery. "I'm sorry you had to find out like that. I didn't want to worry you."

"Too late for that."

Sanders proceeded to make a lot of noise about me showing up, but he didn't fool me for a minute. I saw the smile tease the edges of his mouth; he was genuinely happy to see me. I was relieved to see the sleepy fog in his eyes clearing as he became more alert.

"I meant to call you back about the case—I'm sorry. Time has gotten away from me in here."

I shrugged. "It's fine, really. The case can wait." I didn't want Sanders to worry about the case—he had enough to worry about at the moment. "How are you feeling? Can I get you anything?"

"No, thanks. Tell me what's been going on, Hansen."

"Maybe I could call the nurse for you now that you're awake?"

"If you can't scrub my body clean of this life-sucking cancer, then at least bother me with the case."

"Sanders…"

He closed his eyes and took a deep breath as if to calm himself before speaking. When he opened his eyes, the blue-gray steel of them settled on me. "Hansen, please. I *need* to work."

I understood. Like me, Sanders thrived on work. We both needed active cases to keep our minds busy and to stay grounded in our life's purpose. I understood why Sanders needed work now more than ever as illness loomed all around him.

"David Johnson is still on the lam, but we have a few leads. There could be a tie with the survivalists or preppers. I think Johnson is still in the Simmons County area, but he has help staying off the radar. Sheriff Daniel delivered a press statement this evening. We're moving ahead, though I'm not sure where we're going at the moment."

Sanders smiled. "That's the best way to begin, you know—unsure of the route. I'm proud of you, Hansen. You took that plunge."

"Before you get too complimentary," I warned him, "let me catch that bastard."

"I have no doubt you will. I wish you believed in your abilities as much as I do. Tell me more about your theory."

I laughed. Sanders knew me too well—I always had some kind of theory going even if I hadn't told anyone about it yet. I opened my laptop and displayed a few screens, moving my chair closer to him. "Deadeye has a partner."

"Working with another person would certainly up the stakes," Sanders said, taking the laptop from me. He examined the profile I'd built for Deadeye's partner: Caucasian, male, aged thirty-five to fifty, mission oriented with possible experience in the military.

Ritualistic, controlling, and very neat and organized. Likely had a college education.

Sanders rubbed the stubble of his chin with his thumb. "What is the partner's role in all this?"

"Here it is. I think he helped to plan Deadeye's escape and lined up vehicles filled with necessities," I said. "The nurse, Debbie Turner, could only take Deadeye so far. This person picked up where Debbie left off. Deadeye may be a murderer, but I think it was the partner who killed those brothers. The partner has a stake in this as well. A message, perhaps."

"Interesting. Why not Deadeye? For the murders?"

"He was there," I clarified. "But the shots weren't his. Deadeye goes for the single kill shot to the head. These were both chest wounds, as if the killer was aiming for the heart."

I clicked open the Holdens' autopsy photographs for Sanders. He maneuvered around the photos.

"I don't know why they're both killing," I said. "We've always thought Deadeye picked his victims at random. He chose people based on their location and whether or not he could be alone with them. We've always attributed the cross-gender killing to this idea." It was rare for serial killers to kill outside their gender, just as it was rare for serial killers to kill outside their own race.

I continued, "But we haven't fully addressed the age of the victims. All have been between fourteen and twenty-six—young people, on the verge of lives of their own."

"Lost youth. Regret, possibly," Sanders said. "Do you think he stalked the victims? Followed young people out into rural areas?"

"I'm wondering if he knew each of his victims."

Sanders leaned his head back on a pillow and looked up at the ceiling. "It's possible he did. That would explain why they didn't initially try to get away from the shooter. Deadeye also displays predatory behavior and likely followed them. He loves the hunt, the cat-and-mouse chase—that's what sexually arouses him. In order for it to be satisfying, though, he needs a worthwhile opponent. A younger person certainly fits that bill."

"We've always known Deadeye wasn't local to the Simmons County area," I said. "He drove in on the weekends to Simmons County to kill and then left the area. But"—I held up my index finger like an exclamation mark—"we never had any evidence of a partner. What if *he* is local? Not just local, but a trusted and visible member of the Simmons County community. This gives Deadeye a cover—if he's seen with a prominent local, no one questions who he is or why he's there."

Sanders considered carefully what I'd said. "Wasn't there a recording of this past murder? Any indication the kid knew the killer?"

I shrugged. "Possibly. I'm curious as to why Logan didn't tell his mother in the recording that it was a stranger. He said, *I couldn't stop—*, and then it cut off. "

Sanders rubbed his tired eyes. "So why not call the killer by name? Why the cryptic message?"

"It's only cryptic to us," I said. "I think it's very likely someone in that family knows a lot more than they're telling us."

As night descended, the hospital hallway lights dimmed and a shift change brought in a new nurse. Sanders asked me to stay, to keep him company. Ultimately, he wanted the two of us to continue working through the case together. Fear about his medical prognosis was nearly palpable, and I had to restrain myself from asking any questions. Instead, we both focused on what was my favorite part of the job, puzzling out the why of a serial killer, tracking his movements, and making a best guess as to what his next moves would be. More than once, my father's image flashed through my mind. This had always been his favorite part of his work, too. We'd spent hours together building murder boards and reenacting possible crime scenarios in our basement. I thought again about the murder books—I could almost hear my father turning in his grave over those ridiculous little books. Worse, I felt lost without my standard method of investigation, unmoored without the board to tether myself to.

Eventually Sanders brought up his illness. "I'm sorry I didn't tell you. It's embarrassing, and I'm not sure how to deal with it."

"Cancer? What do you mean, embarrassing?" I asked, moving my chair a little closer to his bedside. "Come on, everyone is pulling for you."

Sanders looked over at me, his eyes now dulling with the return of pain. "It's not just cancer, Hansen. You know that, right? It's breast cancer."

I did know. I'd demanded answers from Bennett, and she'd explained what the surgery entailed.

"It's cancer, Sanders. Cancer is cancer and all of it begins with a capital *C*."

He reached up and rubbed the stubble along his chin, keeping his gaze on the computer screen in front of him. "I've never even heard of a man with breast cancer."

"Don't be sexist, Sanders. Breast cancer is an equal opportunity offender." I tried to get him to look at me, but now he was staring at the ceiling. I figured this would be what would bother Sanders most—the anti-masculinity of his illness. "I bet your doctor cleared that up for you real quick. Even though it isn't talked about much in our society, that doesn't mean it's not happening. It's devastating news for any person."

Sanders shook his head. "It would have made so much more sense for me to have lung cancer, you know? Throat cancer, maybe, with all those cigarettes I've smoked over the years. But breast cancer? Seriously? It's like some kind of sick joke from God." He chuckled even though he clearly didn't find it funny.

Bennett told me the surgeon had performed a double mastectomy on Sanders, and warned me he would be wrapped and quite sore. What Bennett didn't know was whether or not the surgeon had gotten all the cancer or if it had already spread to the lymph nodes.

I nodded over to the uneaten tray of food on his side table. "How much longer will you be in here to enjoy these fancy dinners, anyway?"

Sanders groaned and shook his head. "At least a few more days. They want to get my first dose of chemo in before I go home."

Sanders filled me in on his diagnosis. He had stage 2 breast cancer, and they had located cancer cells into the lymph nodes under his left arm. His surgeon had been hopeful they'd gotten as much of the cancer as they could possibly take in the surgery.

"They can never be sure," Sanders told me. "But I'm going to channel my inner Hansen and say the doc has me headed in the right direction."

I relaxed a little. I put a lot of stock in instinct, and if Sanders felt positive about the surgery and his prognosis, then I should, too. I also knew there was only so much bad TV and true crime podcasts that would get him through this time in his life. His drive, his need to work cases, would help him heal and push away from the hospital bed faster. He knew that at any given time our state had at least a few active serial killers, and it was anyone's guess how many others across the country. This knowledge was what got both of us out of bed every morning; we *needed* to save people who didn't even know they were in danger yet. The Deadeye case could be some of the very best medicine for Sanders's health. He was physically limited, sure, but he had a laptop and a genius knack for trailing killers, no matter where his body might be limited to.

"God, I need a cigarette," Sanders groaned. He winced if he moved his arms too far from his body or if he tried to maneuver his position in the bed. The pain medication was wearing off.

"I wondered how you were doing without your precious smokes."

Sanders patted his chest port, the hub with spider leg hoses spilling from it. "Supposedly they're giving me something for that. I can't tell. Besides, there is nothing that can take the place of the first drag of smoke."

"Yeah, nothing like it." I nearly gagged. "Sounds like you'll be getting used to a tall glass of orange juice in the morning instead of a cigarette." When Sanders groaned, I waggled my eyebrows at him. "I have an idea—how about you join me on Bennett's intense clean-eating plan? We can suffer together."

"Is she still on you about that? Persistent, isn't she?"

Then it hit me—the idea of the century. "Sanders, how about you join us for the marathon in Disneyland after the new year? You'll want to dress as your favorite Disney character," I teased.

"Jeez, a marathon? With these old lungs?"

"Run your way to health, Sanders," I joked, "in a Disney costume of your choice."

Sanders's laughter boomed in the quiet space, a sound I was happy to hear. "Well, now you're getting somewhere. I'll be that blob thing from *Star Wars*."

"Jabba the Hutt?" I asked. "Jabba doesn't run. He can't even walk."

"Exactly. You can look at Bennett's clean living ideas for you in one of two ways, Hansen. She's controlling and demanding," he offered. "Or she loves you so much she can't imagine her life without you." Our fun had loosened Sanders up, which was probably why he felt comfortable commenting on Bennett. He generally kept his opinions about our relationship to himself.

I'd certainly come up with the first option on my own, but I hadn't given much credence to the second. It always seemed to be Bennett's way or no way, and somehow I got lost in that equation.

"Speaking of Bennett, I need to text her." I reached for my phone. I hadn't told her I was going to see Sanders, though I was pretty certain she'd figured it out.

With Sanders. Awake and doing well.

I didn't want to talk to Bennett; the thought of her holding back information on Sanders still stung. It wasn't only that, but also the tension between us—a tension that had increased with the last few days.

Good news! When will you be back to your hotel room?

The bubbles moved along my texting screen and told me Bennett was composing something more for me, possibly deleting it, and starting again. I watched those bubbles a little longer and then closed out with the home button, slipping the phone inside my back pocket.

The overnight nurse pushed through Sanders's curtain barrier around midnight, her rubber-soled shoes whisper quiet against the hospital's linoleum floors. "Time for your meds."

"Thank God," he groaned.

I stepped out of the room while the nurse checked Sanders's bandaging and delivered more medication into the port. She emptied the fluid collection bag and reattached it. I imagined that the bandaging rubbed and the stitches across his breasts itched and the tubes pumping drainage from him hurt. Once she was done, she dimmed the lights and settled his bed back into a lowered position.

"He's doing quite well," she said to me on her way out of the room, "but he really needs to rest."

"I understand." The thought of driving all the way back to the hotel room in Simmons County seemed so daunting. I could have gone to my home in Spring Rock, but it also felt far away. "Is it possible for me to stay the night?"

"As long as you let him sleep," the nurse cautioned. "We generally reserve that option for family members only, but in this case, it seems like you two are very close." She led me into the room where Sanders was already asleep. She extended the base of the oversized chair into a single mattress. "Let me get you some blankets and a pillow."

The hospital room beeped all around Colby Sanders's bed, and I sat down, careful not to wake him. Despite his age, Sanders looked almost childlike in the bed piled with so many blankets and pillows. His white hair fell against his brow, still tanned from summer.

"Hair loss isn't a given so much anymore with chemo, Hansen," Bennett had told me. "Breast cancer responds well to treatment, and Sanders made the right choice going with the double mastectomy. Just give the man some time to heal, okay?"

Heal. I nearly laughed thinking about that conversation. Bennett didn't understand Sanders the way I did; she hadn't worked with him in the field, hadn't had Sanders step in when her life was so far gone to depression and drink that she couldn't hardly see the way out. Sanders was family to me, and both of us were short on people to call family.

While Sanders slept, I sat cross-legged in the makeshift bed and tried to minimize the glow of my open laptop. A second letter had emerged from the Holdens in the press, this one shame-based and full of accusations. Sheriff Daniel and I planned to meet at the Holdens' home first thing in the morning. This time, we would arrive with a search warrant for the grounds.

I continued to search through the BCI databases for reports on any preppers or survivalist groups and found a large one based near Mansfield. They'd been ordering weapons through the postal system, a lot like the David Koresh group in Waco. BCI had intervened, and the majority had disbanded, but enough members still populated that area. Others moved on to follow the advice of Coleman Frank.

It never ceased to amaze me how hungry people were for a leader, how desperate some were to believe in something. It was frightening to see how some charismatic and misguided individuals could derail lives. BCI agents had a color-coded map that tracked cells of these survivalist or militia-style groups in the state of Ohio. I wasn't really surprised to see so much of Ohio highlighted. We were a state of so many complexities and polarizations. We had the thriving business, educational, and cultural area of Columbus within miles of desolate areas like Simmons County where residents struggled with poverty and the departure of industry from the area. Fracking had also taken its toll on Southeastern Ohio, places where Big Oil had come in and promised money and business. They'd left the remnants of their machinery behind, and left everyone struggling to recover. It was in these places that I imagined reality TV guys burying steel containers underground and loading them with freeze-dried food and knives and guns to fend off an attack from zombies.

For Deadeye, it was all about the hunt. He lived for it. Before the pain meds had knocked him out, though, Sanders had been careful to warn me that Deadeye and his partner were most likely feeding off the fear their actions created in the community. Sanders had talked about the connection between a terrorist, a sniper, and Deadeye. Our first experience with terrorism wasn't on September 11 or with ISIS or any other hate group, Sanders claimed, but with the emergence of the lone sniper in our society, the one who seemed to kill at random. This was the guy that opened fire in a full movie theater or a church service on Sunday, the one who shot people at gas stations across the country from dozens of feet away, or the person who opened fire in a crowded fast-food joint. It was the kid who killed indiscriminately in a classroom or a disgruntled employee who shot up his colleagues when he no longer had a job. Sanders believed this sort of homegrown terrorism caused members of a community to change their behavior. "Danger lurks everywhere," Sanders said, "and no one is certain where to direct that extreme fear. It ends up permeating the thoughts and actions of a community, eating away at any confidence they once had in the police to keep them safe."

I wasn't sure where this talk was coming from, the drugs or Sanders's prior training, but I wanted to hear more. He spoke about how Deadeye, like the lone terrorist sniper, operated in a universe where everyone was a potential terrorism suspect. With danger everywhere, these killers maintained the ability to maneuver without detection until it was too late. A sniper predator became almost mythical in the community and in the media, an airy and transcendent figure that was like an all-knowing wolf circling clueless sheep. It was the proverbial monster that slept under the bed, or, in Deadeye's case, the beast that lurked in the forest.

The thing about monsters and beasts was that they rarely left their comfort zones. The more I listened to Sanders's ramblings and reviewed the case, I understood: if I wanted to stop Deadeye, I'd need to meet him on his own turf, wherever that might be.

CHAPTER TEN

Simmons County
Sunday, 8:00 a.m.
Day 3 of the investigation

I waited at the front door of Bad Billy's Hunting, Supply House, and Range with Sheriff Carl Daniel. We'd gotten a call on the tip line in the early morning hours from an anonymous source that believed she'd met Deadeye at Bad Billy's bar the night before. Officers on duty were dispatched to Bad Billy's, but they didn't find Deadeye or the person who'd made the phone call. The caller had used a burner phone, and the IT department had spent a fair amount of time trying to track it down without much luck.

I doubted David Johnson would be brazen enough to visit a favorite hangout filled with hunters, especially with a BOLO out for his arrest. However, Deadeye was very good at meshing in with a crowd, and a place like Bad Billy's Hunting, Supply House, and Range could be a great location for him to be a part of the community and stay anonymous. Bad Billy's was an oversized warehouse on the outskirts of Simmons which served as a combination supply house, bar, music venue, shooting range—basically, a little something for every hunting enthusiast. In the off-season, the locals met up there and practiced shooting on the range behind the building. My colleague Mike Snyder introduced me to the supply store's extensive social media presence. I scrolled through Bad Billy's Facebook and Instagram postings over the last three days, searching through the collection of faces. If David Johnson had been there, he'd managed to avoid the camera.

Surprisingly, I hadn't had a better night's sleep in months than I did on the pullout bed in Sanders's hospital recovery room. Once I finally fell asleep, I slept until the morning nurse came in to give Sanders his meds. When Sheriff Daniel called to say we had a tip at Bad Billy's, I was sharing scrambled eggs and toast with Sanders and watching the sunrise morning news.

Sheriff Daniel gave the heavy steel door another knock. He'd contacted the owner who agreed to meet us on the premises, but there was no sign of anyone save an empty Chevy pickup truck that had seen better days near the back of the lot.

"Sounds like things got rowdy here last night." I passed my phone to Daniel to scroll through the posted photos. "Is this the only hot spot for hunters during open season?"

"Tradition, more or less. They are so far out of town that noise isn't really a factor. Billy has a liquor license, and folks congregate here to talk weapons and hunting. Lots of competition and big stories about who took down the biggest buck, that sort of thing."

I chuckled and stepped over to a small window. Everything inside the large building was dark. Quiet surrounded us without a hint of anyone on the premises. I thumbed around the corner of the massive building. "Let's check out the shooting range."

As we rounded the long block of a warehouse, I spotted a surveillance camera and then one more as we neared the entrance to the range. The facility was heavily monitored, and if the owner played along with us, it could be a great source of information.

When we heard the crunch of the lot's gravel and the spin of wheels, we headed for the lot.

"It's the owner, Billy," Daniel said, and he gave the truck a wave.

Daniel had called Billy before we left the station, and Billy assured us his morning staff would be working and could let us in until he arrived.

Billy jumped out of his truck, hitched up his jeans, and almost simultaneously pulled down the large brim of his hat. The morning sun reflected off his recently polished cowboy boots. With a sun-weathered hand, he shook Daniel's hand and then mine.

"I saw you two on the surveillance," Billy said. "It feeds into my phone and I keep a close eye on things. Joanne is supposed to be here. My apologies."

"Joanne? Any chance she worked the bar last night?" I asked.

Billy turned his gaze on me—piercing blue eyes with the spray of fine crow's feet at their corners. *Handsome.* He had hair longer than mine pulled back into a ponytail at the nape of his neck with multiple bands throughout, spaced about an inch or so apart.

"Yes, ma'am. She's my constant here at the store. Joanne's in charge—she's the general manager and takes care of everything. Even me." He jangled a large key chain until the correct key fell into his fingers. "What's this all about, anyway?"

I hated to be referred to as *ma'am*, such a bold and gendered term, but I let it slide. As much as I wanted to school Billy on the proper way to greet a special agent, the purpose of our visit took precedence. "We received a tip that David Johnson, Deadeye, might have been here last night. We would like to talk to the staff on duty last night and check out the surveillance recordings."

"If you're amenable to that," Daniel added.

I felt certain that Billy knew his rights and understood them well; most entrepreneur bar owners knew exactly what they could get away with and what they couldn't. The heavy surveillance, though, signified something else. Either the place had been ripped off a few times in the past or the owner had someone he needed to watch out for.

"Absolutely, I'll take you to the control area. You're welcome to any footage you need," Billy said. "I wonder why Joanne didn't call me."

"You weren't on the property last night, then?" I asked.

"I needed a break. We've been so busy with events and deliveries, getting ready for the opening of hunting season. But Joanne knows—I'll come in at any time. This place is my baby."

"Is that her truck in the back of the lot?" Daniel asked.

"No, it's mine. Deader than a doornail! I haven't had a chance to replace the battery yet." He pushed the door open and stepped into the building, his gait wide and firm. "Strange. The alarm isn't set."

Sheriff Daniel pulled Billy back by his arm. "Wait outside," he whispered.

Daniel turned back toward the door slowly and palmed it open with his right hand. I reached for my gun and followed behind into the dark cavern of the building. At our first opportunity, Daniel went left into the showroom, and I went right into the bar area. I took long strides along the wall until I'd cleared every corner. I eventually met up with Daniel toward the back of the building, and together we cleared the range area.

"No one here," Daniel said, opening the door for Billy. "Did you try calling Joanne?"

"No answer." He walked through the store looking for anything out of place as he led us to his security center. The system was surprisingly sophisticated with multiple cameras throughout the building. We sat beside Billy as he scrolled through the different angles from the afternoon and night before. The camera showed Joanne closing up at 1:22 a.m. while a man waited on her at the bar. Joanne's eyes glistened with drink, her balance clearly off. She showed no signs of distress in the recording, though, only that she had gotten remarkably drunk.

Billy groaned. "Holy hell. Joanne is breaking just about every rule I have for my employees."

"Who is the guy waiting on her?" I asked.

"That's Coleman," Billy said. "He's been seeing Joanne for a while now."

Daniel chuckled. "Coleman Frank? He's that popular survivalist, right? The prepper who's preaching that everyone needs to be prepped for the end of American society?"

"The one and only," Billy said. "Coleman's got quite a following. They come in here looking for him. Bringing too much attention to it all, if you ask me."

"So he's on our radar," I said. "I've heard of him and his work. We need to talk to him."

I guessed Bad Billy's would be exactly the kind of place survivalists would love for socializing and strategizing about how to take on the end of the world. They were known to stockpile food, ammunition, and anything required for health care needs. Some preppers stockpiled sheds, basements, or garages with essentials, but the diehards built underground bulletproof, fireproof bunkers on their property—every man, woman, and child for themselves.

"Conservatism meets a harsh independence," Daniel said to me. "We certainly have our share of these types living in the county, particularly along the state border."

As I scanned through the recording of the crowd of faces that all looked the same—white middle-aged men at varying stages and degrees of balding—I thought about those underground bunkers.

I turned to Billy. "Any idea how many stocked bunkers there are in the area?"

He shrugged. "More than a few. The thing is, you're really supposed to keep these places a secret. It's a matter of safety when everything goes down. You don't want everyone showing up on your doorstep the minute Armageddon hits." Billy laughed at the image, a deep-chested laugh that caught me by surprise. "You wouldn't believe it, though. Despite all of Coleman Frank's warnings, most guys can't help bragging about what they built. They can't stop themselves from one-upping each other."

"Bragging rights, I guess," I smiled up at Billy. "Coleman Frank is some sort of expert, someone people seek out for advice on the process, right?"

"He's nothing but a charlatan," Daniel muttered.

"Possibly, but I'd like to see inside *his* bunker," I said. "He seems like just the kind of guy that could help David Johnson get from one location to another without detection. And if he's got a fully stocked bunker with food and water, Deadeye could be below ground right now."

"I'll get you in that bunker, ma'am." Billy pulled his cell phone from his back pocket and dialed a number. "Coleman owes me a favor or two."

❖

If you listened to Coleman Frank, he had the granddaddy Cadillac of all bunkers, the safest hole you could possibly find in the ground, this side of West Virginia. I'd never been inside an underground bunker before, but I eventually came to agree with Coleman. His bunker was top-notch with cable TV, a beer fridge fully loaded, and a finagled Wi-Fi system that ran on its own generator.

We'd followed Billy out to Coleman Frank's to look for Joanne and talk bunkers. While Sheriff Daniel drove, I googled Frank. He certainly was a web celebrity of sorts. His blog and podcast had their own sets of avid fans that followed and sent in questions about every possible end-of-world situation you could imagine. And Frank had an answer about exactly what you would need to survive the longest in any doomsday scenario. He prided himself on preparedness and was chest deep into the conspiracy theories which gave the phrase *off the grid* a whole new meaning.

Billy's phone call roused Coleman Frank out of bed, and he was just pulling on his clothes when we arrived. Eventually, Joanne made it to the door wrapped in an oversized robe that she gripped tight around her waist, looking like she was fighting the nausea of an incredibly bad hangover.

"I must have forgot to turn on the alarm," Joanne told her boss, not seeming all that surprised to see him at the door when she was very late to work. "I'm sorry, but I really don't remember."

Frank gave her a knowing look that said, *Hangover hell.*

"I'll get some coffee brewing," Frank said and left Daniel and me with Joanne.

"Someone called in a tip early this morning. They said David Johnson, the escaped inmate, was in Billy's last night. Do you have any information on that?" Daniel asked.

Joanne shook her head. "You mean the guy on TV? The mug shot they keep showing?"

"That's him." I pulled up the photo on my phone to show her once again.

"If he was there, he was hiding," Joanne said. "And he never came to the bar for a drink. It's bullshit if you ask me." She lit the end of a bent cigarette and took a deep drag.

"We checked the footage but didn't see anyone resembling him," Daniel said.

Joanne handed Daniel her phone from the pocket of her robe. "I took a few photos last night of the hunting teams. We had a preseason party last night where many claimed their teammates. You're welcome to look through the photos, but your man isn't there."

"About how many were there?" Daniel asked.

Joanne shrugged. "Over the course of the night? We probably saw close to sixty or seventy."

Daniel held the phone down so that I could see as he enlarged the photos. Each showed a grouping of men, all clad in camouflage, piled around the stuffed head of a buck hanging from the wall.

"Hunting teams?" I asked.

"Many of the hunters compete on teams," Daniel explained. "We have an unofficial night hunt one night every season. The team that takes down the most deer during the night wins."

"Wins what?" I asked.

"Clout," Joanne said, "and some crappy trophy that's been passed around for years." She excused herself to get dressed while Daniel and I continued to search through the event photos.

I stopped Daniel's scroll through the photographs with my hand. "Go back a second."

Daniel held the picture out for me, a grouping of four men who all looked remarkably the same. With my fingertips I enlarged the screen over each of their profiles. Most had camouflage paint on their faces, but I clearly recognized one of the men.

"Hello, John Holden Sr.," I said.

The sheriff took a closer look. "That's him, all right."

"He must be an avid hunter if he's not willing to miss the season after two of his children have been shot." I checked the time stamp. "And not too long after we left his home."

I detected the slightest eye roll from Daniel as I moved on to magnify the other faces in the group.

"I never said John was perfect," Daniel commented.

"Sure. Everyone grieves in their own way, right?" I wanted to make my point, but not come off as condescending. "I just hope you'll keep an open mind, Daniel. That's all I ask."

The sheriff said nothing but fiddled with the phone in an effort to send himself the photographs.

"Do the Holdens have a bunker on their property?" I asked him. "Anywhere else someone might hide out besides those big barns?"

Daniel finally gave up and handed me the phone. "Send us those photos, could you please? As for the Holdens, they have a lot of land."

I worked Joanne's phone to send multiple pictures that featured Holden, when I saw a pair of eyes I thought I recognized. "Isn't that the coroner?"

Daniel leaned down to take a look. "Yeah, that's Mike all right."

"Dr. Mike?" Joanne asked, heading back into the room, buttoning up her shirt. "He's an avid hunter. A solid shot, too. His team has taken the trophy a fair number of years."

I thanked Joanne and handed the phone back to her.

"Dr. Mike might be able to help us in more ways than in autopsy," I said to Daniel. "He could be a real asset in the field, particularly since he's local."

"I'm sure he'd be happy to help any way he can," Daniel said.

"The Holdens have the blue house on their property," Joanne offered, giving away that she'd been listening to our conversation while out of the room.

"The blue house?" I asked.

"It used to be a place teenagers went to party, an abandoned farmhouse that used to belong to his great-great-grandparents or someone like that," Joanne said.

"There haven't been any reports on that house for a few years, since that kid fell through the flooring and broke both his legs," Daniel said.

"Does the blue house have running water?" I asked.

Joanne shook her head. "I spent some time there in my youth." She blushed and laughed. "No water, no electricity. There is a pump for the well water, though."

Her phone beeped with an incoming text. "Coleman wants me to bring you all out back. He's with Billy out back by the bunker."

❖

I had to give Frank props; he was clever about how he'd hidden the bunker, sneaky in that he'd covered its entrance underneath a small shed in his backyard. I wondered just how many people he'd told about it as I watched him move the riding lawn mower to reveal the flat circular entrance that looked a lot like a giant sewer. Family and friends? The crew at Bad Billy's? I wouldn't be surprised if the entire county knew where to find Coleman Frank's amazing bunker. I was willing to bet he couldn't keep his mouth shut about what he'd built, just like the others.

Frank used three different keys to unlock three different locks. An electronic pad turned on and he entered a password. He gripped the three-pronged crank in the center of the steel door and turned until the airtight seal popped. Slowly, the heavy door swung open. Daniel and I peered down into the deep dark hole, neither of us making a move to climb in.

"Awesome, huh?" Coleman nudged the sheriff. "The entire shebang is solar powered. It makes its own electricity."

Running lights illuminated the ladder into the bunker. "Come on down," Frank said, when Daniel and I hesitated to follow him. "I promise, it's worth it."

The multiple-room bunker was impressive. Coleman had built a living space with a bed and TV. A small kitchen led into a bathroom with a toilet and shower. Another bulletproof safety door led to a small room loaded with canned foods, emergency care kits, batteries, and ammunition. Bottles of whiskey lined one row of a supply area.

"How long could you survive in here?" I asked. "Let's say we shut the lid right now. How long?"

Coleman Frank furrowed his brow and pulled at the scruffy length of his graying beard. "It's an issue of water, but I'd say a good two months."

"You said everyone marvels at your bunker—you are the envy of all the survivalists," I said. "Any chance someone could get in here without you knowing about it?"

Coleman Frank laughed and held up his keys, jangling the collection at me. "Not without these and my password."

"Is there an alarm system on it? Cameras for surveillance?"

Coleman shook his head. "I plan to get one of those outfits like Billy has for his place, but I haven't gotten around to it."

I didn't question Coleman Frank further, but it seemed odd that he wouldn't have his prized possession completely wired with eyes all over it.

"Look, Coleman, you're connected with a population that might come in contact with our fugitive," Sheriff Daniel said. "These bunkers are a perfect location to hide someone on the run, especially the ones stockpiled with months of food, water, and ammunition. I'd really appreciate any help you can provide us in tracking down all the underground bunkers in the area."

Daniel and I had already discussed assigning two task force members to investigate any and all bunkers in the area, but Coleman Frank's knowledge and help with the survivalist community could make the process go much faster. Frank would most likely run his mouth about our investigation, I was sure of it, but it was a risk worth taking. I wondered about the other person that had been with Deadeye, the potential partner in his crimes. Was he a survivalist? Could he be one of the men in the group photographs huddled around the buck's head? My gut told me David Johnson remained close and his partner possibly even closer. Deadeye probably gloated over his prison escape and the murders in much the same way others bragged about taking down a deer. It wouldn't be long before Deadeye went back to doing what he did best—hunting humans.

CHAPTER ELEVEN

Sunday, 3:00 p.m.

Sheriff Daniel banged against the old farmhouse door with the heel of his hand. While the solid wood of the door held fast, the weathered ocean-blue paint peeled away in long curls. "Sheriff's office!" Daniel's voice boomed. "We're coming in!"

Detective Donovan had arrived earlier in the day with permission from her sheriff to work one week with our case. She'd found a hotel room on the same floor as mine and, after she dumped her bag, joined Daniel and me at the Holden property. Donovan and I stood at the base of the porch stairs, weapons drawn, in backup position.

While the Holdens had given permission for us to search their land, they hadn't given permission for us to search their home. Officers had been searching abandoned houses, trailers, or cabins for the last twenty-four hours, but no one had been to the blue house yet. Simmons County had more properties than we could contend with— the area had been stripped barren through fracking and so many of its jobs had been lost to major corporations. Vacant properties dotted the Southeastern Ohio hillsides.

When there was no response, Daniel announced our presence once more, and then turned to us. His stern nod said everything he needed to say: *We're going in. Watch yourself.* Donovan and I took the three porch steps at a side angle, both of us careful to avoid the weak sections of the wood and the area that looked like it had been punched in with a barbell.

Daniel kicked the door below its knob and it slammed open with one solid grunt. Dust flew about us as we pushed through the debris and into the foyer of the home. Guns drawn, we each moved into separate areas of the farmhouse. Daniel went toward the living area and bathroom, Donovan headed for the staircase, while I went for the kitchen and back porch. Daylight filtered through the windows, most of them shattered, illuminating my surroundings as I made my way around the lower level. Remnants of furniture had been left behind, most of it broken with its remaining fabric shredded. The home had been one of the original buildings on the property and housed one of the Holdens' long-passed relatives. Joyce Holden explained that they'd used the home for storage, but no one had lived in it for at least twenty years. As I walked through the space, though, I had the feeling that someone had recently been there. I flipped on my small Maglite and shone it into the corners of the small bathroom. Pieces of the busted commode lay across the floor, and I found the discarded tools of heroin—spoons burned into odd shapes and empty syringes scattered about the dark space. There was enough dust and splinters of old wood to bury a small city, so any thoughts of clean drug use went out the window with whoever had last been here.

Daniel and I cleared the first floor. He went up the stairs to join Donovan, and I listened to the boards hiss and creak under their weight, crackling above my head as they slowly moved from room to room. I stood for a moment at the top of the cellar stairs, the beam of my light shining down into its cavern of darkness. I couldn't imagine anyone hiding out in that hole where the smell of mold was enough to make me gag. I descended each step slowly, testing the wood with my weight before stepping down. It turned out those stairs might have been the most solid wood left in the house. When my feet hit the cement floor of the cellar, I swung the light beam quickly from corner to corner looking for any sort of movement.

"Hansen, you clear?"

I about jumped out of my skin with the boom of the sheriff's voice. "Just finishing," I yelled up the stairs, catching my breath. I heard him descending stair by stair with Donovan following behind.

"Lord! It smells like a few animals died down here." Daniel zeroed in his light beam on the area behind the stairs as the three of us ventured out to the corners of the cellar.

"I'm sure the Holdens had no idea a part of their property was a known drug house." I tried to keep the cynicism from my voice.

Daniel grunted. "This place is so secluded in the woods. Without electricity and its dark blue exterior, it's hard to see any movement out here unless you're very close to the house."

"I'm sure that was the point," I added. "Everyone who used this spot for drug activity wanted the place to be off the grid."

"We have no reason to think the Holdens had any knowledge anything was happening out here except natural decay."

"Decay," I said, noticing a half-moon cellar window. "That's one way to put it. Why was the house painted navy blue? Seems an odd color for an old farmhouse."

Donovan chuckled from somewhere across the cellar as I reached up and wiped away an area of the dirty window. The glass was thick and warped but looked out over a hillside.

"Can't explain it," Daniel said. "My guess is it was someone's favorite color, or something like that. I heard a while back the family was thinking of restoring the house and using it as a bed-and-breakfast."

"How many drug houses like this one are in this area, anyway?"

"Hard telling," Daniel said. "We have a scattering of abandoned farmhouses and cabins. They meld into the forest, or in some cases, the forest takes them back."

I tipped up onto the balls of my feet and peered out the window. There, hidden among the tall trees, I saw a dark trail of smoke snaking up through the branches and leaves.

Taking the stairs two at a time, I hollered over my shoulder about the fire behind the house. I was out the front door and rounding the side of the blue house before Daniel and Donovan had even started up the cellar stairs. The undergrowth and tree roots of the woods had grown wild. Branches nipped and smacked at me as I ran toward the fire. It didn't take me more than a few feet beyond the house to smell it—the piney hot scent of a fire pit blaze that had spread.

Donovan and Sheriff Daniel trailed behind me, all of us crashing through what wasn't meant to be a path until we found the clearing beneath a copse of large trees. Beside the fire pit, I found all the makings of someone hiding out from the world—bags of processed food, clothing, blankets, and a sleeping bag—all in various stages of burning. I grabbed one of the full gallon jugs of water and doused the burning backpack beside me. The open bag whooshed with the sudden drench of water, smoke sizzling up as I poured one more gallon on it. With my foot, I nudged the bag and a smoking shirt tumbled out of the open seam. The burning button up was stamped with HARTFORD CORRECTIONAL INSTITUTION.

"Johnson can't be too far," I told Daniel, who reached for his radio to call for backup. Donovan followed my lead and poured what was left of the water jugs onto the burning objects—evidence of Deadeye.

"Close off the perimeter," I directed Donovan. "Don't move anything else until we get a team out here."

Daniel didn't respond until after I'd moved much deeper into the woods. "Wait, Hansen!"

I stopped, my footstep caught in midair. I'd heard this warning more times than I cared to admit in my career—*wait for backup.* I'd been reprimanded at length for not following that direction. *Hardheaded* was the word Sanders used to describe my insistence that I could go it alone.

Only this time Sanders wasn't there to back me up.

"Hansen…wait!"

In the distance, not far from where I stood, I heard the distinct *whoosh, crack* of footfalls tearing a path through the forest.

Whoosh, crack. Whoosh, crack.

I didn't look back.

❖

I followed the frantic sound of footfalls that couldn't have been more than a few hundred yards in front of me. I came upon snapped branches with their exposed white wood still seeping. I squinted to protect my eyes from the swat and sting of the trees while I attempted to hold my weapon in front of me, ready to take aim, but it bounced around in front of me with the uneven ground.

My heart slammed inside my chest. It was a feeling I recognized, a combination of panic and pure oxygen tearing through my system. It had been a while since I'd felt this kind of a rush, and it always brought me back to Marci and the run I'd made out of the wooded quarry to phone for help. We didn't have cell phones yet, and I believed Marci still had a chance to live. It was a couple of miles back to where I found Marci in one of the limestone caves that pockmarked the land around the water. I couldn't carry her back to the car, but I could run for help. I whipped along the wooded path that day, my feet sometimes feeling as if they didn't touch the ground. I'd gotten about a third of the way out the woods when I felt it—the presence behind me. The killer chasing me.

Now, I slipped into that space somewhere between the past and the present, a dreamlike state that tossed me back and forth into the run to try to save Marci's life. I looked down and actually saw the Tretorn tennis shoes I'd been wearing as a fifteen-year-old, the frayed edges of my cutoff blue jeans. I blinked hard and saw it was actually the steel toe tips of my Frye boots that kicked through the underbrush and hurled me forward. Before I knew it, I was once again back in the wooded quarry, certain the man would catch me as he closed in the space between us. I heard his grunts with each step, the slap of his shoes against the earth, eventually feeling the edges of his fingertips reach for my shoulders but instead only graze the fabric of my shirt. My breath completely stopped with the phantom feel of his touch, and my heart seemed to stand still for a few seconds.

I so clearly remembered—it was the thing I didn't see coming that saved me that day—the quarry so far below. I leapt off the edge of the path, my arms windmilling through the air on the way down, and I waited for him to plunge into the water beside me. He never did. Instead, he vanished back into the woods.

The thing I didn't see coming. The water of the quarry saved me that day, but it just as easily could have killed me.

What couldn't I see coming now? The figure running from me now had the speed of Bennett, and I struggled to catch up. We were well within the hunting area boundaries, and I thought about the other hunters who might fire when they saw our rapid movement. But the woods were quiet, save for the two of us, and I pushed myself to run faster.

A hillside emerged. As the figure started up, I called out to him, "David Johnson, stop before I fire!"

He didn't slow down, and I saw his fists pumping hard at his sides to help push him to the crest of the hill. A long black rifle was strapped to his back, a powerful weapon with which he could easily have sprayed gunfire in my direction. Instead, the runner continued until he crested the hill and then dropped over its side and out of my sight.

I screamed, letting all the sound and air and frustration spew from my body. My thighs burned and my chest clenched with the final push I gave. I knew the thing I wasn't expecting was over that ridge, but I needed to see it. I just needed to get there.

It wasn't long before there was a sudden screech of tires echoing through the forest.

I finally crested the ridge in time to look down on the scene below. An old truck sat with its engine rumbling at the crime scene where the Holden brothers were murdered on County Road 571. The runner darted over the place where the Holden brothers passed and jumped into the passenger seat. The door hadn't even slammed closed when the driver pressed the gas pedal to the floor.

I stumbled and fell to my knees while my chest heaved with the hard run and the sight of what transpired below. There, on the two-lane rural route not more than a few hundred feet from where I knelt, the truck sped around the curvy country road and into the forest that seemed to consume it whole. But not before I recognized that old truck. I'd seen it before in Bad Billy's parking lot. What was that he'd said about the abandoned truck? *Deader than a doornail. I haven't gotten around to getting that old thing up and running again.*

❖

"Dumb-ass move, Hansen." Sheriff Daniel paced back and forth as his radio crackled against one hip and his phone sat dead with lack of reception against the other. The heels of his boots smacked against the road—he was agitated because I'd scared him. Daniel was used to being in control, to calling all the shots. And then he met me.

I sat in the open back end of an emergency squad wagon, my legs dangling over the bumper. An EMT daubed the scrapes and cuts to my face, neck, and arms with antiseptic. Less than thirty minutes before, I'd chased a man to this exact spot where he'd found a ride to safety.

"Good thing you were wearing pants," the medic said. "It saved you from some brutal injuries." He dabbed the edge of a gauze pad on a wound on my right cheekbone. "Sorry—this one really needs a few stitches. It's going to bruise pretty good, too."

I shook my head, thinking about the branch as thick as my wrist that tore across my cheek. I hadn't seen it coming.

"Just butterfly it," I told the medic. "I'll be okay."

"Ah," he said. "You're one of those strong and silent types. At least let me get you an ice pack."

The truth was, I didn't have time for a hospital. Every minute I sat on the EMT's wagon was another minute Deadeye and his partner had on us.

The medic did his best to bandage me up while Daniel turned his attention back to me. "Sanders said you were bullheaded. He said you'd take risks, but I thought we were doing pretty good as a team."

"We are," I agreed.

"That," Daniel pointed at my face, "was not teamwork."

I watched the sheriff pace and thought about Colby Sanders. I needed to check in with him, to make sure he was on track to leave the hospital soon. I was grateful, however, that Sanders wasn't in Simmons County to see me. He would have torn me up one side and down the other over putting myself in danger and disobeying protocol. Sheriff Daniel tried his best in Sanders's absence, but he couldn't come close to giving a chewing out like Sanders.

"Hansen, are you listening to me?"

I looked over at Daniel. "Sorry, no."

"You're sure it was the truck from Billy's lot?"

I nodded, and Daniel radioed back to an officer to let a new model pickup truck go. Once the medic finished his work, the sheriff took a seat beside me on the edge of the wagon. He looked out over the scene before us—emergency vehicles lined the road while officers combed the forest for any signs of Deadeye. "He could have killed you, you know."

"But he didn't," I said, letting my fingertips graze over the places where the butterfly bandages held skin together. "And they got away."

"A person cannot run forever. Even Deadeye."

"The partner," I said, watching Detective Donovan walk toward us from across the road. "He's just as quick and smart as David Johnson. How did they know we were here, anyway? It's not like Deadeye could have called him."

Daniel nodded beside me. "They could be using a radio system like us. The range is shit, but it does allow some contact."

I'd always imagined Deadeye as the brains and brawn behind the entire operation, but after seeing the vehicular rescue, I thought it was very possibly the other way around.

"We need to find their frequency." I sighed. "They've found ours, obviously."

Our radios crackled to life. Officers and detectives detailed their findings.

"We need to keep our chatter to a minimum," I said. "Code words, all that."

We couldn't continue to give Deadeye and his partner a roadmap to stay ten steps ahead of us.

CHAPTER TWELVE

Simmons County Morgue
Sunday, 7:00 p.m.

Postmortem examinations were an essential part of my work but my least favorite part of the duty. I'd never grown used to the cool, sterile smell of chemicals and bleach that I'd come to associate with murder. Once Bennett came into my life, I thought the morgue might take on new meaning for me. I'd hoped to grow more familiar with the dead room and learn some of the ways death detectives like Bennett worked with bodies as they tried to uncover their secrets. No matter how much time I spent in Bennett's office, though, I hadn't been able to shake the feeling that the two of us were never really alone—those filled coolers and ghosted white sheets over the dead lingered noisily outside her door.

It had been less than seventy-two hours since the Holden brothers were murdered, and most of the task force gathered around John Holden's body for the postmortem. His brother, Logan, occupied another steel table nearby.

Unlike me, Colby Sanders seemed to like the postmortems. It felt strange without him next to me at the body, and I wondered if Dr. Mike Duncan knew he'd get off easy with this crowd. Sanders would have questioned everything he had to say and then questioned it once again. Sometimes those questions led to more information than the coroner felt comfortable listing on the report. The entire postmortem had to be recorded for evidence, so Sanders would be able to catch up with the case when he felt up to it.

Mike Snyder would be Skyping in to fill us all in about Deadeye's weapon and ammunition.

An overhead light hummed in the cavernous room. Duncan stood at the head of John Holden Jr.'s body that had already been prepped for our examination. Exhaustion cloaked Duncan, and I imagined the pressure to complete the autopsies and make the findings public so quickly weighed on him. Precision was essential, and he knew as well as we all did that his findings would be scrutinized at length both inside and outside the courtroom, assuming we ever got that far with the case. Dark circles lined his eyes, making him look much older than his late fifties. Even though he'd been doing the job for decades, there had been the heavy influx of bodies from the opioid crisis in the last few years, which had hit his office hard. He regularly had a backlog of cases with bodies waiting for his knife in multiple refrigeration units.

Duncan double-checked the recording equipment and asked, "Everyone ready?"

We gave our approval, and he pulled the white sheet down over John's face and chest, cinching it at the waist. We all wore the required garb of autopsy—gloves, facial masks, hairnets, and goggles. In some ways, the uniform helped me to separate from the body before me. In other ways, the protective barriers we used only served as a constant reminder that the deceased had been the victim of a failed system. Our hope now had to be placed in the justice system, that the killer or killers would be apprehended and stand trial for their crimes.

Dr. Duncan began: "John Henry Holden, age twenty-two and four months. Resident of Simmons County."

Duncan pointed our attention to the exposed flesh and the hole only a little bigger than a quarter. "The only way to sustain this type of injury is through a point-blank shot to the chest. Based on the gunpowder stippling, I'd say the rifle was no more than a foot or so from the deceased."

At intake, Dr. Duncan had taken extensive photographs and some of them filled the large screen on the wall. Duncan zoomed in on the bloodied wound, detailing the tiny black markings across the chest. The gunpowder tattoo against his pale skin, only left through the weapon's close exposure to the body, sealed the cause of death. A gunshot wound through John's chest tore the right side of his heart and instantly killed him. John might have had time to register that a rifle was leveled at him and that his life was in danger, but nothing more.

"Other than slightly elevated blood sugar, John Holden was in perfect health," Duncan told us. He turned to the screen and clicked over to where my BCI partner Snyder waited on Skype. "I'll let you fill them in on the weapon," Duncan said.

"My favorite part!" Snyder grinned at us. "We've pulled all the known Deadeye cases, and what we can verify is that the same weapon used to kill those victims is the one used for the Holden brothers."

Snyder flashed a photograph of a semi-automatic rifle on the screen for us, the exact same type of rifle I'd seen on the back of the runner I'd chased only a few hours before. "This is an MR, standard issue for the military. We know that Deadeye used a civilian AR, built very similar to the MR. They have matched the weapon from these two murders with the previous murders committed by David Johnson through the striation marks."

Two close-up photographs showed what Snyder referred to—marks left on the sides of the bullet as it rifled through the barrel. Each gun had a specific marking it left behind, lines and grooves striated into the metal. In this case, all of Deadeye's proved to be an exact match. No weapon had been recovered when Deadeye had finally gone to prison for his previous murders. No matter the deal offered in exchange for the weapon, David Johnson refused to give it up. Now, here it was, resurrected to kill once again.

"We know David Johnson served in the Army, and the M4 is standard issue. For civilians and those who have cycled out of the military, the closest equivalent is an AR," Snyder said. "Previous analysts determined that he was most likely connected to his weapon from those years, a bond he couldn't let go of."

"No surprise, this type of assault rifle is also banned from hunting areas across the country," Daniel added.

"Let's not forget that John Holden Sr. served time in the military as well," I said. "He would have had just as much access to this weapon as Deadeye."

Dr. Duncan spoke up, surprising me. "We have no evidence the two men worked together or even knew one another, Special Agent."

"You're right," I said to Duncan, "but we cannot rule out the possibility. We have a member of the task force trying to get clearance for military records. It's quite an ordeal."

"As it should be," Duncan said. "The military in our country is under enough scrutiny as it is, don't you think, Agent? Connecting a serial predator and his partner to them is the last thing they need."

A silence settled around us for a second, and I felt the heavy accusation in the air. They thought I was simply gunning for Holden Sr.'s guilt. I held back from defending my thoughts for fear I might appear too myopic.

"I did some digging into the survivalist movement," Snyder said, thankfully changing the subject. "Coleman Frank advises all of his followers to obtain the AR. He claims it's the most reliable weapon, and its bullets will one day take the place of our paper currency."

A chuckle circulated around the death room.

There was one point I wasn't clear on. "You said there was something special about Deadeye's bullets, right?"

"Ah," Snyder said. "Not the bullets, but the casings. Here's where things get interesting. Just like in the past, Deadeye is using the hollow point bullet. It's built to stay together but expands on impact inside the body, causing more damage than a standard bullet."

Snyder held up some casings to the camera so we could see them. "These casings were found at the Holden brothers' scene. What our guys found is that these NATO casings are being reused. Deadeye is *not* using the standard core bullet. This allows him to refill the casings and reuse them."

NATO as in the North Atlantic Treaty Organization. Many survivalists sought surplus from this organization because NATO was held to an outside standard. Their ordnance was seen as more reliable.

"These bullets come cheap, though," I said. "You can buy them by the bag. Why go to the trouble of reloading?"

"That's the million dollar question, Hansen. I can tell you that we have seen this trend with the survivalist groups. Some preppers believe that manufacturers are purposefully limiting the supply of NATO casings in order to weed out the unprepared." Snyder's voice came a few seconds after his mouth moved, an eerie delay due to the slow Wi-Fi connection.

Daniel whistled in disbelief beside me. "Now that is some paranoid thinking."

"It is," Snyder agreed, "but it fits in with the preppers' line of thinking. They aren't the average Joes, right? They have their fingers on the conspiracy pulse, and they want to keep as many NATO casings as possible for their perceived safety."

"Which means we are dealing with someone who is precise and patient in the process," I added.

"That's part of the survivalist manifesto, according to Coleman Frank," Daniel said. "He claims manufacturers are working with the government in an effort to disarm the American public. It all ties back to Frank's basic message—trust no one but yourself."

I understood Frank's line of thinking. Was it paranoid? Absolutely. But it also reflected the deep mistrust so many members of the survivalist movement dealt with. They'd lost faith in America in many different kinds of ways—these thoughts about ammunition manufacturers and corporate America were only the tip of that well of mistrust.

"Let's go ahead and move on to the second body," the coroner said.

We followed him to the next gurney where Logan Holden's body waited for us.

Duncan pulled back the white sheet to a much different scenario than the first body. "This young man wasn't so lucky. He suffered."

Duncan matched Logan's intake photos to various points on the cleaned body. Some of the fingernails had torn off with Logan's struggle to pull himself up. Abrasions lined the palms of his hands. He'd tried to claw at his chest, perhaps looking for an exit wound, scratching and bruising his skin with long red marks. And then there were the multiple cracked ribs. Our killer had taken the time to kick a victim barely clinging to life, proving he wasn't in any rush to leave the scene.

"Logan Simon Holden, age twenty years and two months. Resident of Simmons County." Duncan had Logan placed on his stomach so that we could see the location of the gunshot wound. The entrance wound shattered Logan's shoulder, missing the edge of his heart by centimeters.

"Given the severity of the gunshot wound, I'm surprised he was able to hold consciousness and move to the location of his brother's body. He would have been bleeding heavily and most likely choking on his own blood." Duncan referred to the pierced lung. "I can only credit his ability to remain alert to his will to survive."

In light of Duncan's analysis, I thought about the message Logan had left on his brother's phone recording. Logan had quite literally *stayed alive* in order to leave the message—it was that important to him. If only I could have deciphered its meaning.

Duncan continued, "We have a clear cause of death for both individuals. Given all the surrounding circumstances and the recording left at the crime scene, I've determined both John Holden's and Logan Holden's cause of death to be death by gunshot wounds."

Duncan reached behind him and pulled a stainless-steel dish from the shelf. The dish held two bullets, one mangled and the other in slivers. In another dish, two casings rolled around with a bright red flash of color inside the silver and white room.

"This is the bullet that entered and exited John's body," he said, pointing with an instrument. "Forensics found it intact at the scene. But this one lodged inside Logan's shoulder."

Duncan reached into the dish with a pair of tweezers and held up the mangled bullet for us to see. One shot for each victim, just as the sick rules of the game permitted.

I turned to Sheriff Daniel. "We need to keep canvassing the area for bunkers and abandoned properties."

BCI had created topographical maps of Simmons County and its surrounding area. There was no way to find bunkers from the aerial maps alone, particularly since the goal was for them to remain hidden, but the maps at least gave the property lines and a way to mark the ones that had been checked. Billy had denied the knowledge that his truck had been used by anyone he knew or that it even ran. I found it odd that a place of business that worked hard to use surveillance footage didn't have a camera that captured the back part of the parking lot—the very section where the dead truck had been taken. My spidey sense was screaming; everything in me said that if there was a ground zero to this case, it was Bad Billy's.

"We also need to question some of the local hunters again to see whether they have seen anyone hunting with an AR." Sheriff Daniel checked his watch. "I cannot put off the public much longer. They need a strong message that assures them we are working hard on the case, something to ease the growing fear out there. I've scheduled a press conference for first thing in the morning."

Internally, I cursed Colby Sanders and his absence. The case was shaping up to be one which I wasn't sure I could close without his help.

Chapter Thirteen

Sunday, 10:15 p.m.

The hotel parking lot teemed with hunters arriving and leaving. Trucks and SUVs had their tailgates kicked open. Spirits ran high, and I felt like I'd stumbled into some kind of college reunion celebration instead of what the joy was really all about—bonding over the slaughter of animals.

Inside, I passed the front desk and headed for the elevators when I saw her sitting in the hotel lounge waiting for me with an overnight bag at her feet. I did a double take. A book rested in her lap, and the overhead lights glinted off the lenses of her glasses. She looked up at me through the dark fringe of her bangs and a smile teased her mouth in a way that only Dr. Harper Bennett's could.

"I'm still mad at you," I told her as we waited for the elevator. "You should have told me about Sanders."

"And I'm mad at you for not responding to my messages. You said you would call. I didn't know if you were okay."

I frowned. "Are you saying that makes us even?"

The elevator door slid open and we stepped inside.

"Not at all, Luce. I'm saying we'll get through it—whatever it is."

The floor numbers flashed above and I watched them, wishing I had Bennett's conviction. She kept her word. If Bennett didn't do something she said she would, you knew everything was falling apart.

In a culture where so many tossed around promises and commitments as if they meant nothing, I admired her dedication to her word and that she'd come to Simmons County directly from her flight in from South Carolina. I wasn't so in love with her to think there couldn't be other reasons for her presence than Sanders and me. Bennett might not have been as obsessed with her job as I was, but she was certainly dedicated and wanted to catch bad people just as much as the rest of the team.

A pang of guilt shot through me when I remembered the beer I'd had without Bennett, the beer that had turned my thoughts on the path to getting another one and soon. "Problem with the case?" I nudged her for information about why she'd come to Simmons County just before my floor dinged.

"I want to help," she said. "I've called in to see if Mike Duncan will allow me to work with him until we catch Johnson and whoever else is helping him."

I looked over at her.

"But first, tell me all about Sanders."

The cleaning crew, thankfully, had been through my room. Bennett was saved from my scattered mess, and the crew had replaced all the wadded up towels with neatly folded ones. The bed had been made with fresh sheets, and we sat cross-legged together on one of the queen beds sifting through the reports on her laptop and the folder full of papers she'd brought with her. She'd gone through all the victims associated with Deadeye through the use of the weapon. Bennett spread out the autopsy photos of the known victims in a half-moon around us.

"We also have the two from Longston County," I told Bennett. "It has to be the partner's work."

I scribbled the names *Kara* and *Jessica* onto separate Post-it notes, adding them to the half circle. We continued to build the spread around us, filling Post-it notes with information.

"It's a makeshift murder board," Bennett said.

I laughed when I realized she was right. I hadn't used the murder books much, and I suddenly understood just how much I'd missed a working murder board. Without one, I felt hitch-less, unmoored, like I was floating aimlessly through a river of random clues. I needed something to tether my thoughts and ideas to. The case felt like we were in flux, both shifting and changing with every challenge before us.

❖

Bennett slept in the bed beside me, while I continued to work on the murder board and my laptop. Sleep had long been my nemesis, particularly during a case, but tonight my brain churned with possibilities of Deadeye's goals and where he and his partner might be taking us.

Bennett slept in an old *This is what a feminist looks like* T-shirt that she'd taken from me when we started dating, a shirt washed so many times the decal had mostly worn off. I didn't fight Bennett for the shirt—it fit her well, the stretched-out collar yawning wide against her collarbones and the fabric hugging the swell of her breasts.

Bennett's dark hair spilled over the pillow, and I brushed the corkscrew curls out of her face with my fingertips. I envied Bennett's ability to sleep so well. I never understood her abandon of the senses and her trust of the night to keep her safe. We both saw some of the worst acts of humans in our work. It was hard for me to turn those images off because a sound sleep put me at my most vulnerable—that was something the killers I chased also understood too well.

As Bennett slept, I didn't let myself think about the Bennett that I'd come to know in the last few months—the bossy Bennett, the Bennett who wanted me to be ultra-healthy. Instead I thought about the Bennett I fell in love with—the woman who showed me a new way to be a part of water in kayaks and canoes, the woman whose skin smelled of fresh rain that could calm me with only a few breaths. I thought about the woman who wrote poetry in her spare time and made statements like *When we get old, I want us to be avid bird-watchers* or *This time next year, let's go to Arizona to see the Red Rocks transition into summer.* She tossed out some great random questions, too. My favorite, after we'd slept together for the first time at her place: *Do you think Dr. Phil would approve of our relationship?*

I'd laughed extra hard at that one and wondered when Dr. Phil had become an authority in Bennett's eyes. *Well, he's more open and supportive than Judge Judy, don't you think?*

And I tried not to feel guilty. I told myself the beer had been nothing, that it wouldn't happen again, and that Bennett didn't need to know. It would only worry her. The paradox of it all was I told myself *not* to think about drinking, and it was all I could think about.

Since I couldn't sleep, I researched. I wondered what it would take for a person or a family to become so fearful—so paranoid— as to actively prepare to go to war with everyone around them for survival. Survivalists and preppers feared a blackout during which all the electrical grids and other infrastructure would go down across the country. They blogged about how this could be a result of a man-made disaster, a weather-related issue, or simply an act of God. No matter the cause, they argued everyone needed access to two water sources, both well and stream, and a stockpile of ammunition which would one day become our currency. Backup generators and hand-cranked radios were in high demand, and multiple sites rated the best ones for preppers in a doomsday scenario. Coleman Frank's extensive blog advised preppers to learn the fine art of reloading casings and how to make their own bullets. Multiple sites listed directions for how to make your own bugout bag with at least three weeks of supplies packed and ready to go at a second's notice.

The heart of this movement was an intensely deep mistrust of authority. The language in all the sites and articles was clear: *We cannot trust those in power to keep us safe. We must fend for ourselves.* These messages resonated with me; I couldn't deny I still had trust issues, though my Berlin Wall had crumbled quite a bit in the last few years. The fact that this structure still remained inside me helped me to understand the pull toward self-reliance and isolation. Before I discounted everyone in the movement as crazy, I had to consider how many times I'd wanted to ghost on society, to bug out and find my own plot of land near water and take care of only myself. What I absolutely couldn't relate to were the racist and bigoted beliefs many of these sites spiraled down into and some of its prominent leaders promoted, including Coleman Frank.

These pockets of doomsday preppers were overwhelmingly white and ultra-conservative, and some of them lacked any understanding when it came to people different from themselves. That self-centered righteousness angered me.

More tips flashed onto my screen: invest in gold, not currency or stocks; bury or hide your cash and don't trust the banks; invest in a standalone freezer and stockpile freeze-dried meals; build an underground bunker—and on and on.

I could see how someone who already struggled with authority issues and who didn't feel secure in their community could tumble down this rabbit hole. Fear infiltrated the language of these sites. Instead of addressing that fear, they hyped it up with flashing warnings of doom and advertisements about how to save yourself and those you love from the end of the world.

I closed the laptop and examined the ceiling above me. I hadn't found anything in my search that addressed the real issue at hand. What allowed the survivalist movement the space to thrive in our culture centered around a few pertinent questions: What exactly did it mean to feel safe? What did it take to have security for one's family and loved ones? And was it even possible to control the murderous rages of another person?

CHAPTER FOURTEEN

Monday, 8:30 a.m.
Day 4 of the investigation

There's nothing like a double murder on Thanksgiving Day to bring on a media firestorm. While Simmons County had been the focus of the Deadeye case for some time, it had lost traction in the media once David Johnson was found guilty and went to prison. The sudden return of reporters and cameras overwhelmed the small town, particularly with the increased hunting population. The attention was a double-edged sword—the area certainly needed the economic boost, but the entire region had had enough bad press to last decades with the lingering opioid crisis.

BCI's media relations team helped the Simmons County sheriff's office prepare for the public statement and placed a podium outside the picturesque building, at the base of its stone staircase. There weren't enough chairs set up to seat all the reporters, and camera grips stood along the sides with their equipment set for the best angle.

Inside the building's foyer, Sheriff Daniel moved into the small makeshift waiting area just inside the main doors. The plan was we would all walk out of the building together, descend the stairs, and take our positions around the sheriff at the podium. We'd decided that Daniel should lead the statement—it was his county and the residents knew him best. They were looking to their sheriff for answers, not a stranger who had come in from the big city.

When Daniel saw me, he lit up with a big smile. "Don't you clean up well."

I smoothed the fabric of my dark business suit jacket. The media representative had called my dress shirt mauve, but it looked pink to me. No matter—you could clean up this special agent, but you couldn't take her away from the Frye boots. "Looking stellar yourself, Sheriff."

In his dress uniform, Daniel looked even taller. Wider. His white hair and beard had been freshly trimmed. His blue eyes seemed to swim behind the thick lenses of his glasses reminiscent of Santa Claus. While I stood with him, the media representative handed Daniel his final touch—the sheriff's hat with the brim brushed clean and its gold tassel polished.

"Let's do this, gang. Get in, get out, so we can get back to chasing our tails." Daniel pushed through the heavy wooden doors.

The sudden click of cameras assaulted us as we descended the stairs and formed a semi-circle behind Daniel at the podium.

"Good morning," Daniel began. "Our community has suffered an immeasurable loss. We mourn the passing of John Holden Jr. and his brother Logan as their deaths have formally been ruled as homicide. Our thoughts and prayers are with the Holden family as they navigate this trying time."

Daniel stopped for a breath, and the only sound was the click of cameras capturing every second of the press conference.

"The Bureau of Criminal Investigation has joined our task force, and we are asking for anyone who might have information to please contact our hotline," Daniel said. "If we all work together, this predator doesn't stand a chance."

As Daniel promised to re-apprehend David Johnson as quickly as possible, he was careful not to directly blame Deadeye for the two murders. We'd discussed the issue at length, but I wanted to keep Deadeye guessing as to what we might or might not know. I also hoped that withholding credit would send a message of inferiority to him—*You are not the center of this universe, Deadeye...*

Daniel advised all hunters and members of the community to use the buddy system. It hadn't worked for the Holden brothers, but there could be safety in numbers, he said. He then dropped a new piece of information for the reaping: "At the time of the Holden murders, our suspect drove a Chevrolet pickup truck, a model from the early 1980s. The vehicle was abandoned, but we think the killer might have some connection to the truck."

Photographs of a old pickup truck flashed on a media screen set up beside us with the task force number underneath it. "Remember, people: Report. Do not approach. Safety first."

The sheriff paused giving his message a moment to sink in. "In light of the tragic murders and the continued dangers present in our area, we advise everyone to not take part in this season's unofficial night hunt in Simmons County. Everyone is on edge—accidents can and do happen. It may be tradition in these parts, but the night hunt is certainly not worth losing your life. I caution every hunter to be on high alert and follow all safety regulations."

I scanned the crowd, but everyone looked the part of a reporter or media representative—heads bowed taking notes and faces hidden behind cameras.

Daniel thanked everyone for their time and motioned he was ready to leave the podium. A chorus of *Sheriff Daniel!* rang out as each reporter tried to catch his attention before he walked away. We had already determined that he wouldn't answer any questions from the media. They would want to know exactly what we wanted to know— was this person still in the area, if the community was at risk, and when might we finally catch him. We weren't in a position to answer these questions; rather than show our hand, we planned to say nothing.

"Sheriff Daniel, what do you have to say about the second letter released to the press?"

Daniel's confident stride hitched.

"The second letter from the parents," another reporter called out. "Are the Holdens working with you, Sheriff? Did you advise them to publicly write to Deadeye?"

After we took refuge from the cameras inside the building, Daniel hollered for everyone to meet in the task force office. We'd been blindsided, yet again.

❖

The task force office door had been sealed shut to keep anyone from overhearing anything they shouldn't. We arrived to find legal notification from the Alec and Blaylock firm declaring that all future correspondence with the Holdens must go through their law office.

"Fantastic," Daniel said, tossing the letter across the table. "This will help us find their children's killer, for sure."

I ignored Daniel's sarcasm and continued pulling up the latest press postings regarding the case. I displayed them on the multiple screens in the room, and it was more than clear that the mass media had gotten ahold of the letter, or at least a portion of it. The full letter was set to publish in the evening's *Simmons Tribune*'s front page.

I read the published part of the letter aloud to the team, slowly. You never knew when a word or a phrase might resonate with someone—a resonance that could lead us in a new direction.

To the person or persons who killed my sons,

My God (and yours) is a merciful being—I know this much to be true. Many members of my family have been praying for you. They pray that you come forward before it's too late. There is a time limit on our sins, as they say, and yours is running out. My family wants you to confess, as much for the safety of our community as for the forgiveness of your soul.

My prayers for you, however, are of a different sort. I pray that the hand that held your rifle burns—that it literally falls off your body—and that the wound never heals. I pray that the very weapon you used on my boys sends multiple bullets through your own heart. I pray that Jesus takes your tongue and your eyes so that you may know darkness and loneliness—darkness so deep there is nothing to pull you back from the nightmare that is now mine.

You took my boys from my family and the world. They were kind and loving, men that were on the verge of making their way in this world. They were young men who would have changed our society for the better. We will all suffer because of your cowardly actions.

I read this sentence over and over again: *I pray that Jesus takes your tongue and your eyes so that you may know darkness and loneliness—darkness so deep there is nothing to pull you back from the nightmare that is now mine.*

"If he's trying to stop Deadeye from killing again, I doubt his spew of anger is going to do the trick," Detective Rachel Donovan said. "If anything, this tone will only piss off the killer, not convince him to stop."

"Unless Holden is using some sort of reverse psychology," Daniel said. "He's trying to elicit empathy, sympathy for the family and their loss."

"As I told Holden in our last meeting, it's pointless," I said. "Deadeye and, most likely, his partner are incapable of such feelings."

Daniel groaned. "You cannot fault a man who has had two children murdered for being angry and then making that anger public."

"It's possible this letter was written by Joyce Holden," I said. "Given the change in tone and diction, it's possible we are dealing with a second writer. John wrote the first one. This time, Joyce gets her say."

Discussion of my theory's probability broke out among some of the officers in the room.

I read the key sentence aloud again in an attempt to get everyone focused. When I had everyone's attention, I said, "There are two ways to look at this sentence in the letter. *I pray Jesus takes your tongue and eyes*—why these two specific body parts if it's about inflicting pain on the killer? Sure, that is a tremendous amount of pain, but we could also read the letter as a warning. Don't talk to anyone and close your eyes to something that has already happened or will happen."

The room fell silent around me as the group thought about what I'd said. After a minute or so, an agent said, "You could see this as an indication the two are in on something together, or at least know one another."

Others agreed.

"It's not proof, by any means," I said, "but it is something. Until we find something better, let's work under the assumption that at least one of the Holdens has been in communication with Deadeye and his partner. Put a tail on them."

Daniel shook his head. "I can't figure out why they decided to lawyer up now. Is it because of the second letter? And *why* is the letter being published today? What's the significance?"

I shrugged. "I guess we need to go with the assumption that Holden wanted to get the message to Deadeye before someone else is murdered."

Sheriff Daniel seemed to accept my explanation, but I felt just as uneasy about the Holdens' behavior as he did. Something had changed. I felt the gears of the case speeding up, shifting directions.

❖

The steel door slammed behind me as I made my way onto the loading dock. I'd found the area behind the sheriff's office when I was looking for a quiet place to think, and I liked the seclusion of it, save for the staff that took their smoke breaks on the dock.

The temperature hadn't climbed above forty, and the cool air felt good against my face and neck.

"I love the cold weather," Sheriff Daniel said. He surprised me; I hadn't seen him come out the side door. "Looks like we're going to get a blast of it tonight. Frost advisory."

"The turn in weather might keep a few away from the night hunt." I leaned against the concrete wall of the dock beside him. The building backed up to a cornfield where the tall stalks had gone winter-brown.

"You doing okay, Sheriff?"

Daniel took a deep breath. "I wanted to extend an apology for my sensitivity about the Holdens." His fingertips played with the edges of his mustache. "It's hard to put aside personal relationships in these types of investigations, you know?"

"It is hard, and I hope I'm proven wrong about them."

"I do, too," Daniel said. "But the last few days...I don't know this version of the Holdens."

I understood. People could be the most confounding creatures on earth, particularly those you thought you knew. "What can you tell me about Mrs. Holden?"

"Lord, what can I say about Joyce," Daniel started. "She's quiet most of the time, but she's a fiercely devoted mother—she'll do anything for those kids. Logan and John are her youngest two, but there are two other children who are married and have their own kids. She volunteers at the church every week with the kids' program and cooks meals for those in our congregation who are homebound."

Joyce's activities made her a regular fixture in the small town, then. "Has she ever worked outside the home?"

"She worked with our coroner's office for quite a few years. Secretarial duties, you know," Daniel said. "She also took reports to different offices before we went digital and had email, PDFs, and electronic signatures. That's been some time ago."

He stepped away from the edge of the loading dock and twisted to the side. His spine gave an audible pop. "Oh, that felt good. I need to get in to see the chiropractor. This old man has seen far too much in these last few days."

"Come on," I chided. "You're far from old."

"That's debatable," Daniel chuckled.

My phone buzzed against my hip. I checked the screen. "BCI forensics," I told Daniel and pressed the phone to my ear.

"Agent Hansen, we have the report completed on the samples we received yesterday. The subject is positive for pregnancy," the specialist said.

So, Debbie Turner wasn't delusional—about the baby, anyway.

"But the additional sample you sent—David Johnson—does not match the paternal DNA."

"No match, huh? Let's run the sample through the system, then. See if we get a hit."

The specialist paused while she flipped the paper in front of her. "I'll get it started right away. The minute I get anything, I'll contact you."

I thought back to the way Debbie had rubbed her belly when we met, that proud and possessive hold she'd had on her growing baby bump.

I hung up and told Daniel the news.

"Thank God that slime won't be procreating after all," he said. "We don't need a Deadeye Junior anywhere in this world."

I agreed with him, but it didn't change the fact that Debbie *believed* she'd been impregnated by Deadeye. She struck me as a person who could be easily manipulated, though, a person with weak critical thinking skills. I was certain David Johnson recognized that as well. He only had to tell her it was his semen—no proof necessary.

"So then, who's the father?" I asked.

"Lord only knows." Daniel whistled.

I slipped the phone back into my pocket. "What do you say about a drive up to meet our favorite prison nurse? She's had some time to stew in a lonely cell. It might have been enough to jog her memory, to have remembered something in those long hours."

CHAPTER FIFTEEN

Hartford Correctional Institution
Monday, 1:30 p.m.

Remnants of Doritos, Cheetos, Snickers, Paydays, and M&M's scattered across paper plates. A small table separated Debbie Turner and me, and she rubbed her belly filled with the selection of junk from the prison vending machines. She'd washed everything down with Dr Pepper, and I watched her while she cracked open a third bottle.

"I take it prison food isn't your thing."

She shook her head, stuffing another Dorito in her mouth. "I feel so bad for David. He told me the prison food was enough to make anyone go on a hunger strike. I never understood just how bad food could be."

"Don't fool yourself, Debbie," I said. "He'll be back to it soon enough. We're close to capturing him."

She gave a bark of a laugh. "That's why you're here talking to me, right?" Her gaze settled on me. "You really should have that cheekbone looked at. Nasty cut." She popped the chip in her mouth.

I'd about reached my limit with Deadeye's fiancée. I'd been with her for over an hour and hadn't gotten very far. An offer had been placed on the table. Debbie hated her solitary cell and had begged the guards to move her to general population. We'd make that happen if she could provide direction to David Johnson's whereabouts or information on the partner he was working with.

"You have kids?" she asked through a mouthful of food.

I shook my head and checked my watch. I wasn't willing to play much longer, and I was over buying her mounds of junk from the vending machines.

"I never really believed all those pregnant women who said they had cravings, you know? I just thought the baby was a convenient excuse to eat whatever they wanted. Now I get it."

I took a drink from my own bottle of Mountain Dew. I'd given up on the prison coffee and needed the caffeine to keep me going.

"I never thought I'd be a mother," Debbie said. "I thought that opportunity passed me by. Then David came along."

"Well, he didn't just stroll into your life," I reminded her. "You sought him out, remember? In prison."

Debbie grinned at me like a child, her lips shiny with the sticky sweet of soda pop. "It was meant to be."

"*Right.*" I leaned back in my chair. The last thing I wanted to do was get into meant-to-bes with this woman. "Which brings me back to why I'm here. What information do you have for us?" I tapped the face of my watch. "You've got exactly fifteen minutes more of my time, and then the offer expires."

Debbie ripped open a package of chocolate chip cookies and popped one in her mouth.

"Who is David working with?" I asked once again.

Debbie laughed and a few crumbs of cookies flew out of her mouth. "Did I tell you about how I got pregnant? It was beautiful. Completely magical."

"Magical, I bet. Particularly since the baby isn't David's." I tapped my watch. "Twelve minutes."

Debbie eyed me and considered her options. She'd wasted as much time as she possibly could, but solitary was her weakness, as it was for most inmates. For Debbie, the isolation felt like it was smothering her—she might have been mentally unstable, but Debbie was social and outgoing. She needed others around her to keep her head on, and the eight-by-ten box was wearing on her.

"I can go to general population as soon as I leave here?"

"If your story checks out."

Debbie's arraignment had been delayed; she had another week to wait to see the judge and determine charges. Debbie's lawyer was new to the game and the prosecution took full advantage of that. Since Deadeye hadn't been captured, they wanted to keep her behind bars and away from any sort of bail possibility that might reunite her with David Johnson.

"I don't know who's helping David on the outside," she finally said. "All he told me is that they've known each other a long time. David said no one else in this world has ever had his back like this guy."

"David is most likely in Simmons County," I told her. "Why return to the place of his crimes?"

Debbie shrugged. "He always said that place had the best hunting in Ohio."

I considered the word *hunting.* "The night hunt."

Debbie nodded. "He's talked about it before, how there are so many clueless hunters out alone in dark and isolated areas. It tempted him. He told me that if it hadn't been for the rules, he'd have taken many of them down."

One bullet per target. That was what we knew about the rules so far. I wondered if there were rules about hunting during the daylight hours as well. Still, it made sense. Sheriff Daniel had said that Deadeye was known to mingle with the hunters and share in their celebrations. Why wouldn't he be drawn to the highlight of the week? He'd never taken a victim during a night hunt. Then again, he'd never taken two victims at once, either. Deadeye was evolving, and I wondered how long it would take before he decided the rules of his game didn't matter anymore.

I screwed the cap on my empty Mountain Dew bottle and signaled the guard. "Time's up. I'll be in touch."

"What about my move to GP?" The guard locked her wrists together.

"I told you, the information must check out." I thanked the guard and walked out, ignoring Debbie's screams. I had every intention of moving her once we found David Johnson. Until then, I needed Debbie Turner uncomfortable. We'd need her statement, her testimony against David Johnson when we captured him. She wouldn't do that hanging in the prison gym with all her new girlfriends chiding her to ignore us.

❖

Sheriff Daniel drove toward Simmons County, his wrist cocked over the steering wheel. "We can't really trust her."

"Nope. But what else do we have?" I flipped through the guards' and warden's notes regarding Debbie's stay in the prison. While I'd been sitting with her, Daniel had been meeting with Warden Spen.

"We need to plan for an attack during the night hunt. If she's right, you know?" Daniel said. "I just worry she could be leading us into an ambush."

"It's possible," I said. "Despite Debbie's delusional thinking, she's not stupid. She sees that she's losing David Johnson. She wants Deadeye back, and I don't think it matters if he comes back to her in handcuffs or as a free man. She just wants him back. So why mislead us when we can give her what she wants?"

Daniel couldn't argue that point. Debbie Turner might have been hurt by the lack of contact with David Johnson, but she was still smitten. Her fiancé alive and in prison would at least allow her some level of control over Deadeye. She now realized she couldn't control him in any way outside prison bars and the possibility of losing him was too much for her to take.

"The night hunt will happen, despite my warnings," Daniel said. "We have a little over twenty-four hours to position ourselves and call in additional officers. I'd like to get our people posed as hunters and scattered throughout the field long before night sets in."

I agreed. "We have to meet Deadeye in his own element. We go to him, not the other way around."

"We still have no information on the partner," Daniel said.

"If we take Deadeye, the partner falls, too," I told him. "He's weaker than Deadeye, not as deadly with the rifle. *He's* the one scrambling to catch up in the game."

As we neared the exit for Simmons, Sheriff Daniel pointed out a billboard advertisement for Bad Billy's: *The headquarters for all your hunting season needs*. "Most of the night hunters meet up at Billy's," Daniel said. "They share drinks and pump each other up for the hunting contest. Looks like you're going to experience the infamous night hunt after all, Special Agent."

"Looking forward to it," I said. And I was—Deadeye and his partner wouldn't be the only ones out in the thick of the Simmons County woods hunting humans.

CHAPTER SIXTEEN

Monday, 5:00 p.m.

The station hummed with activity, and every task force member chipped away at her assigned duty. Tension over the upcoming night hunt was palpable; some regarded it with fear while others looked to it with excitement. The possibility of danger had a way of amplifying everything at stake. We worked any loose ends of the case, attacking the frayed edges that needed trimming.

Two detectives worked the military angle and continued scouring records from any base where David Johnson had been stationed. We knew that his rifle skills had been honed in the military and that Deadeye felt very comfortable—and was very accurate—with this type of weapon butted against his shoulder. We knew Deadeye served two tours in Afghanistan and most likely would have served a third if detectives in Simmons County hadn't caught him and put him in prison. Some members of the team worked under the theory that Deadeye met his partner while serving; they ran searches on the long list of military personnel names that matched Deadeye's movements in the military. A few believed their connection might have been made in Afghanistan; however, I wasn't sold on that theory. While David Johnson was at home shooting his rifle, the partner had a record of missing shots. If the partner had to rely on the weapon to save his life in battle, he would have understood the rifle better. That didn't mean the two couldn't have met during basic training or while they were on leave.

The military theory only gained strength when we learned that John Holden Sr. was a retired Air Force general who had been stationed near Dayton. He worked with and trained soldiers for years. I'd requested a second interview with Mr. Holden through his attorney, but hadn't received any acknowledgment.

Officers had been dispatched to interview anyone who made a call to the tip line no matter how absurd some of them sounded. Road crews had set up a checkpoint near the area where most hunters parked their vehicles. Drivers were stopped and shown Deadeye's mug shots, but there had been no leads yet. It was as if Deadeye had simply vanished. Or, as I suspected, he vanished into a well-made, smartly hidden bunker.

Rachel Donovan and a local team of officers used aerial maps and gridded search patterns to locate possible bunker locations in the county. Most owners willingly let the officers in and then gave directions to other bunkers in the area. It was slow going, though, given the vast rural county, and everyone was surprised to see just how stocked and prepared their neighbors were for the end of times.

Bennett had gone into the sheriff's office with me that morning to offer help to Dr. Mike Duncan. She looked smart and sexy in her dark business suit and dark-rimmed glasses, and I couldn't imagine any coroner telling her no—or anyone for that matter. When I saw her around the office, my heart filled with a sudden gratitude—I'd been the one to share a bed with her the night before, a woman I never imagined would be interested in me. I was happy to have Bennett near me despite all the mounting pressure. We certainly had moments in our relationship. At work, though, I always knew I could count on her to have my back. Such loyalty in the law enforcement world, I'd found, was as rare as it was beautiful.

As I finalized a plan to leave the office with Sheriff Daniel, Bennett gave me a nod toward the door. I followed her to one of the staff bathrooms where she checked the stalls to be sure we were alone. One of the hardest things about having a relationship with a colleague, I learned quickly, was the constant effort it took to keep that information private. In a roomful of detectives, crime investigators, and law enforcement at the top of their game, it was a very difficult secret to keep.

"We need to talk," Bennett said, her heels clacking toward me.

I leaned my hip against the sink counter and stretched my neck. My muscles felt tight enough to snap, and I needed a strong shot of caffeine. The case was catching up with me, and nothing sounded better than a long afternoon nap.

"What's up?" I asked.

Bennett reached for my hand. "You look so tired." With her other hand, she reached out and tucked a stray curl behind my ear. "I have some news about Sanders."

"Everything okay?"

She gave me a sad smile. "The surgeon thinks he might have an infection in one of the surgical wounds. His temperature is running high and they have him on antibiotics."

"Oh no," I said. "Will that be enough to kill the infection?"

"Hopefully," Bennett said. "There's a real danger of sepsis—when a bad infection gets into the bloodstream. The surgeon wants to take Sanders back in to surgery and clean out the wound."

I dropped my head into my hands, totally frustrated with nowhere for those feelings to go.

"Hey," Bennett said, her hand squeezing my shoulder. "He'll get through this. Sanders is a fighter."

Maybe it was her touch after the news about Sanders, or maybe it was the quiet safety of the bathroom, but I needed to feel Bennett against me. I reached for her, hugged her close, nearly falling into her.

"Whoa," Bennett said, catching my weight. She asked again, "You okay?"

I tucked my face against the base of her neck, that space near her collarbone that seemed to be fitted just for me. I felt Bennett's tension and readied myself for her warnings that we could not have any physical contact at work. Instead, her tension released, and she hugged me back. We stood that way, silently holding one another. And I realized that I'd been longing for a moment like this with Bennett since I'd found out about Sanders's cancer. I felt all the emotions I'd stuffed down during my overnight visit with Sanders, and they flooded back with the relief of Bennett's body against mine.

"It's all going to work out," Bennett said. "They caught it early."

I nodded against her silky blouse and listened while she told me about the miracles of medicine and surgery and about how we needed to trust his medical team.

"I'm going to the hospital to be with Sanders," Bennett said. "I'm not getting anywhere with Duncan, and I don't want to get into any sort of argument over territory."

The bathroom door swung open. As the officer walked in, Bennett dropped to her knees. "Dammit. I know it's here somewhere."

I pretended to search the area around the sink. Looking into the mirror, I caught the woman's gaze. "Lost contact lens."

It was a tired move, one that Bennett and I had used before when caught in some kind of physical embrace at work.

The rules would have been the same even if we'd been a heterosexual couple—sexual relationships on a team could hinder our ability to think clearly or objectively on a case. If the relationship came out in court, it could be used to argue against the hard work of the entire team. I understood the rules and respected them…most of the time. Bennett and I worked well together, and what we did outside of work didn't hinder that. The fact that we were a lesbian couple only heightened the danger of the relationship being revealed.

The woman sympathized with the lost contact and shut herself inside a stall.

"Found it!" Bennett stood. "These suckers cost too much to lose on a bathroom floor."

I flipped on the water, and Bennett stood beside me, the fake contact lens forgotten. We considered one another in the wide mirror above the sink. My fingers intertwined with hers under the spray of cold water. We held them there, the water cascading over our skin.

"Thank you," I mouthed to her reflection.

Bennett smiled in a way that softened her eyes. She gave me a quick wink, and I wanted to catch it in my hand to keep in my pocket. I wanted to hold on to that wink and pull it out later to examine it.

When the toilet flushed, Bennett gave me the slightest of nods, our eyes meeting in the mirror one long second before we both turned away from one another, moving in separate directions.

Chapter Seventeen

Monday, 6:30 p.m.

Sheriff Daniel and I spent the evening working with Billy so that we could secure his surveillance equipment and synchronize it with ours. BCI's technical support team wired in additional surveillance for Billy's extensive parking area, given that somehow Deadeye and/or his partner had apparently stolen Billy's old truck from the lot. Officers found the truck abandoned at an interstate rest stop within the county. Again, no surveillance video—I was skeptical, as usual.

During hunting season every year, Bad Billy's boomed with business. The megastore filled its makeshift bar and sold more hunting gear than the entire rest of the year. Some made Bad Billy's the base camp of their hunting experience and met members of their party at specific times at the bar. And those who didn't have the money to rent cabins or hotel rooms in the county, they slept in their vehicles in Billy's parking lot. The property reminded me of a concert venue in a major city awaiting a big show.

"Rumor has it that Billy started the infamous night hunt years ago," Daniel told me as he threw the cruiser in park. "It certainly worked as a marketing strategy—the entire hunting season revolves around his place."

"How much do you know about him?" I asked.

"Old Billy? We've never had any trouble with him. Some folks in town don't like having such easy access to weapons in our backyard. Then again, these people don't think about the ease the internet provides. We've heard he can play loose with the sales rules, but he's never been caught doing anything illegal." He opened the door to step out, and then turned back to me. "Why?"

"He has a lot of access to hunters. You'd think he would have heard something about the partner. Or possibly where Deadeye is hiding out."

Daniel grumbled behind me as I led into the building. I ignored him. For all of Sheriff Daniel's excellent work habits and strategies, he had an undeniable blind spot when it came to the people of Simmons County. He trusted them inherently, and in his defense, very little crime occurred within the county outside of meth and opioid abuse and sales. As far as I could tell, Daniel wasn't completely sold on the idea that Deadeye had a local partner. We would need undeniable proof to make this hard sell to the sheriff.

Inside Billy's private office, we huddled around his security station. Mounted heads of deer lined the walls, and when he took off his hat, he revealed a bald patch at the crown. He was conscious of it, combing his fingers over the pale skin while he considered Daniel and me. "I don't mind telling y'all, this whole thing has got me a bit nervous."

Sheriff Daniel laughed. "I heard that."

"I want you to know I have officially canceled the night hunt," Billy said. "These guys are so pumped for it, though, and they aren't listening to me. I have taken away all the rewards we've used in the past to hopefully put a stop to it."

"We're grateful for your support," I said. "You are our best connection to the hunting community."

Billy said, "I'm nervous because I'm not sure who we're looking for. Every time my door swings open, I'm wondering if it's him."

We talked about the probability of Deadeye altering his appearance for the hunt. We also talked about the chances that he wouldn't be alone, and that whoever he was with would partner as his cover.

"Everyone is a suspect at this point," I told Billy. "Be cautious of any person who enters the premises, whether you know them or not."

Billy paced the length of his office while the specialist worked on the equipment. He looked anxious with his hands fisted inside his jean pockets and head bowed in thought.

"We have an alert code for you," the tech specialist said. "Worse comes to worst, wave into a camera. Officers will be monitoring them at the sheriff's office while everyone else is either patrolling or working undercover."

"And we will have undercover officers scattered throughout your property," Daniel assured Billy. "Someone will always be close."

"It's really important our hunters stay undercover," I added. "Don't change anything else in terms of the way you do things here. We don't want to alert anyone that you are nervous about law enforcement or anything else."

"Hunters?" Billy asked. "You're going to have people in the night hunt?"

I pointed at my chest. "My first night hunt."

He chuckled. "We need to outfit you for it, then. You need the clothes and gear of a hunter."

I agreed, envisioning myself clad from head to toe in camouflage with a hat made out of tree branches to boot.

"Most of the guys we picked are real hunters," Daniel said. "They can and will talk the talk with the best of them. They'll blend in with the crowd."

Our tech specialist finished wiring a feed into Billy's security system so that we could monitor all the cameras in real time.

"The media keeps hanging around," Billy mentioned.

"And they will be here until the night hunt is over," Daniel assured him. "They've heard about it the same as us. Just treat them like any other customer and don't say anything on the record."

"We actually *want* the media around right now," I said. "Deadeye loves the attention. There's a thrill that comes with fooling everyone while hiding right beneath their noses. We know he has an ego the size of the United States. Deadeye believes he is above capture, smarter than everyone else, and I'm certain his partner is of the same mold. They will test our system, and it makes sense they would put themselves in a lively place to try and fool us."

While Daniel and the specialist worked with Billy, I watched the business's monitors. One camera showed the action from behind the bar and another featured the tables. There was no other word to describe the mood in the place other than celebratory. I scanned the other cameras and caught a glimpse of Detective Rachel Donovan entering the building. She'd been on a call to check bunkers in the area and offered to meet us. I sent her a quick text so she could find us, and then I watched in the screen as she received it. I detected the hint of a smile before she set off to join us in the office. Our undercover work was set to begin.

❖

It turned out shopping for hunting clothing and accessories could be fun, especially when someone else was paying for it. Billy had given me and Donovan access to all his top line hunting wear, and by the time Donovan and I made our way to Billy's bar, you couldn't have detected that I had only been hunting twice as a teenager.

Donovan tipped her glass against my beer bottle. "To a safe and swift hunt," she said, careful not to broadcast what exactly we were hunting for. She'd untied the knot of hair at the nape of her neck and dark hair fell across her shoulders.

I was dressed in a variety of thin but mighty layers, and my new cargo pants crackled when I bent at the knees. Billy swore that sound would dissipate if I wore them all night to break them in. The insanely comfortable pants were quickly shaping up to be one of my favorite pairs.

The bar pulsed around us with an anxious energy. Teams gathered, and it was clear that very few were willing to follow the sheriff's advice to avoid the night hunt. Donovan told me that many hunters teamed up for the night hunt and moved in teams of four to six people. It was a safety measure—hunting in the darkness of the forest unsettled most folks, but it also increased their chances of bringing down deer. In Bad Billy's unofficial contest, teams were permitted, and so men and women camoed to hell and back sat with land maps and GPS as they built a plan together.

Bennett had texted me throughout the night to update me on Sanders's surgery. He'd been placed in ICU afterward to allow his body to gain strength to hopefully fight off any of the remaining elements of the infection.

Bennett had described the surgery: *Think of it like a big vacuum. They'll suck out the infection, clean the wound, and close him back up.*

Texts like these nearly made me gag, but at least Bennett had gotten my message that I wanted to be kept informed about Sanders. She was trying—I had to give her that.

Bennett had always found humor in my inability to hear the gritty details of medical procedures. "You're a woman who deals with gruesome deaths every day," she liked to tease me, "yet you cannot handle a discussion of organ removal or surgery."

"Dead people, Ben. There's a big difference," I liked to point out. "They aren't feeling anything that happens to them anymore."

Throughout the night, I tried not to think of Sanders, instead focusing on the undercover work ahead of me. I'd paired myself with Donovan for the night hunt, a partnership that made me feel better about my lack of hunting skills. Sheriff Daniel would stay behind at the station and monitor all the incoming radio feeds. He'd make sense of it all with our tech specialist and send us any needed information. We decided that Daniel was so well known among the local hunters that he would draw too much attention in the field. Quite possibly, his presence could hinder the investigation. Donovan and I were able to fly underneath the radar—we hadn't come into contact with enough people to be recognized as law enforcement in Simmons County.

As the heavy country music beat pulsed inside my chest, I couldn't stop my thoughts from turning back to Sanders. I worried about how well he would recover from this second round of surgery once he left the hospital. He claimed he didn't want to worry anyone, and because of that, he still hadn't contacted his grown kids, or anyone else for that matter. This spoke volumes about the embarrassment Sanders felt about his breast cancer. I recognized that Sanders was trying to use a really good avoidance tactic, and his current plan seemed to be that he'd ride out his recovery and future treatments at home alone. I didn't like the image that left in my mind—an image that felt so incredibly lonely to me. This only made me want to be at the hospital with him even more, but we were less than twenty-four hours away from the beginning of the night hunt. I needed to be in Simmons County with Donovan making connections with the different hunting teams.

I drank with Donovan and scanned the growing crowd. I told myself the drink was needed in order to penetrate the different hunting teams. There weren't many women in the crowd, and they were the ones we targeted first. Most welcomed us and pulled us into their group, but nothing struck as suspicious. When I switched from beer to whiskey and Coke, I told myself it was for the welfare of the case—we needed to be enmeshed within the hunting community. The excuses for my behavior continued, and because no one in Billy's bar really knew me, I was able to pretend that I also didn't know myself.

Somewhere after 10 p.m., I stepped outside to call Bennett for another update on Sanders. The cool air smacked against my warm face, and I leaned into the brick wall for support. Exhaustion washed over me—I needed a few hours of solid sleep and a long, hot shower.

"He's doing fine, Hansen," Bennett said. "The surgeon was very positive. He thinks Sanders is on the right track now. He's on some powerful antibiotics, and they reissued the pain meds."

"I hope they got everything."

"Me, too. He's really groggy from the anesthesia. Stop worrying—there's nothing you can do for him here."

I knew Bennett was right, but it didn't stop my feelings of guilt.

"I've been thinking about this night hunt," Bennett started. "Are you really prepared for that? I mean, have you ever even been hunting?"

I laughed. "Briefly," I admitted. "It didn't go well. Everyone is lucky I'm hunting serial killers and not deer."

Bennett chuckled. "Ah, your specialty. This thing sounds... intense. No phone service, spotty radio connections. It worries me, Hansen."

"Please don't. I have a great team and Donovan will be with me the entire night. She's Katniss Everdeen in disguise," I said, my words tumbling out with the alcohol warm in my belly.

"It's hard not to worry," she said. "I know you're used to these things, these missions, but I almost lost you in the Wallace Lake case when you nearly drowned. Promise me you'll keep in touch at all times. If you find yourself in a poor reception area, move!"

I explained to Bennett that we couldn't alert any hunters to the possibility we were there for any other reason than hunting, so they decided to limit our radio use and instead plant tracking devices inside our jackets and our packs. We also planned to carry emergency radios, just in case. As we talked, I heard a voice in the background. A female voice.

"Is that a doctor? Or a nurse?" The phone jumbled as Bennett seemed to be walking. "Have you told someone about Sanders's surgery? He's so private, Ben. I'm afraid of the news getting out before he's ready." The female voice again. I recognized it. "Is that... Harvey? *Alison Harvey?*"

"I'm sorry, okay? Harvey called to find out about the case..."

"She's there because of the *case*? Come on, Bennett."

No matter how good the last twenty-four hours with Bennett had been, I couldn't shake the nagging fears that haunted me from the moment I learned of Bennett and Harvey's past relationship. Harvey was nearly perfect, with her chiseled, handsome face and body. I'd never been able to compete with her.

I paced back and forth with the sudden burst of energy and nowhere for it to go. I wanted to tell Bennett that Harvey needed to go, that our conversation was done. Instead, I said, "His own family doesn't even know yet."

"Apparently others do," Bennett argued. "Harvey heard about it from someone else, not me. She admires Sanders, you know, the same way she admires you."

"Please." I held my arms close and my shoulder harness pulled tight against my collarbone. "She's only there for the case, though, right? A case you aren't even *officially* involved in."

"It's not about me," Bennett said. "She's looking for you. She wants in on the Deadeye case."

"Of course she does."

I hadn't known Harvey very long, but you got to know a person well when you were partnered with them, even for only a short length of time. Harvey was the type of law enforcement employee who focused all her current job duties on activities that would help her move up the ranks. Her sole focus was how quickly she could climb to the top of the law enforcement food chain. Someday Harvey wanted to direct it all, and her goal seemed quite achievable, given her personality. It made sense that Harvey would have stayed in contact with Sanders in the hopes of one day working with BCI. Harvey hadn't been able to maintain contact with me, but Sanders and Bennett had softer hearts for these kinds of things. I didn't want to admit it, but with Sanders out of commission, it was possible Harvey'd relied on Bennett to get her foot in the door.

"I'm worried you aren't over her."

"It doesn't matter how many times I tell you I am, does it?" Bennett asked. "You're not hearing me."

We both knew she was right, that I was much more inclined to follow the pull of my instinct over anything that she could ever say. The problem was that sometimes my instinct could be misdirected by fear.

From the start of our relationship, Bennett and I rarely saw the behavior of colleagues, suspects, or criminals similarly. Justice didn't always look the same to us. For Bennett, there was a clear distinction between right and wrong. For me, though, there were so many variant shades in between.

When Bennett and I walked away from Wallace Lake, our first major case, we carried its lingering effects with us. Sure, we'd made a dent in the opioid and human trafficking trades in that region of Ohio, in a town that screamed of some of the highest opioid death rates in the country. Our team had also celebrated the end of a serial killer's career. But there were many disturbing elements to the case, and I still had contradicting emotions about the way it all went down. Sadie Reid, a teen I'd fought to save from drowning herself in Wallace Lake had been arrested for murder; evidence showed she had been manipulated to kill. I wanted to be the one person in her life who wouldn't walk away, the one who wouldn't forsake her. The law, however, had other plans.

The Wallace Lake case had been massive, with its crime ring spreading deep and wide throughout the region. Attorneys were still building their cases. Because I was the lead special agent on the case, my testimony would be subpoenaed. I couldn't have any contact with Sadie until the trial was over.

"You do the crime, you pay the time," Bennett often said.

I saw Sadie as a product of her environment and a lack of guidance. I believed the weight of a person's past, along with abuse and neglect and psychological issues, should be considered in one's sentencing, particularly a teen. Which was another reason why Bennett's excuses for Harvey's behavior, so out of character for her, rang suspect to me. What exactly were they doing together, anyway? How long had the two been in contact without my knowledge? But what really bothered me was I never would have known Harvey was with Bennett if I hadn't surprised her with a call. Yet another secret Bennett would have tried to keep from me.

I'd heard enough—I ended the call after a quick good-bye. And I wanted a drink so bad I could nearly taste it.

CHAPTER EIGHTEEN

Monday, close to midnight

The bartender kept the drinks coming while Donovan and I worked the crowd. We shared beers and stories with so many of the hunting teams over the course of the evening, joining in their discussions about best hunting locations or what type of weapons worked best. Donovan had skills—she could match any self-proclaimed hunter in the bar's talk of hunting.

The night wound down, and Donovan sat beside me on a bar stool, her eyes still clear and bright. I was pretty sure she'd finished only her second beer, but I'd lost count of how many drinks I'd consumed.

"I've been on an enforced health kick," I said, thinking of Donovan's weight lifting regimen.

"Oh yeah?"

"Yeah," I slurred. "I've been good about not drinking. Looks like tonight I've blown it." I didn't tell Donovan that I'd more than blown it—my plan was in smithereens. My usual disasters began with me drinking alone, a favorite MO of mine. This time, I'd reasoned that the crowd at Billy's and my work with Donovan would save me from myself.

Donovan changed the subject. "Do you live in Columbus? Near the BCI office?"

"Bought a little house. A bunga*looow*." I stretched out the word to show her how fun it was to say. I handed her my phone, and she scrolled through the photos.

"Nice place. Where is it?"

"Spring Rock. Out in the country."

"Good for you. I love living in the country," Donovan said, eying my empty glass. "There's no place I'd rather be."

I signaled the bartender. "One more."

Time—it moved in the strangest ways once my belly filled with alcohol and it fired through my veins. I couldn't tell how many hours had passed in that bar with Donovan or how many drinks I'd actually consumed. It was enough that when I left the bar with Donovan, I relied on her to hold me up. We made our way to the parking lot, and because I hadn't driven, she gave me a ride back to the hotel. Her long thin arms goose-pimpled in the cold night, and she guided me into the passenger seat. She spoke on her phone as she drove, and I sang something about the darkness and hardness of life. Back at the hotel, she held me up in the elevator and led me down the hall to my room. Even though I'd shared that room with Bennett the night before, it felt like centuries had passed. When Donovan and I stepped inside and the heavy door clicked shut behind us, I hugged her tight and swore I'd never let her go.

CHAPTER NINETEEN

Tuesday, 10:15 a.m.
Day 5 of the investigation

I woke to the incessant ring of my phone and the obnoxious morning sun streaming through the hotel window. Squinting, I rolled over too fast. I held my pounding head as I tried to find my bearings. I recognized where I was immediately—in the throes of wretched hangover territory. I'd been here way too many times to count, though my mind had the uncanny ability to forget just how bad it really felt. My tongue felt like cotton superglued to the roof of my mouth. Somewhere in the room my phone kept up its obnoxious ring, which didn't help.

Then I remembered Donovan. She'd brought me back to the hotel the night before, and I remembered her arm around me helping me to bed. I turned over, terrified I might find her asleep beside me or in the bathroom. Still in my new hunting outfit, I was sweating through the layers of thin shirts Donovan had picked out for me. Thankfully, I was alone in the room.

I searched for the phone as I pulled off all the bedding. The hotel floor was quiet—a complete change from the other mornings I'd spent here. Other guests were up and ready to hunt no later than six a.m. most mornings, and the stillness unnerved me.

The phone rang again and I snatched it up. "Hansen." My voice sounded like a dry rattle.

"Finally," Sheriff Daniel said. "Where are you? Did you get my messages?"

"Messages?" I put him on speaker and checked the missed calls. Eleven from Daniel.

"It's ten fifteen, Hansen. The lawyers will be here any minute."

I had no idea what he was talking about but knew I'd screwed up. "I wasn't aware of a meeting. I have a friend in the hospital," I started, as if I could blame Sanders for my behavior.

"We need you here," Daniel said. "Now."

I ended the call and changed as fast as I could into my work clothes that had been tossed over the back of a chair. My stomach churned and threatened to explode. I didn't have half the energy I needed to face the day. And the night hunt was only hours away.

Stupid, stupid, stupid. I chastised myself as I chugged a glass of Alka-Seltzer and then ran the toothbrush through my mouth. I couldn't let myself think about Bennett—her reaction to my behavior last night would not be fun to deal with. But as I pulled shut the hotel door behind me, I realized that things could have been so much worse. Donovan could so easily have stayed with me—I wasn't in any frame of mind to say no. And these were the exact frames of mind that regularly sank me in relationships.

"No truck." I stood in the parking lot, dropped my bag, and let a ribbon of curse words flow. My truck was still at the sheriff's office. "Great start to the day," I said to myself, dialing for a ride. Despite the chill of the air, I was sweating and shaky. I needed water and someone much smarter than me to completely smack some sense into me. As I waited, I went back in the hotel for a bottle of water. But I felt shaken—my lapse in sobriety, if you wanted to call what I'd been doing sobriety—had happened so fast. But I'd had a plan, I reminded myself. I could control it. Instead, the ease with which it all happened rattled my nerves.

❖

Coleman Frank brought an entourage to the sheriff's office—three lawyers and a spokesperson from a national organization representing survivalists—and had alerted the media to his visit. When the Uber driver dropped me at the front of the building, I chose to avoid the reporters huddled around the entrance and came in through the back. I found Sheriff Daniel in his office.

"It's some kind of ambush," he told me on the way to the conference room. "A ploy for the media's attention."

We each took a seat opposite Frank and his crew, who eyed us carefully as we entered the conference room.

"We're here to file a formal complaint about the invasion of private land by this investigation," Frank said.

It took me a few seconds to register what he'd said. Daniel and I didn't know exactly what to expect from the meeting, but this wasn't it. "Please clarify for us," I said.

"This sheriff's office has been through the county, breaking in to bunkers and survival sheds without the slightest thought about privacy," Frank said. His puffy cheeks burned red with a fresh shave. He'd proudly shown me his own bunker that was the envy of all the area survivalists. This was certainly a drastic change from that guy.

The spokesperson, a man with an unmanaged beard, jumped in. "We get that there is a search going on here, and we want to help. But our people have the right to build and protect their own bunkers. They have the right to keep those spaces to themselves for the purposes they were built. Officers have been demanding entrance to many bunkers without a search warrant."

Donovan groaned beside me, and I sensed the sarcasm before it left Daniel's mouth. "All you want to do is help, right? That's why you brought the media along with you?"

"Sheriff," one of the lawyers said, "it's simply a matter of courtesy. We're here to file the complaint and let you know we will take legal action if the searches continue."

"I'd say your people are lucky," Coleman Frank said. "Survivalists are armed and prepared to kill to keep their family and land protected."

"Coleman, you know threats like that don't work with me. Period." Daniel turned to the lawyers. "If, and that's a very big *if,* one of my officers was too aggressive in his request for access,

I apologize. The safety of our community is at risk. My job is to protect it."

"You have no idea where he is, Sheriff. No one does. Canceling the night hunt isn't going to make one hill of beans difference in that," Frank said, standing. The lawyer handed Daniel the paperwork. "I've instructed my website followers to shoot to kill any intruders to their private property. We have the right to protect ourselves, Sheriff. Our world demands it of us."

The entourage followed Coleman Frank out to the main entrance of the building where the media waited, microphones turned on.

Daniel and I watched through the tall plate glass windows as the spokesperson for the survivalists gave a statement, whipping the reporters into action.

Daniel crossed his arms over his big chest and sighed. "Hansen, I don't understand much about this world anymore. Not a lot of anything makes sense to me." He hiked his pants up by the belt loops, the paperwork crinkling in his hand.

"I suspect this has very little to do with the searches and everything to do with your formal call to end the night hunt," I said.

Daniel reached up and stroked his thick white mustache. "I'm sure that's the case, Hansen. They're anxious we'll put this on someone in their organization, which makes me think David Johnson and his partner have ties to this group in some way. But I don't believe survivalist thinking caused the murders."

I agreed. The victims hadn't threatened anyone's safety. They'd simply been in the wrong place at the wrong time.

"Besides," Daniel said, "it might do us all some good to be prepared for what could be coming."

"Such as?" I asked.

"All you have to do is turn on the evening news. It's filled with all kinds of tragedies that folks didn't see coming. School and workplace shootings. Floods and tornadoes and freaking hurricanes that sink whole towns. And those fires out in California and Colorado? Let's not even get into the politics of our day. It's a minefield out there, Hansen."

I rubbed my pounding temple. Once Coleman Frank made his way to the parking lot, the media dispersed.

"Haven't you ever just wanted to gather all the things you need and lock yourself inside your home with the people you love most? Just shut this insane world out?" Daniel asked.

"Yeah, I have." I followed Daniel back to the task force office. "My home feels like one of the only places I can control in this world. But even there, bad shit can happen. There's no safe place, Daniel."

The thing I didn't see coming.

An invisible trip wire. A hair-trigger explosion.

I understood all too well what it felt like to have a bomb go off in your life, something so big and so unforeseeable that it literally rocked you to the core of your being. I understood what was behind the sheriff's words, that feeling of vulnerability and the need to protect those we love.

I survived many assaults that first year after Marci's murder, attacks that I never anticipated could possibly be in my path. Once the police had cleared me as a suspect, both my father and I thought all questioning surrounding my involvement would end. We didn't take into account the town where we lived. We didn't count on the persistence of Marci's mother and the pain she felt that left everything very far from over. She argued that I must have seen something out in the quarry that awful day and blamed me because her daughter never would have been in the caves that day if not to meet me. While Marci's mother didn't say these things directly to me, I was always close by when she had my father on the phone yammering into his ear. These phone conversations generally ended with my father saying, "For Christ's sake, Sharon, they're just kids. Let it go."

The blame from Marci's family rolled over to school—everyone had heard about what happened, and I found myself friendless and hiding in the library to avoid the horrible reality of school lunch and no one to sit with.

The hardest truth I had to face after Marci's murder, though, was that she was really gone. It was like some twisted form of magic. *Poof!* She was here one minute and vanished the next. I never saw it coming, the tragedy that changed my life. Then again, did anyone ever really see tragedy looming ahead? That's what made it all so tragic, the inability to stop it.

"There might not be a safe place," Daniel interrupted my thoughts, "but maybe it's the feeling that we *can* control something that's so important. Maybe we have to believe we have some control over our homes. It keeps us sane when a random house burns down or a family is robbed in their home or a murder happens between partners."

I nodded and sank into my chair as he stepped outside to make a call. I reached for another bottle of water and some aspirin. I needed to hydrate before the night hunt and get rid of my looming migraine.

That's when Detective Donovan pushed through the door. She was already dressed to hunt, her hair perfectly slicked back into a tight bun. She gave me a grin and held up a take-out bag to me.

"Chicken noodle soup and as many saltines as I could grab," she said, handing me the bag. "Eat up."

My mouth watered with the smell of fresh soup. "Thanks," I said, digging into the bag. "And my deepest apologies about last night."

I concentrated on opening the steaming soup and packets of crackers. I deserved to be embarrassed, but that never made it any easier. After I made sure no one else was in the room, I said, "I never meant to drink so much."

"I understand," Donovan said. "We never mean to drink that much."

I looked over at her. *We?*

Donovan reached into her pocket and produced a silver Celtic cross the size of a half-dollar. She pointed out the engraving on it and handed the cross to me: *seven years.*

"Seven years, three months, four days, and"—she looked at her watch—"four hours sober."

"You're in recovery?" I asked, dumbly. Donovan was so well put together, so organized and bright, I never would have guessed. I picked up the weighty cross and held it in the palm of my hand.

"I am an alcoholic, and I'm grateful for these clean days," she said.

"But you had beer last night," I said, turning the cross over and over in my hands. I was reminded of the Celtic cross around my neck—Marci's cross that her family had given me once we closed her case.

She nodded. "Like you, I saw alcohol as the only way in to the groups we needed to talk to. I held the beer. I dumped it out at some point and got another. I dumped that one out, too."

I rubbed the cross between my fingers, and then handed it back to her. "Seven years," I said. "Impressive."

"It could be yours, too," Donovan said, slipping it into her pocket as another officer pushed through the office door. "Let's talk more tonight."

I focused on my soup and the way it soothed my throat on the way down. I didn't really want to talk to Donovan about sobriety, but I was intrigued. There was a story there, I knew. A painful story, and one I couldn't help but be curious to know.

CHAPTER TWENTY

Simmons County Forest
Tuesday, 5:00 p.m.

Detective Rachel Donovan steered her Jeep onto the shoulder of the single lane road. The gravel under the tires crunched as we rolled to a stop near the trunk of an enormous maple. The sun had begun to set behind the forested land, and the temperature had dropped about ten degrees.

"Ready for your first night hunt?" Donovan asked, killing the engine.

I pushed open the passenger door. "As ready as I'll ever be." I meant it, too. My hangover queasiness had subsided and taken the edge of my migraine away with it.

"According to this year's hunting guide for Simmons County, we are in the best area for deer."

"Good to know." I shut the door. "Except we're hunting people who aren't hunting deer."

"Shouldn't be difficult, right?" Donovan teased, jumping out of the Jeep.

Billy had brought by the sheriff's office a few pairs of some fancy new hunting pants that promised to withstand every type of weather possible. "Winter squall or rainstorm from hell," Billy had said, "these pants have you covered."

The olive-green cargo pants made a soft swishing noise with my every step, something I was still getting used to. The day before

I'd spent a good two hours with Donovan at Bad Billy's with the intention of coming out looking like a real hunter. My gauge of whether or not I succeeded rested on Donovan's reaction. If I pleased her hunter's eye, I'd pass in the field. While I did receive her approval, I hardly recognized myself in Bad Billy's full-length mirror. Donovan helped me pick out a cream-colored utility button-down shirt covered with enough pockets and hooks to declare me legit. She also picked out thin shirts for underneath, layers meant to keep warmth inside and enough compression to give my muscles energy. A deep brown canvas field coat with flannel lining was my favorite—oversized on my slim frame and warm, it felt like I'd wrapped myself in a blanket. Everything was topped off with a camouflage wide-rimmed hat and night-vision goggles that hung around my neck. Thankfully, I still wore my lucky Frye boots with thick wool socks. I couldn't imagine trekking into any type of field operation without them.

Donovan had come up behind me at the mirror at Billy's. "Looking good, but lose that coat," she said.

I stared back at her in the mirror. "What? It's so warm."

Donovan shook her head. She reached for the bottom of the coat and pulled the bulk away from my body. "See this? Nothing but cold air will find its way in there. You need a down jacket that cinches at the waist and wrists."

"But I love this coat," I told her. "It's so cool."

She shrugged and handed me the required blaze-orange vest. "Be cool, then. I'm going with warm."

I chuckled. "Putting this neon orange on seems so out of sync with all the camo."

Donovan patted my shoulder. "It does, doesn't it? Good thing deer can't see color."

"Let's just hope all the tired and possibly inebriated hunters will spot me as their own," I only half joked.

I'd fashioned my hair Bad Billy style by starting with a long ponytail pulled tight at the base of my skull. I then used an elastic band every inch or so down until the end of my mousy brown hair flipped up like the tail of a snake.

Now, as we entered the forest, I followed at Donovan's back and helped to mark tree branches near our entrance point with neon orange surveyor's tape.

"We can always follow our GPS back to the Jeep, but there's the question of whether or not we can get a signal. Tagging is a surefire way to find the Jeep no matter the situation. If we make it through the night," Donovan said, "we'll be tired as hell by the time we get back to the Jeep. This just makes it a little easier on us."

"*If* we make it?" I asked.

Donovan grinned. "I'm hoping we catch these two chumps before midnight, Special Agent. I want to spend the rest of the night in my warm hotel bed."

"I hear that." I was grateful I had Donovan as a hunting partner. She knew the ropes, and I needed as much help as I could get.

"What do we do now," I asked. "Just walk?"

Donovan laughed. "Pretty much. We'll cover the area and case out any spots where there is evidence of deer. When darkness hits, we'll find a place to settle until the night hunt un-officially opens at seven thirty."

"And then we walk around some more pretending we're looking for deer through our binoculars. Fun." I couldn't help but make light of the hunting sport; it felt so pointless to me. Then again, I felt the same way about fishing, and the two sports both featured a lot of waiting without much to do. The more I thought about it, it wasn't all that different from a long-term suspect stakeout. I'd spent too many hours camped out in an unmarked car waiting for a suspect to do something…anything.

"It's all about the hunt, Hansen—that's what people love. Hunting is about outsmarting and conquering the deer. A show of mental strength."

I couldn't see how shooting a defenseless animal showed any sort of strength, but I'd encountered numerous people on this case thus far who felt differently, including the woman next to me who looked like she'd stepped out of the pages of some *Field and Guide* magazine.

"Taken to its extreme, I can see how hunting is a statement about independence," I said.

Donovan pushed through a thicket of branches that led us to a main trail. We settled in to walk side by side. "It's about sustainability, too. Absolutely no waste from the animal." She chuckled. "See, you're getting the hang of this, Hansen! You can't have a good hunt without a lot of philosophizing."

Donovan and I had planned for about fourteen hours in the field. That didn't sound all that long to me, so it was a surprise to discover all the supplies Donovan insisted we'd need. We each carried a quart of fresh water along with a small first aid kit, waterproof matches, a butane lighter, a Swiss Army knife, a heavy duty flashlight, a roll of surveyor's tape, a bandana, a brick-like and most likely unusable radio, and the rifle strapped to our backs. We each also had three protein bars and a banana. When I first heard everything we would need to carry, I imagined we'd put them all into a backpack. I soon learned the packs easily snag against tree limbs and slow the hunter down. Instead, we each wore a bag around our waists that reminded me of a much larger version of a fanny pack.

Even with all of this clothing and accessories, I felt naked. I'd taken off my shoulder holster, and I missed the constant reassurance its straps gave me. I liked knowing at any moment I could reach my right hand across my chest, grab my Glock, and take aim in less than fifteen seconds. I still had the Glock with me, only it was strapped to my ankle, and somehow that made it feel a million miles away. I wasn't as familiar with the rifle on my back as I was my service weapon, and I hoped that over the course of the night I wouldn't have to use either one. I was grateful for BCI's tracking devices planted on us—another layer of security. They promised to find us if we stayed stationary too long or got lost and couldn't find our way out of the forest.

"I think we've prepared for almost anything," I told Donovan.

Donovan gave me a smile. "What I've learned from doing these hunts is that you never have everything you need. Each time that pack gets bigger and bigger, but there's always something you need that you don't have."

We moved through the forest, and suddenly I fell back in time to the second hunt I took with my father. The two of us were alone on that venture, and I stumbled through the undergrowth next to my dad. Since my first attempt at hunting hadn't gone so well, he decided to take me out once more on his own. Leaving behind Tyson, his partner, had been my dad's idea, and he sold me on trying hunting one more time because it would give us the time to spend the day together. My dad really wanted me to like hunting, that much was clear. Then again, he'd also really wanted me to like and do many things that I'd rejected in my life. My father had a different relationship to Ohio's land than me—fishing and hunting filled the long hours of his summer days. The outdoors became as much a part of him early on as his breath.

"Where exactly do you think our food comes from? We don't even have a garden." My father's voice cut through the hushed quiet that surrounded us. An owl hooted somewhere in the distance.

Honestly, I hadn't given the answer to that question much thought. I'd eaten meat for almost every meal in my thirteen years, and hadn't thought too much about where that meat had come from. I had a few friends who were raised on farms and took part in 4-H, but how our food made it to our plates was far from our conversations.

"Hunting shows responsibility," my dad told me. "It's taking ownership of what you eat and honors the animal it came from."

Shooting a bullet into an animal didn't sound much like honor to me, but I liked spending time with my dad. It was a rarity I had his full attention, and while hunting he was away from the scanner and radio that so often called him into work after he'd just gotten home. I also knew most of the guys I went to school with hunted, and my dad had generally treated me like the son he never had.

"Besides," my dad said, "one of my goals as your father is to be sure that you can fend for yourself—no matter what the circumstance." He nudged my shoulder. "You never know when you'll need these skills, Lucinda."

We moved through the quiet forest for at least two hours before I finally asked my dad the question I'd wanted to for some time. "Why won't you take me to the station with you anymore?"

The station had always been a place I loved to go, but since we'd taken that first hunt with Tyson, it felt like my dad was keeping me away from the station, as if he was trying to protect me from something.

"You don't want me to be a cop, do you?" I asked.

My dad laughed. "Detective work is in your blood, my dear. I think you're kind of young to make a career decision, that's all it is."

"I can be a cop and still take care of myself," I said.

"I'm sure you can. I'd much rather see you in a job where your life isn't in danger every day, though. I don't want you to have to move through life with a bull's-eye on your back. I want you to be secure in the world. Happy."

I'd been trying to keep up with his wide stride, but when I heard his comment, I stopped in place. "Let me get this straight. You don't want me to track people doing bad things, but you do want me to learn how to track and kill a deer who isn't doing *anything* wrong?"

My father stopped and turned to face me. "Capturing some crazed outlaw won't feed you or keep you warm, Lucinda." He nodded back to the path. "A deer will."

I watched him walk away from me on the path. After a moment, I called after him, "I'm very happy, Dad. Aren't you?"

He didn't turn around or even acknowledge that he'd heard me. He kept walking. Once he started down the crest of a hill and almost left my sight, I ran after him, closing that widening gap between us.

CHAPTER TWENTY-ONE

Tuesday, 7:00 p.m.

Night descended on the forest like a blanket, thick and weighty. The night brought the cold with it, and the wind chill put the temperature in the lower teens. Donovan and I had followed the trails deep into the woods and come across numerous hunters beginning the night hunt early. I hadn't considered that everyone out here would virtually look the same—camo clothing along with the boxy cut of the hunting clothing took away gender markers and personal style. Some hunters wore military hats pulled low, hiding their features even more. Donovan and I had walked into a strange, removed world where virtually anyone could hide in plain sight.

At 7:30 p.m., a horn sounded in the distance, the unofficial marker of the opening of the night hunt. The *pop pop pop* of gunfire up into the tree branches was followed by cheers. Fireworks for hunters. I found it eerie, all these voices rising up from the growing darkness, and the sound of so many weapons firing from locations I couldn't quite place. It was any law enforcement officer's worst nightmare, particularly when an active serial sniper was on the loose.

Before darkness had completely descended, Donovan led me to an empty deer stand. We'd decided to wait out the opening of the hunt seated in the trees where we could unfold our paper map and strategize locations together. Donovan had already marked points where we might find stragglers from the hunting groups—exactly the ones Deadeye and his partner would be looking for. But we'd forgotten the map in the Jeep, and Donovan wanted to grab a blanket. She'd seen me wrap my arms around myself for warmth.

"You should have listened to me about the coat," Donovan told me. She rubbed the arms of her down-filled puffy jacket. "This coat may not look as cool, but it's definitely warm."

I sat on the hard-planked wooden ledge of the deer stand to wait for Donovan in the frosty evening, and I knew I should have listened to her.

According to Donovan, there were many different variations of a deer stand. The empty one we'd found had a lot of height, at least ten steps up to the landing. Someone had spent a good deal of time on it, and whoever built it would be returning sooner rather than later. I sat with my back against the trunk of the tree as the rough bark dug into my shoulders. A silence had settled over the forest, a quiet I would have otherwise found comforting if I wasn't alone in a dark forest looking through my NVGs for a serial sniper and his partner. Every once in a while, a hunter passed on the trail below me, sometimes alone, sometimes a group of them. I kept my small flashlight off so as not to draw attention to my location and fought against the sleep that wanted to take me.

Without so much as the rustle of leaves or the snap of a branch, a figure suddenly crested the top of the deer stand, their pack jiggling against their waist. I jumped, my heart rocketing into high gear until I recognized Donovan through the goggles.

"I wasn't sure you were coming back," I teased her.

"We're farther from the Jeep than I thought we were." She shook the folded paper in her hand. "Hence, the map. We have over one hundred acres in the designated hunting area. It's a lot of ground to cover."

She spread out the map on the planked wood between us and flipped her flashlight into the torch mode. She pointed to the area where we were located. "We aren't too far from Deadeye's campsite behind the abandoned farmhouse," she said. "The edge of the Holdens' property is only about a mile away." Donovan looked up at me. "You're cold, aren't you?"

"I'm okay."

She shook her head and mumbled something about telling me so. She unzipped her jacket and slipped out of it. "Let's trade."

"No way, you need that coat."

"Clearly, you need it more. Besides, I have three layers of heat gear on my body to your one layer. Hand it over."

I hated to admit it, but Donovan was right. I took off the field coat and traded with her. I was grateful for the down jacket on my arms.

"I brought you something." Donovan handed me a Snickers bar from her pack.

My growling stomach responded. "Yes! I'm so hungry."

"A sugar rush to keep your energy up," she teased.

I ripped into the bar, while Donovan drank from her water bottle.

"I say we start there as soon as it's completely dark," she said.

"The abandoned house?"

She nodded, the glow from the flashlight highlighting her eyes. "I'm thinking he was doing exactly what we are while he was out at that old farmhouse—scouting for pockets of land to hide in. If we start where he did, we might be able to track him."

I polished off the candy bar and shoved the wrapper into my pocket. "You're not taking into account the game aspect of this all for him. His partner will also be hunting. They have to know we're out here—it's only going to heighten the excitement for them."

"And excitement brings on trigger-happy hunters," she added. "The good thing is we don't have any reason to believe they hunt in separate locations. It's an odd game tactic, to be attached at the hip to your opponent, but I think that's what they're doing."

I nodded. "Whoever takes the target down with one bullet gets the point and the bloody shirt as proof."

As we waited for the last of the day's light to end, Donovan marked places on the map we needed to walk through. Eventually, she leaned back against the tree trunk beside me, occasionally taking a swig from her water bottle. Her booted foot bounced against the floor of the deer stand, and I understood her overplanning was due to anxiety rather than a control issue. I liked that anxiety, that realness of her.

Donovan shook her bottle of water at me. "You know, back in the day, this would have been a flask of whiskey, not premium purified mountain spring water."

The image of a leather-bound flask popped into my mind, and I wasn't prepared for the way my body responded—my heart thumped hard against my chest, my breath shallowed out, and my mouth almost watered for a drink from that flask. I tried to joke those feelings away.

"I'm a beer girl through and through," I told Donovan, "except for the occasional wine from a box while on the road. Out here, though, I'd take a shot of about anything."

Donovan chuckled, and then we both fell silent, alert. There was a rustling below us. Donovan reached for her night-vision goggles and scanned the area below us. We both caught a whiff at the same time. "A skunk." She reached for her flashlight. "These bastards are nocturnal. They run from light." She aimed the light beam down on the ground and held it there until we heard the animal scuttle away.

I was grateful for the reprieve, to have a moment to myself when her focus was elsewhere. I twisted my own water bottle around in my hands and thought of Detective Alison Harvey. One drunken night during the Wallace Lake case had led me into bed with her and had almost cost me the opportunity to be with Bennett. I always blamed the drink. I wanted to think that never would have happened if I hadn't been so drunk I could hardly hold my head up. Now, though, Harvey's name brought with it so many other questions. She'd been Bennett's soft spot; I'd always known that. But was there something more going on? Why were they alone together at the hospital? Meeting up to discuss our relationship? All of these unknowns drove me crazy.

"Everything all right?" Donovan asked.

"I'm just thinking," I said. Maybe it was the darkness and the way it hid everything within it, but I surprised myself when I actually told her. "I slept with one of Bennett's exes after a night of drinking. It almost cost me our relationship."

"Hmmm. Sounds like the fallout of a night of drinking. I've had too many of them myself."

I chuckled. "The worst part is she's a detective. One that we come into contact with occasionally."

"So there is always the reminder."

I took another swig from the water bottle. "Harvey is always there, you know? I understood that Bennett had a soft spot for her, but I guess I didn't realize their split wasn't a mutual agreement."

"You think there's something still going on between them."

I shrugged. "I don't know. I'd like to think not."

"This is why I don't do relationships."

I laughed out loud at that comment. It reminded me so much of myself, reminded me of the promise I made myself over and over again. And then I met Rowan. And then there was Bennett when I least expected it.

"I'm serious! It's the secrets. Everyone has them."

My hand shot up to my throat to make sure the necklace was still there, Marci's Irish cross. My fingertips traced the edges of the pendant.

"Since you shared a secret with me, I owe you one," Donovan said.

"Thank God," I said. "I love hearing other people's secrets."

Donovan reached into her pocket and pulled out the engraved Celtic cross. She rubbed it between her hands. "My alcoholism cost me everything. And it very nearly cost me my life."

I'd been curious to hear Donovan's sobriety story since she'd revealed her issues with addiction. I listened as she recounted the ride she'd had with her best friend and biggest nemesis, whiskey. She'd learned the acquired taste early on from her mother, she said, something she swore she'd never take up once she saw how it ruined her mother's life. Donovan and her siblings had been removed from her mother's custody only to cycle in and out of foster care homes in the Cleveland area. Foster care wasn't completely terrible, Donovan had told me. "It gets a bad rap, but there are good people in the system." Besides, without the foster care system, she wouldn't have met Christy Vallentini.

When Donovan turned eighteen, she had been assigned to a brand new social worker to help adjust to her life outside of foster care.

Christy Vallentini was almost twenty-two years old and pregnant. She'd completed a two-year social work program in a little over a year, and the county needed her services immediately. So she dug in with one of her very first clients and helped Donovan learn living skills and find a job. In the process, Christy and Donovan fell in love.

"It was really about us needing each other," Donovan said. "She was going to be a single mother and was terrified. I was on my own and unsure of how to make it in this world. Christy and I…well, we sort of fell into each other."

They eventually moved in together. It wasn't until after a year into the relationship and after the baby had been born that Christy confronted Donovan about her drinking. That's when the secrets began, the hidden bottles, the late night runs to the grocery for milk. A year and a half later, Christy took the baby and left Donovan.

Not long after, Donovan got word her mother died. It turned out she hadn't totally forgotten about her daughter. She'd left a small fund in her will for Donovan to attend the local community college—just enough money for Donovan to start over. To rise up from the ashes of the mess she'd made. Once Donovan enrolled in the community college, she was able to get help for her addiction through the counseling center, and it wasn't long before she was enrolled in law enforcement classes. She was well on her way to a badge.

"They helped me solve that great paradox in my life. I cannot drink but I must drink. Mind-numbing, you know?"

"A lot has changed for you in seven years," I said.

Donovan agreed. "Once my body finally rid itself of the years of alcohol, my life opened up. I never got back what I'd already lost and what mattered most—Christy and my daughter."

We sat quietly beside one another for a time, the full night's darkness taking hold, breath puffing white in the cold. A sound came from below us.

Donovan leaned forward on her knees to scan the area again for movement. She settled on one location.

"Do you see that?" she asked.

"What?"

"That light. Over there."

I followed her pointed finger and stood. I soon saw it, a light flickering in the distant sway of the branches. The glow was singular, and had to be on the outskirts of the main hunting area.

"Is that a campfire?"

"I think so," Donovan said. "A group of hunters must have set up camp there. Not the smartest thing to do in a hunting competition," she said, "given that fire drives deer away."

"We've been up here awhile and haven't seen much," I told Donovan. "What do you say we head in that direction?"

CHAPTER TWENTY-TWO

Tuesday, 11:00 p.m.

The night-vision goggles gave everything a greenish cast, otherworldly and alien. It felt like my feet were a hundred miles away. I lost my step more than a few times, whether from the binoculars or the strange disassociation with the land, I couldn't tell. The fire had been much easier to see from the deer stand. The closer we came to it, the more the flames messed with the accuracy of our night-vision goggles, and we'd had to remove them.

We'd had to make our way by the smell and the rise of the smoke through the trees. The farther we moved toward the flame, the fewer hunters we encountered. Most were in teams and out in the hunting field for fun and drinking; very few seemed too intent on actually taking down any animals. Others made light of the situation with Deadeye and had signs with messages for any possible serial killers they might encounter. My favorite read: *Pick me, Deadeye—I shoot back.*

As we crested the final hill and the fire came into full view, I realized I knew this place. I'd been there before. We were entering the property from a different angle, but it was the Holdens' place.

"Do you think Holden is part of the night hunt?" Donovan asked.

I shrugged. "Possibly, but why camp out when you could stay in the warm house not more than a few hundred yards away?"

John Holden had just lost two children. It didn't make sense that he would be taking part in the night hunt. Unless…

"He's hunting Deadeye and the partner," I said. "Just like us."

Donovan wore a black beanie cap with her hair tucked underneath. Only the whites of her eyes were visible. "It's possible someone else is using the Holdens' land."

Possible, yes. But something felt off.

For the first time since we'd been in the forest, I took the lead as we neared the campsite.

"Heads-up," I warned Donovan, but she already had her rifle in the low-ready position.

We approached the fire with caution, Donovan going left as I went right. The fire had been recently tended to, the flames bright, but no one was in sight. As the fire popped in the cold night, my hackles rose—was someone watching us?

A shot fired—I saw the muzzle flash before I heard the crack of the bullet as it hurled past me.

"Donovan, behind you!"

She dove downward just before the second flash of the muzzle. The length of Donovan's body curled into a ball on the other side of the fire, and I ran for cover behind a tree. We'd willingly walked into some sort of trap and landed dead center of a makeshift bull's-eye. Another bullet snapped past my shoulder just as I took cover in the thick underbrush.

Using a tree trunk for cover, I kept my back pressed tightly against it and rounded slowly to get a better look at the camp. I couldn't see anyone, but I felt eyes on me coming from everywhere. Donovan and I were trapped with nowhere to go.

Blood thrummed in my ears. We'd gone from zero to five hundred in minutes, and I was thrown off by the darkness and the eerie quiet of the forest.

Donovan had also used the cover of a large tree. We stared at one another across the circle of the fire. We had to get better coverage before someone took a shot at us.

Crouched, Donovan rounded the tree and motioned to me. *I'm going in.*

Wait, don't move, I wanted to scream at her. *Not yet!*

It was too late.

Donovan circled the tree and called for me to split off from her—flanked in opposite directions. My boots crashed through the undergrowth until I found a path headed directly toward the Holdens' home. I hoped to find cell reception; I needed to call for help. Then I remembered the sheriff's statement that they would send help to any location where the tracker stood still. Using an oak tree for cover, I found the tracker in Donovan's coat pocket. It was no bigger than a quarter, and I snapped it in half. I reached for the radio on my shoulder.

"Shots fired," I said into the microphone. "Send backup to Holdens' property." The response was jumbled with only fragments of Daniel's words coming through to me. Then, suddenly, the radio shattered to pieces on my shoulder.

Deadeye. The sharpshooter was playing with me, taking away every strand of connection I had to the rest of the team. "Donovan," I said aloud. "No!"

A round of shots broke out followed by the sound of a heavy thump. A body had gone down somewhere near the fire. I turned too fast, my boot slipping against the frost-covered foliage. In seconds, I'd face-planted and plunged the muzzle of my rifle into the hard ground. It was a rookie mistake, one made out of sheer panic, and I'd destroyed the accuracy of my AR. I had no choice but to reach for my backup Glock strapped to my ankle. My fingers fell into its grip.

A tirade of thoughts ran through my mind: *Idiot! Pull it together, before you both get killed. Focus on the mission, not the mistake.*

Slowly, I made my way back to the fire. In its light, I saw David Johnson. Another figure stood over a body.

Detective Donovan was down.

The figure leaned down and grabbed Donovan by the ankles. Deadeye scanned the area with his AR. A bunker had opened, and the figure pulled Donovan toward its wide steel lid. Donovan was almost to the opening of the bunker, and I had to do something before all three disappeared into the hole inside the earth.

"Ohio BCI! Drop your weapons!"

I couldn't wait any longer. I stepped out while Deadeye and the figure went rigid for a moment before a sudden storm of action. As I anticipated, Deadeye stepped back from Donovan to take aim at me.

It was what he'd been dying to do all day—he wanted nothing more than to take down the agents who'd been sent by the state to track him down.

"David Johnson, drop the rifle now!"

I felt him eyeing me through the scope, sizing me up, certain he'd get the most points for taking me down—head agent of the task force. When a bullet ricocheted through the trees, I fired. My first shot hit Deadeye in his shoulder. When he fired again, I shot him square in the chest.

The other person, who I assumed was Deadeye's partner, pulled Donovan into the opening of the bunker, her body falling and smacking against the ladder on its way down. Deadeye's body had crumpled facedown to the ground. He choked to catch his breath. He stretched his arm wide to reach for the rifle that I had just kicked away from him. Stepping on his wrist, I crunched the bones of his hand against the earth.

"Who are you working with?" I demanded, grinding the heel of my boot into his hand. "You only get one bullet for this to count. Call off your man so I can get you some help."

There was only the sound of breath between us.

"David, think of your unborn child," I said.

In the end, Deadeye tried to break his own rules. He kicked at me and used his other hand to produce a small Glock. Before he could pull the trigger, I shot David Johnson.

Like a portal to deep inside the earth, the round steel hatch of the bunker had slammed closed taking with it the last sliver of light. The Holdens had a bunker after all, and somehow we failed to find it on the aerial maps of Simmons County. Easy enough to do, with a bunker hidden so well, but it raised the question for me once again: Whose side of this thing were the Holdens on, anyway?

That's when I felt it—the high-powered bullet from an AR slammed into me. It plunged into my body armor vest, hitting the tip of the plate over my right shoulder blade. It took a few seconds for me to register I'd actually been shot, and then the anger hit. A guttural growl came from deep inside me, as I whirled around with my gun drawn. Who'd shot me? David Johnson was dead at my feet and someone had slithered into the bunker with Donovan. As the pain set into my shoulder, I thought about the bullet's location, a shoulder shot from the back. The same shot one of the sisters had taken, and then again the shot that took down Logan Holden. A third person had pulled Donovan underground. It was the partner who hunted me now.

I tried to locate the origin of the shot. I'd been shot in my shooting arm and barely had the strength to bend at the elbow. I switched my Glock to my left hand, my aim completely thrown off, and felt the eyes of my hunter on me. Was I square inside his scope? Was he readying for a kill shot? Exactly how far away was he, anyway? It was possible the shot had come from near the Holden home. It wasn't safe to head in that direction—I couldn't trust that I wouldn't be running into yet another trap. I had no choice but to run back into the forest I'd just trekked through with Donovan, to charge deep into the belly of it with the hopes of throwing off Deadeye's partner.

At least he'd taken his one shot. As I ran for the cover of the trees, I thought about how many points I might be worth now that he'd seen me kill Deadeye. The partner would most certainly break the game's rules to take me down—he'd use as many bullets as necessary to take my head so he could mount it alongside my bloody shirt on his wall.

Chapter Twenty-three

Wednesday, 3:40 a.m.
Day 6 of the investigation

Under any other circumstances, I would have found an old abandoned cabin deep in the woods utterly terrifying. I would have seen it as a location where I'd possibly need backup for whatever I might find living—or not living—inside those rotting log walls. Instead, it was like finding gold inside my ten thousandth pan of dirt.

I'd been walking for what felt like hours. The forest seemed to go on forever, thickening in places while thinning out in others. I was disoriented inside its thick darkness, and I couldn't understand why I hadn't encountered any other hunters. I wondered if it was possible I'd walked outside the designated areas for hunting. The wet mud clung to my boots and nearly sucked them off with each step. I pushed my way through the thick underbrush, and when I finally saw the wooden frame of the cabin looming in the distance, I thought it must be a dream. Relief washed through me; I needed a safe place to rest while I determined my location and how to get help. By the time I reached the cabin steps, shock had set in. Next thing I knew, I was collapsing on the planked wood floor of the cabin. I hardly remembered making my way up the front steps, stepping through the broken front door.

I felt like I'd been hit with a sledgehammer below the collarbone. The sheer force of the bullet had broken at least one of my ribs, and it felt as though shards of glass dug into my side with each step. I couldn't twist my torso without excruciating pain, and the injury limited my speed of movement to a slow walk. A distance I normally could have covered in fifteen minutes now took me at least thirty. At least I was able to take deep breaths, and I was grateful that my lung hadn't been punctured.

In the beam of the flashlight, I made sense of the cabin that surrounded me. Cold air streamed in through two broken windows. The cabin hadn't been properly cared for in years, but I was willing to bet it had been a squatters' paradise. Broken plastic lawn chairs littered the front room. A crumbling brick fireplace added to the thick dust. Night in these parts was paralyzing for city folk like me, and I was engulfed in a profound blackness. Without streetlights or cast-off light from buildings, homes, and vehicle beams, I was literally thrown into a darkness I'd never experienced. Without the small circle of light from my flashlight, I wouldn't have been able to see my own hand in front of my face. I didn't have a clue how to get back to where Donovan and I entered the forest, or even an idea of how to find the nearest road.

I'd never worked a case where I felt more unprepared or undertrained. I couldn't shake the feeling of the wide-open exposure, as if my body was simply *waiting* for Deadeye's partner to shoot me again, and this time take my life. It wasn't only the unfamiliar terrain or working with a team I didn't really know; the Deadeye case had given me trouble from the start with my lack of hunting experience. When I was honest with myself, I had to admit Deadeye and his crew had always been at least a few steps ahead of me. Each time I got close, Deadeye and his partner had only laughed and defied me even more. Sanders had been clear from the start—serial snipers could be the worst cases to work. I'd known that from my training, but I didn't really *understand* that until I'd collapsed on a cold cabin floor holding my side in pain.

What knocked off my equilibrium most, though, was that all the tools I'd grown so accustomed to in other cases were simply useless to me now. I had a phone that couldn't land any reception and waivered dangerously close to dying. I had teammates but couldn't locate or contact them because of a broken radio. I had no bearing on my location because my GPS couldn't find reception. Other than my firearm, a flashlight, and a few rounds, I'd been stripped clean.

A howl sounded in the distance and spurred me into action to find cover. I stood and used the beam of the flashlight to find a corner in the small room that had a clear line of visibility to the door. The wooden floor planks creaked beneath my weight, and I worried a weak spot might give. With my shoulders pressed against the wall, I slid down into the safety of the corner, flipped off the flashlight, and let the darkness engulf me once again.

I breathed through the pain radiating from my body and thought about my training with Sanders for BCI. He'd practically ground this principle into all of us: *It's not over until it's over. As long as your heart is beating, there is something you can do to survive your circumstance, no matter how bad it may seem. There is hope with every single breath.*

The sun rose with its light filtering in through the broken windows. Warmth slowly spread across the cabin floor. I slept in spurts when the ache of my shoulder and ribs quieted down. What started as a dull burn in my upper torso had worked its way into a raging fire. I sat with my back against a cornered wall with my legs spread out in front of me. I planned to begin walking again at daybreak, but I'd been sapped of my energy. I realized with a start that it must be well after noon, and I hadn't yet tried to move outside the abandoned cabin.

My thoughts floated as I filtered in and out of a restless sleep. I wondered what Daniel and the rest of the task force was doing with our lack of communication. I thought about how Donovan and I had been so easily pulled into the trap of the campfire. I'd broken the tracker in the hope it would bring Daniel and the others to the Holden property. Maybe by now they'd found Donovan and whoever pulled her body into the bunker. *If they found the bunker*, I told myself, *they should be able to track me to this location.*

Time rolled on only as far as each of my breaths could take me. My mind flipped back and forth between images and memories, then back to the situation where I found myself. I thought of Sanders in his hospital bed and of Daniel taking charge and leading a search crew through the forest. I thought about swimming and the way the water would be able to absorb all my pain and frustration. And I thought of Bennett. Bennett would have known exactly what to do—she wouldn't have gotten lost in the first place. For all the times her warnings and her insistence on details had bothered me, I now wished for that careful, cautious mind more than anything.

No matter how hard I tried not to think of Detective Rachel Donovan, she was always there reminding me that she'd lost her life on my watch. I couldn't lose the image of her lifeless form or the sickening sound of her body falling into the bunker.

"Sorry, Donovan," I said, the scratchiness of my own voice echoing throughout the empty cabin. Her death was my fault—I'd brought her on to the case, and ultimately, I'd been the one who couldn't protect her.

I adjusted myself against the cabin's corner, and a lightning shot of pain coursed through my shoulder. I closed my eyes and let my thoughts turn back to the hunt my dad and I had taken.

He'd wanted me to learn to protect myself. More than that, he'd wanted me to learn how to *fend* for myself.

"You never know what might happen in this world, Lucy-girl," he'd said to me many times in my life. "Nothing is guaranteed, including the air we breathe. You need to be prepared."

As I followed him along the trails, I understood what was beneath his words. He regularly worried that if something happened to him on the job, I'd be left alone. And I would've—we didn't have any family. My dad always said his brothers and sisters at the police station were our makeshift family. They shared in most holidays with us, and many of them had fed me dinner and tucked me into bed on nights when my dad worked an extended shift. He felt better knowing one of them was caring for me instead of a stranger he'd hired through some babysitting company.

I'd always sensed there was more to my father's paranoia about my aloneness in the world. He'd seen and heard a lot throughout his time on the force, and one of his worst fears was that his own child would be abducted and held captive. About the time he pushed the hunting experiences on me, there had been a highly publicized child abduction case in rural Ohio. The teen had been held for months before she finally found a sliver of a chance to escape. She took it and fought for her life. Even though the girl lived and the abductor was prosecuted, the situation heightened my father's concern. He didn't want me to only know how to survive. He wanted to teach me how to *thrive* in any given situation. That's exactly what I was thinking about when he didn't return from stepping away to relieve himself inside a grove of trees.

He'd left me.

Alone in the woods.

"Dad?" I called out, searching the woods and everywhere around it. "*Dad*, where are you?"

Eventually, I gave up the search. I had no idea where I was, and my dad had left me behind with only a rifle, a few bullets, and the clothing on my body. I had two choices: sit down and wait for him to return or start walking.

I chose to walk.

When darkness fell, I sat down with my back against a large tree. The blackness of night scared me, and I frantically searched my pockets for anything that might help. I found a half-eaten candy bar and quickly ate its remainder. I emptied all my other pockets and found something tucked away inside the breast pocket of my coat that I'd never placed there—a book of matches.

"Yes!" I hollered with excitement. I knew my dad had tucked the matches inside my pocket, and that this was all some sort of weird survival test he'd devised in order to teach me something important.

I built a small fire. After I had the rumble of a blaze going, I sat down beside the fire's glow and waited—for what, I didn't know. Still, I warmed myself in the glow of that fire.

And I waited.

Inside the abandoned hunting cabin, day turned to night. My shoulder throbbed, and I'd spent most of the evening falling in and out of a fitful sleep. With the darkness, a shiver had set in, and I couldn't stop my body from shaking despite the warmth of Donovan's down jacket. At least the shakes kept me alert, and for the first time in hours, I felt a wave of energy. I unzipped the side pockets of Donovan's jacket and slipped my hands inside for warmth. I thought of my father. What if Donovan had put supplies inside the lining of the jacket? Donovan was more than prepared for our time on the night hunt, and it would be just like her to plan for the possibility of losing her pack.

I winced as I pushed the jacket off my hurt shoulder and let it drop to the floor. My arm felt like it weighed three hundred pounds, and every movement of my hand or arm sent a firestorm of pain across my chest. Still, I leaned forward and managed to pull the jacket around to my lap. I ran the fabric of the jacket through my hands, searching. My touch became my eyes as I squeezed every few inches of the jacket. Just when I was about to give up, I felt something in the back lining. Tearing the fabric, my fingers found three items embedded in the down. The first took me a minute to recognize, but once I did, I felt immediately comforted by its shape and weight. It was Donovan's engraved Celtic sobriety cross, the one she'd shown me in the deer stand. She'd wrapped it inside a well-used bandana. Once I unfolded the cloth, the cross fell inside my palm. I thought of all the times it must have gotten Donovan through a scrape, all those times when she had nothing else to hold on to but the Celtic sobriety cross inside her pocket. That thin cool weight of hope against the world.

I faltered at the third object. At first I didn't believe it when my fingers revealed a small tin full of matches. It seemed too good to be true, and then it felt like something so much bigger than Donovan preparing for the possibility of losing her pack. Maybe Donovan and my father conspired and reached beyond the grave. *We're here to help*, that tiny tin seemed to say to me. *You can't give up—we won't let you.* I held the cross in one hand and the tin of matches in the opposite hand. The matches and the cross felt like the perfectly balanced weight of survival.

I finally stood using the wall to help me up. My knees nearly gave way beneath me—my body ached. I couldn't run in this condition. I had to use another way to find help. In the small glow of the flashlight, I pulled open the front door and stumbled down the few rickety steps.

Pffft! The sound of a match striking to fire. I held it with my good hand and used the light to navigate across the porch and down the steps. The flame burned out against my fingertips, but not before I was able to determine that the cabin was made of virtually all wood. By the smell of it, most likely pine.

Pffft! I lit the edge of the bandana, watching the fire catch. Then I dropped it on the edge of the porch in a pocket of dead leaves that had blown together. It only took a moment to ignite.

Pffft! I set a burning match on the other end of the porch. And then I proceeded to light every match but three, watching the porch take to the fire. I felt its heat, and when I was certain it would catch, I stepped away from the cabin. The fire was hungry, and it soon moved across the porch and reached for the cabin walls.

Soon the fire roared to life. I took cover behind a thicket of trees. I thought of Donovan's comment when we'd seen the fateful campfire: *Idiot move—deer are afraid of fire.* My eyes burned with the thought of her and the thick smoke that filled the air.

The flames licked away more cabin, engulfing it whole. I clutched Donovan's sobriety cross inside my fist, and I waited.

The morning light woke me, and I curled into a ball next to what remained of the fire waiting for my father to return. A few burning embers refused to die. Shivering, I tried to wipe the wet dew off my clothing and hair. Silence surrounded me. I wasn't sure what to do next. I kicked dirt onto the remaining embers, slung the rifle over my shoulder, and did the only thing I could think of. I started walking again.

The afternoon sun eventually warmed me, but once the sky began to darken with the sunset, I realized I needed to cause a disturbance. I needed to do something to get someone's attention. Otherwise, I reasoned, I'd be stuck in that thick forest forever.

I came upon a lean-to, most likely where hunters had taken refuge from the cold at some point. The planked wood was rotted in places and the detritus left by humans littered the ground: an empty water bottle, a colorful candy wrapper, a dead battery.

"Hello?" I called out. "Dad?"

When I didn't get a response, I used the matches again, this time, lighting the lean-to ablaze.

I stood back and watched it burn.

Within twenty minutes, my father appeared with a fire retardant. I watched him hose the blaze down and began to cry.

"Don't cry, Lucy-girl," he told me. "You used your brain to get you out of a bad situation. I wish you wouldn't have burned something so large, but you definitely got my attention!"

Thick smoke filled the area. He handed me a fresh bottle of water. As I gulped mouthfuls of it, he leaned down next to me. "I'm sorry, but I had to see where your instincts would lead you."

"I didn't mean to burn anything," I said.

"It's okay, the fire is out. You use what you have, Lucy-girl. You make a plan, and you use what you have. Nothing is more precious than life. Do whatever you need to do to get help and stay alive."

I handed my father the empty bottle. "I never want to go hunting again. Can we go home now?"

My dad laughed. "Help me to throw dirt on this fire, and we're out of here."

CHAPTER TWENTY-FOUR

Wednesday night

Engulfed in flames, the cabin kept me warm. I used the fire; its light helped me survey the area. I'd been out of touch with my team for more than a day now. They had to be searching, I reminded myself and hoped the roaring flames would draw them to me.

I held my T-shirt over my nose and mouth in an effort to keep out the thick smoke. Even at my distance from the flames, my eyes watered with its smoke.

Thwack, thwack, thwack.

The sound was faint at first, but distinct all the same. A helicopter flew low against the tree line. I jumped up and ran toward it, the sound luring me into the thick of the forest and its darkness.

Thwack, thwack, thwack.

I raised my flashlight to the sky and waved. I screamed for the driver, but the flying machine dwarfed my tiny beam of light and voice. The helicopter was still too far in the distance to see me.

"Special Agent Hansen? Is that you?"

I turned at the sound of the voice, frantic to find its source. I held my gun steady, sweeping the area as I moved. "Identify yourself!"

"Hansen, we've been looking for you." A figure stepped into my line of sight. He flinched when I shone the light in his face. My weapon aimed for his chest, and I tried to make out the face beneath the brown and green camo paint that covered it. I *knew* the shape of this person, didn't I? I'd seen him...

"Duncan?" I called out. "Dr. Mike Duncan?"

He held up his hands as if to say *you got me*. "We have a search party out looking for you. Glad to see you're still with us."

I remembered Duncan with his golf shirts and his tanned face. He looked formidable clad in hunting gear, but his easy grin and relaxed stance disarmed me. As the *thwack* of the helicopter drew closer, I lowered my gun.

"I thought you'd never find me," I said, letting relief finally fill me.

"Are you injured?"

I nodded. "I was shot, right of center mass. My vest caught the bullet, but I have some internal damage."

It made sense that Sheriff Daniel would send Duncan out with the search party—he'd lived and worked in the area for decades. He was also an avid hunter and knew the land. What didn't make sense was why Duncan would be searching for me alone.

He pressed the button down on his shoulder radio: "I've got Hansen. West at grid marker ninety-seven."

"I'm not sure how you managed to get all the way out here," Duncan said with a smile. "Hang in there. It won't be long now, Hansen."

The helicopter's searchlights canvassed the area, and its thick light beam moved closer to us.

I moved closer to Duncan to be heard over the chopper's blades that whisked away the smoke from the fire. "Did you find Donovan and the bunker?"

Duncan gave me a look of reproach. Or was it anger?

"Duncan? Where is your search partner?"

When he didn't immediately respond, I took a step back. I thought of the Holden brothers and the message Logan had tried to deliver to his mother before death: *Love you. I couldn't stop…*Logan and his mother knew exactly who the killer was. Logan didn't need to use Mike Duncan's name because he was certain his mother would recognize the situation and know exactly who killed her sons.

"Duncan." It felt as if my heart dropped into my stomach. "You're Deadeye's partner."

He leveled his rifle at me. "We always said there would be no restrictions for the person who killed one of us. The rules no longer apply."

The wind from the helicopter lifted up the foliage around us, whipping it in circles.

"No rules will be the only way you can hit your target, Duncan. I've never seen a more terrible shot."

My clothing flapped against my body, and Duncan lost his footing. He fell off course for only a second, but it gave me the time I needed to run for cover.

The crack of a shot felt like a ball of fire tearing through my right thigh, and I dropped. I'd been hit from the back, and I guessed the bullet broke the only thing in its way: my femur. I forced myself to roll in order to get an angle on Duncan.

A voice boomed from above: "Police! Drop your weapons."

Duncan paused to consider that his actions would be seen before he rushed me. Duncan fired again, this time hitting the trunk of a tree only a few feet from me, as the bullet sprayed bark to the ground. I fired, but my hands shook with a pulsing adrenaline and the bullet missed him.

"Why?" I screamed. "Who was Deadeye to you?"

"Family." He raised his weapon to me. "He's always been my family."

A voice boomed from the helicopter. "Drop all weapons *now!*" It lowered in the sky and hovered not far from us as if searching for a place to touch down. There was only the heavy *thwack, thwack, thwack* of the helicopter's blades and my own shallow breath.

I saw the twitch of Duncan's trigger finger. I shot him, two bullets to the dead center of his chest as I'd been trained to do in an emergency. Even if Duncan had a safety vest on, the impact of the bullets so close to one another would be enough to keep him down for a while. Then I saw the blood blooming around his fallen body.

Thwack, thwack, thwack.

I rose to my knees but the pressure gave way. Violent shivers set in, and I couldn't stop the thought loop in my mind: *Duncan. I killed Duncan.*

I heard a voice. And then another. The task force had finally found me.

Daniel's voice stood out from them all: "Sheriff of Simmons County on scene."

Chapter Twenty-five

Thursday, 5:00 p.m.

My eyes opened, and I was quickly assaulted with the bright overhead fluorescent lighting of a hospital room. When I tried to move, I felt a warm, familiar hand take mine.

"Surgery is over," Bennett said. "You did great."

When I looked down, I found that I'd been wrapped in a soft cast from the knee all the way to my hip. I couldn't feel my left leg. The nerve blocker was holding strong.

"Much damage?" My voice croaked.

When Bennett heard my hoarse voice, she poured some ice water into a cup for me. "All good. You have a metal plate and two screws holding that femur together." She helped me hold the cup to my lips. "The surgeon says that with some physical therapy, you'll be stronger than ever."

Bennett's words were a relief, but she hadn't mentioned my shoulder.

"The vest saved your life, but you have two broken ribs. The good news is there's no permanent damage to your shoulder or arm," Bennett said. "Your body just needs some time and space to heal, Hansen."

I closed my eyes and let the cool water run down my parched throat. So much had happened in the last forty-eight hours. Snippets of memory flashed through my mind: the deer stand with Donovan, the campfire, the shootings—hers and then mine.

"Donovan?" I asked. I already knew the answer, but a glimmer of hope welled up inside me.

Bennett shook her head and looked down at her hands. "I'm sorry, Luce."

There was no way Donovan could have survived the gunshot wounds, but the news still took my breath away. In my mind, I saw flashes of what had happened—Donovan's limp body pushed into the opening of the bunker followed by a figure who slammed the lid closed. From the distance and the safety of my hospital bed, I recognized that figure. Their shape had been familiar all along.

I groaned. "The third person was Joyce Holden."

Bennett nodded. "Duncan, Johnson, and John Holden met while serving. Joyce and John were already married, and she bonded with Duncan and Johnson. The bond was so tight, they formed a pact to stay near one another and back one another up, no matter what. The game didn't start until after Johnson returned from his second tour in Afghanistan. Duncan couldn't resist the action, but Joyce says she was only in it to try and help them both."

"John Holden?" I asked. "Where is he in all of this?"

"He swears he didn't know anything about their pact or the game, but I find that very hard to believe."

"Family," I croaked.

"What do you mean?" Bennett asked.

"Duncan told me Deadeye was his family right before I shot him. He must have included Joyce and her husband in that family as well."

"Interesting bedfellows, huh?" Bennett said, digesting the information. "Joyce was apparently in full support of these men until they killed her two boys."

"Did Duncan and Deadeye know the boys?" I asked.

"We have no proof, but it seems likely." Bennett tucked a dark curl behind her ear. "The three had some kind of argument over the timing of Deadeye's break from prison."

Thanksgiving. Joyce Holden had mentioned how much she loved the holiday and hosting many family members. As if losing two of her children wasn't enough, they chose to kill the boys on Thanksgiving.

So much of the last two days' worth of chaos could have been avoided if Joyce Holden had just come forward. If only she'd given us Duncan's name, Donovan would still be alive. We were left with the one question that never seemed to have an answer: Why?

"I read the report, and Joyce has already been questioned extensively," Bennett said. "The only comment she gave is *Family takes care of their own.*"

I wanted to say something about the audacity of attributing the word *family* to the three people who destroyed so many lives, but my ribcage exploded with pain.

"Take it easy," Bennett said. She leaned in to kiss my forehead, and her lips felt cool against my warm skin. "You were out there for almost two days. You're lucky to be alive, Hansen. *I'm* lucky you're still alive."

Then I remembered what Sheriff Daniel said once he'd found me. He leaned over my bleeding body and hollered over the sound of the helicopter while he tied off my leg near the groin. I filtered in and out of consciousness, but I distinctly heard him say Bennett had been the one to track me.

"You found me, Bennett," I said. "You saved me."

Bennett smiled. "I wasn't sure if anyone told you. It was difficult—those aerial maps were a pain to work with, but we did it. You led us to the Holdens' property with the broken tracker, and the aerial maps revealed the possible remnants of dwellings within a ten-mile radius. Some of the sites that showed up on the maps were nothing more than a fallen tree and the bushes that grew around it. It took some time weeding through that area to find the place you'd taken refuge."

"It felt like I walked forever. How far was I from the Holdens' property?"

"That's what threw us off, Hansen. We knew there was a high probability you had been shot because of all the bullets found at the scene. We never expected you to make it almost eight miles, even if a shot didn't penetrate your vest."

"I felt like I was walking in circles," I admitted. "I couldn't find my bearings. I hoped I'd meet someone who'd help or eventually wind up on a road. Instead, I found myself deeper and deeper into isolation."

"It was a smart move, Hansen. At least the cabin kept you safe. If you hadn't, things could be very different for you right now." A visible shiver ran through her body.

"Thank you," I said, squeezing Bennett's hand.

"The fire helped us pinpoint your exact location much faster, but it was a big risk, you know."

I silently agreed with her. The fire had brought Duncan right to me, and if he had better aim, I wouldn't have survived.

"Ready for the bad news?" Bennett asked.

I groaned. "There's more?"

"Debbie Turner's baby. I'll give you one guess who the father really is."

"The warden." I tried to laugh, but it hurt.

"Close, but no. Dr. Mike Duncan, head coroner and so much more. Some members of the team are grateful Deadeye wasn't reproducing. Personally, I don't think this is any better."

I smiled at Bennett. "You've always had a feeling about Duncan, but I thought it was some kind of professional jealousy. It sounds like I need to listen to your spidey sense a little more."

"Please." Bennett rolled her eyes. "You know I don't give much credence to such things."

Debbie had wanted David Johnson's baby. In some twisted way, her wish was granted. By their own account, Duncan and Johnson were family. The baby would be born in jail. It seemed a tragic fate for a baby whose mother wanted it so badly. Debbie's crimes would cost her the privilege to care for her own child.

Dr. Mike Duncan had been Deadeye's partner in the murders and in so much more. David Johnson might have been the sharpshooter of the two, the one who played their game too well, but Duncan had been the mastermind behind it all. He held the answers and played us all while we listened to his findings and expertise. He fooled us all in his golf shirts and with his complaints of career exhaustion. All of us, that was, except Bennett.

"How is Sanders?"

"He's been worried sick about you," she said. "The infection is clearing, thank God. They're releasing him from the hospital tomorrow."

Sanders's health and Harper Bennett—these were the bright spots for me with the fallout of the case.

A nurse returned with more pain meds, and I closed my eyes as the medicine filtered in through my IV. When I opened them, Bennett had settled back into her seat. An open book lay folded over the arm of the chair.

My thoughts turned to Rachel Donovan once again. Her body would be in the morgue, most likely next to Duncan's. "Do you need to get back to work?" I asked. I didn't have the strength to voice either of their names.

Bennett shook her head. "I'm staying with you, if that's okay. We've called in another forensic pathologist."

I had mixed feelings about that news. Part of me wanted the person who examined Donovan to be someone I knew and trusted. Another part of me was relieved Bennett didn't have to take that role on; it would save her from testifying in court.

"Go to sleep, Hansen. I'll be here when you wake up."

I'd always hated allowing myself to fall into the vulnerability of sleep, but sometimes the body simply won out. This time, though, I fell into the arms of sleep with the comforting knowledge that someone was there to watch over me. Harper Bennett would keep me safe.

I woke to find Sanders sitting at the bedside table. An open newspaper rested in his lap, and he'd filled the table with goodies from the vending machine down the hall.

"There you are!" He tossed the paper onto the table. "Don't worry, I checked with the nurse. You don't have any food restrictions." He tempted me with too salty Pringles and pretzels and Snickers bars.

"What would I do without you, Sanders?" I joked, reaching for the chilled bottle of Mountain Dew he'd cracked open for me.

"It would be difficult, but I think you'd survive, Hansen. You're quite the fighter."

Sanders decided to humor me and eat some of the collection of junk food. He chipped off the corner of a Dorito and popped it into his mouth.

"What do you think they use to make this cheese dust?" he asked.

I laughed, delighted that Sanders and I were having our own version of a bed picnic, something I used to share with my ex, Rowan. "Not sure, but I love it."

Sanders picked up another Dorito. "Doesn't it make you wonder? I mean, it stains your fingertips. That can't be good."

I shrugged. "Blueberries stain your hands, too, and nobody accuses them of ingredients that can harm you."

Sanders laughed. "As usual, you have a point there, Hansen."

A frantic spate of announcements came over the speakers, codes for a certain room, some sort of medical emergency.

"Ah, I'm glad to be rid of those calls," Sanders said. "It's funny—doctors tell you to get some rest in the hospital, but it's probably the least restful place I can think of."

Darkness had fallen outside, and I'd completely lost track of time. Bennett must have gone back to the hotel for some rest.

"How are you feeling, anyway?" I asked.

"I'm ready to go back to work," Sanders said. "All this time off leads me to too much thinking."

"Thinking about what?"

A rolling medical cart zoomed past the open door and soon a nurse peeked in. "All okay, Ms. Hansen?" She hardly waited for his thumbs-up before she pulled the door mostly closed behind her.

Sanders sat back in the chair and crossed one leg over the other. "Did I ever tell you about why I went into law enforcement?"

The question took me by surprise. Sanders rarely spoke of his life outside work, let alone his younger years. I reached for more Pringles. "You've told me stories of your dad. About the abuse. I guess I always figured you wanted to become an agent because of him—that you wanted to get all the fathers off the street who treated their children the way you were treated."

A quiet settled between us for a few moments, such a quiet that I thought Sanders might have dozed off on me. Then he cleared his throat.

"I was a rough kid, Hansen. The kind we like to get while they're young, while they still have a chance to make a turn for the better. Know what I'm saying?"

I did. We didn't work with kids too often, but when we did, those cases made a big impact on us all. We worked hard to get children to the correct resources, to people who could help them turn their lives around.

"A few cruisers rolled up to my house one night. I was eleven. My father was so drunk, he'd passed out in the hallway of our small apartment after he'd punched his girlfriend purple and bloody."

"That's tough," I said. "I'm sorry."

Sanders waved off my apology. "One of the young officers took me out to his cruiser to keep me away from all the fighting. He sat me in the passenger seat and shut me inside. He told me he'd only be a minute, to sit tight and touch nothing. He went back in the house to find out where I needed to go."

Sanders smiled thinking about it. "Boy, I loved that car! The radio squawked with all these codes and voices. There were lights everywhere, and I can still smell the smoke from the officer's cigarettes that had been absorbed into the upholstery of that cruiser. But there was something else, Hansen. I loved the inside of that car because it was just like a hideout—I felt so safe in that cool cavern of the car, the call of the officers' voices over the radio, the flash of the lights that swam red and blue across my yard. It was the safest I'd felt in my whole life—I wanted to just stay there, to never go back to my father, his fists, or his screams."

"What happened?" I asked. "Did they take you to your grand-mother's? Arrest your dad?"

Sanders nodded. "Not before I found exactly what I wasn't supposed to."

"Oh Lord."

Sanders giggled, again so childlike. "I was looking for the officer's cigarettes."

I rolled my eyes. Already at eleven he was insufferable with his smokes.

"I looked in all the usual places—the console, the glove box, under the driver's seat. And that's where I found it. I felt the cool metal of a handgun under the passenger seat."

God, what a nightmare scenario for a cop. "Was it the officer's personal piece?"

"Yeah. In those days, they could carry whatever, you know? His issued weapon was on his belt, but I had his personal. I wrapped my hand around that gun. So heavy! I wasn't expecting it, you know? And then I held that piece up to the light, let the red and blue swish of the lights color the weapon. That's when I knew."

"Knew what? That you wanted to be a cop?"

Sanders shook his head. "I knew I'd found my home. That safe place I'd been dying to find. Home, you know?"

I nodded. I did know. I'd had those feelings of recognition, epiphanies full of belonging and love that generally happened at the most unexpected moments.

"When that officer opened his door and found me with his gun… boy howdy! But I'll tell you one thing, Hansen. I've been trying my whole life to get back to that minute, that…feeling. I finally felt it. Home."

I reached over and took his hand. It felt leathery inside mine, the skin cracked and dry. I wondered if he was thinking about his upcoming round of chemotherapy and all the unknowns it brought with it. "We're going to be okay, Sanders. I'll be beside you every step of the way." When he said nothing, I added, "Besides, you're family. There's nothing I wouldn't do for family."

Tears welled at the corners of his eyes and threatened to spill over. Would Sanders ever let another person see him cry? I doubted it, but I knew Colby Sanders had been moved.

He squeezed my hand. "You've always felt like home to me, too, Hansen."

CHAPTER TWENTY-SIX

Ohio State University Physical Therapy Center
December 14

Will, my physical therapist, pushed me hard for two hours, and my muscles ached as I made my way down the long hall toward the waiting area. At first, I'd been embarrassed to be reliant on a walker, even if it had only been ten days since my surgery. I couldn't deny it, though; the sturdiness of the walker beneath me brought such relief. Because the orthopedic surgeon had basically welded my femur back together with all kinds of interesting hardware, the walker allowed me to put varying degrees of my weight on the leg. Thankfully Mike Duncan was a piss-poor shot. My injuries could have been worse—much worse.

Will didn't allow anyone back in the therapy areas while we worked, and I was thankful for that. I wanted to gain back my strength without an audience. Bennett always waited for me in the waiting area in front of the television with an open book perched in her lap. On most days, I found her reading something by her favorite author, Virginia Woolf. Today, though, things were different. As I rounded the corner, I saw that Bennett was not alone. No book rested in her lap.

"Dr. Eli!"

Eli Weaver stood to greet me. At well over six and half feet tall, he had a long way to look down at me.

"Good to see you, Luce." Eli's large hand squeezed my shoulder, and his gentle voice relaxed me. I'd never met anyone who triggered such an instant soothing response in me. "It's been much too long."

Like me, Eli was a survivor of an ex-gay ministry—it was one of the shared experiences that brought us together. Once the Willow's Ridge case closed, Dr. Eli and his partner had reached out to me numerous times to attend their support group north of Columbus, but I'd never gone. It didn't feel right to me—I'd only taken part in an ex-gay ministry for a short time, and there had been so many other people who had been hurt worse than me by people like Pastor Jamison. When I offered up these thoughts to Bennett, she didn't buy them.

"No one ever thinks her experiences are worthy of support," she'd told me. "Our perceptions of ourselves can become so skewed. Sometimes you have to trust someone else's opinion, Hansen."

When I saw Bennett and Dr. Eli together, it wasn't hard to figure out what the two of them were up to. Even though the meeting felt contrived, I couldn't be angry with either of them, especially Bennett. Since the shooting, I decided to take on Sanders's view of Bennett's controlling behavior. I could see that she was trying to be helpful and to care for me in the way she knew best.

"I've thought a lot about you," Eli said. "When I heard about the Deadeye case and your injury, I felt in my heart I needed to see you. May I interest you in a cup of coffee? There's a small hospital café on the next floor."

I couldn't say no to Eli's invitation—he was always so polite. It had been much too long since our last visit.

Bennett gave me a smile. "I'll let the two of you reconnect. I need to run a few errands, anyway." She leaned in for a quick kiss. "I'll be back to get you later."

Eli Weaver took the seat across the table from me. The small coffee shop on the medical campus was a welcome relief—therapy days were incredibly helpful but also exhausting. The smell of fresh coffee along with the whir of the machines brought me back to what life was like before the shooting, before the hours of therapy and leg braces, and all the talk of healing.

Eli crossed one matchstick-thin leg over the other and settled his gaze on me.

"You've been through quite an ordeal. We need to stop meeting up around serial killer cases, don't you think?"

My laugh was short-lived when the movement of my core muscles pulled against my ribs. They were healing, but laughter still hurt.

Eli filled me in on what he'd been doing since we last met and how steadily his group was gaining membership. "We're filling a real need in the queer community," Eli said. "So many of our members feel like the world has let them down. Worse, some feel their own people have betrayed them. I'm working hard to bring hope back into their lives."

I took a sip of steaming coffee and decided to ask—I couldn't avoid the topic any longer. "Bennett told you, didn't she? About the relapse?"

Eli looked surprised at my words, but only for a second. He shook his head. "Colby Sanders called me. He's worried about you. From what I gather, Harper is, too. She's the one who told me where I could find you."

Sanders! I never saw that coming.

"You can't run from it, Luce. Colby and Harper care about you. I do, too."

It felt strange to hear all of our first names, something we so rarely used.

"Thanks, but I'm doing okay."

I reached up instinctively for Marci's cross. Then I remembered— Bennett had taken it off my neck and put it on her own when they prepared me for surgery. I'd never gotten Marci's Celtic cross back from Bennett, and it was the longest I'd gone without wearing it.

Eli braided his fingers together and rested his hands in his lap. "They're never far from us, are they? The ghosts of our past."

I nodded and looked over to a table beside us full of older men and remembered my father. I thought about how much he would have liked Eli Weaver, this gentle soul who wanted to help everyone around him find peace within themselves and their world. I missed my dad. I missed Marci. And sometimes these holes in my heart caused me to miss what was right in front of me, the family I'd begun to form—Bennett, Sanders, Eli. There was even a place in this makeshift family for my ex, Rowan. They'd all become vital elements of my life, and I couldn't see myself surviving without them. Maybe, I reasoned, this would be my year to do the nesting thing, to build a home and a family, no matter how nontraditional it might be.

"I want to show you something," I said.

Detective Rachel Donovan was never far from my mind. I slipped my hand into my pocket and set Donovan's cross on the table between Eli and me. "I'm not sure if Bennett told you, but I was shot and alone in a cabin for some time before the team found me. This helped me get through it," I said.

Eli reached for the Celtic cross and held it up to the light. "It's beautiful." He turned it over in his hands. "It's a sobriety cross," he said, noticing the engraved date.

"Not mine, obviously." I took a drink of my coffee. "It was Detective Donovan's. I wore her coat during the night hunt because I'd been too stubborn to listen to her advice earlier that day. After we were attacked and I found the cabin…well, let's just say I felt a nudge to check the lining of her coat. I found the cross with a packet of matches and a bandana. Donovan's survival kit." I grinned at her choice of objects.

"A kit that helped to see you through the nightmare," Eli added. He set the cross down. "I'm glad this brought you hope and comfort. What will you do with it now?"

I shrugged. "It doesn't really feel like something I should keep. I didn't earn it, after all. But I'm so glad I had it in the cabin and through my recovery so far. It's felt like Donovan was with me somehow, like a part of her stayed behind to see me through it all."

"We certainly have helpers, Luce, people who have passed on and then lend us a guiding hand when we need it. I believe she was there with you, and I have no doubt your father was, too." He reached across for my hand and gave it a squeeze. Then he reached into his pocket. "You'll find the right place for Donovan's cross. In the meantime, I brought you something else to add to your party of protection."

He reached out and dropped a silver coin into my hand. About the size of a half-dollar, it held the image of a woman with wings holding a lantern. The words *Guardian Angel* ran along the upper edge.

"I figured if anyone needed a little extra protection in this world, it's you. There's a prayer on the back."

I thanked him and flipped the coin over. An angel prayer was engraved there.

"Just a little something for your well-being," Eli said. "You do so much to keep our world safe—something needs to be keeping *you* safe in return."

"I love it, thank you." Fisting the coin, I chuckled. "For a minute there I was worried you'd brought me a newcomer's sobriety token."

Eli shrugged. "No one can make that decision for you, Luce, and nothing can earn you a newcomer's token but attendance at a twelve-step meeting."

I rubbed the etchings of the coin, and I liked the way the wings of the angel felt against my fingertips.

Eli watched me closely. "This doesn't have to be all about sobriety, Luce. We could simply say this coin marks a fresh beginning for you, if you like."

I thought about it a moment before I said, "I like the sound of that."

Eli held up his mug of coffee and waited for me to cheer his. "To a new beginning."

"Absolutely," I said. "It's funny you brought something for safety. This case has made me really think about that—not just my own, but the safety of those I love."

My own feelings of an unsafe world helped me better understand the folks I'd met in Simmons County who were actively preparing for the end of days. They longed to go back to a simpler time, and their entire philosophy centered on holding those we love close in order to keep them safe. Many people shared those same concerns but expressed them in different ways.

"We're living in difficult times, Luce, that is for sure." The café lights reflected off the lenses of his glasses so I couldn't see his eyes. "The truth is we aren't safe anyplace or at any time. In some ways, I understand what the preppers are doing, but it's a futile exercise. They are preparing for something no one can really prepare for."

"No one wants to acknowledge that safety, at least in our modern world, is nothing more than an illusion," I said. "So what's the answer? We do nothing and hope everything will be all right?"

Eli shook his head. "We do our very best and we trust, Luce. We must trust that our efforts matter, that our lives are worth something much bigger than we can ever imagine."

We sipped the remainder of our coffee and considered together some of the ways life could be bigger than anything we could imagine. When it was time to go, I slipped the guardian angel coin into my pocket where it rested safely against Donovan's Celtic cross for the rest of the day.

CHAPTER TWENTY-SEVEN

Kirtland, Ohio
December 20

I pressed the doorbell, and I peeked in through the bay window of the large suburban home. A circular staircase wound its way down to a landing of polished wood flooring where the lights dimmed for the evening. A child's face popped into the lower corner of the window. A blond girl screamed, "Mom! Door!"

She looked at me through the window, sizing me up. I'd moved on from the walker to a cane that looked a lot like a giant stick. I gave her a smile along with a small wave with my free hand.

The heavy wooden door opened. "Can I help you?" The edges of the woman's button-down shirt were untucked against her dark slacks, and a pair of reading glasses sat on top of her head. The woman's smile was friendly, but she couldn't hide the surprise in her voice.

"Hi, Christy?" I started. I held my ID open for her, a difficult task to accomplish while leaning on a cane. "I'm Luce Hansen, from the Bureau of Criminal Investigation. I was hoping I could speak to you for a moment alone." I eyed the little girl who was still staring at my badge.

"Wow, is that real?" she asked. "Can I hold it?"

I laughed. "Sure." I handed her my badge. The weight of it bobbed in her hand.

"Someday I want to have one of these. Rachel has one kind of like this, doesn't she, Momma?"

"Yes," I told the girl, happy to hear that she knew Rachel was a detective. "Rachel is one of the best detectives I've ever met."

Christy prompted the child to give the badge back. "Go finish your dinner, pumpkin. I'll only be a minute."

Once the child's blond head was out of sight, Christy turned back to me, careful to guard the door with her body. "What is this about?"

"I worked the case in Southeast Ohio with Rachel Donovan. I have something for you."

With the mention of Donovan's name, Christy's face fell. "My God," she said. "You were the one with Rachel. Come in."

While Christy cried, I tried to recount the last few hours of Rachel's life for her ex-partner. "Donovan was brave," I said. "She stood up to her supervisor once she found a connection between the cases. She didn't back down, and I admired her commitment—that tenacity saved lives. We couldn't have closed the case without her."

I handed Christy the sobriety cross, which brought on a fresh wave of tears. I watched Christy turn the Celtic cross over and over in her hands. "She was so proud of this."

I nodded. "Donovan wasn't sure if you or your daughter knew she was still sober. I wanted you both to have it. Donovan worked hard to get back on her feet, and she apparently carried the cross everywhere."

"I gave her this cross," Christy said, her voice barely above a whisper. "I gave it to her when I left with the baby. I told Rachel to consider that day a brand new slate in her life, the mark of a fresh beginning. It was the date I hoped we could start over."

"She certainly heard you," I said. "She made profound life changes from the date etched into that cross."

"How is your recovery going?" Christy asked me, eyeing the cane against the couch.

"I'm getting there, but it's been a long haul," I said. "I'm sorry I couldn't be here for Donovan's funeral."

The mention of the funeral brought tears to Christy's eyes. "It was a beautiful day," she said, holding tight to the sobriety cross. "She touched so many lives. I always knew that Rachel was brave, but I didn't understand just how brave she really was until she was gone."

I placed my hand over Christy's that held the sobriety cross, and a wave of tears fell from my eyes. "Save that sobriety cross to give to your daughter one day. And you'll tell her about Donovan's sobriety won't you? About how much Rachel loved her?"

Christy gave me a sad smile. "I tell my child every night, Luce. I always have. We've forgiven Rachel. It's always been Rachel who couldn't forgive herself."

Later that night, I lay wide-awake, clenching the guardian angel coin in my hand, and thought about shame. I'd spent my own fair amount of time with that wild animal that so easily infiltrated the mind, that peculiar beast that caused me to always look back over my shoulder. Wherever Rachel Donovan found herself in death, I hoped it was shame-free and that she found herself only moving forward.

EPILOGUE

January 11, 8:45 a.m.

The morning sun penetrated my hoodie with the promising start of a beautiful day. Cheers and excitement lined the race route where Sanders and I stood behind the blockade set up at mile marker fifteen for marathon observers. We'd spent the previous night making a colorful banner to cheer Bennett on, and we planned to meet her with our banner along the way until she completed the marathon.

While we waited, the banner began to sag in the middle between us.

"You doing okay?" Sanders asked.

The irony of his question wasn't lost on me; I should have been asking Sanders if *he* was okay, given that he'd just finished his most recent round of chemo seventy-two hours ago. I'd been worried about him making the trip with us, but Sanders had no hesitation when Bennett and I asked him to join us for a Disney vacation to watch Bennett run the marathon.

"The change of climate will do me good," Sanders insisted until we believed him.

In the tangled jungle of chemotherapy, Sanders had faced some issues with nausea and exhaustion, but ultimately fared quite well. He was on medical leave, as was I.

"I'm praying for the Gods of Serial Killers to keep them all hidden inside the darkest of caves until we return, Hansen," Sanders told me every day of our leave. So far, everything on the Ohio serial killer front had remained quiet. But Sanders and I knew it was only a matter of time before another case blipped onto our radar.

The crowd around us swelled as the front pack of runners came into view, and I reached up and hit the button on my Chewbacca mask to let out a roar that said *Yes, I'm fine.* When Sanders reminded me that the batteries in the damn mask didn't have a long life to them, I added one more roar for good measure. Everyone around us wore Disney gear and rainbows as Disney characters of all sorts filtering through the crowd. Before the trip, I'd looked for a Jabba the Hutt costume for Sanders. That was the only character he could conceive of dressing as, but I'd had no luck. Sanders stood beside me on the sidelines of the race as himself.

I'd graduated from physical therapy only about a week ago and no longer needed a cane for support. The bullet and the repair had changed my gait, and I struggled to learn the new movements of my body. I was adjusting, though, and I hoped to be running alongside Bennett soon. It was funny to think about how much I dreaded running with her before I'd been shot; now it was one of the activities I missed most. Running would never be my thing, that was for sure, but I longed for that time with Bennett and our playful competitions.

My leg wasn't the only part of me in recovery. I'd taken on the ninety meetings in ninety days challenge with Alcoholics Anonymous. I'd been encouraged to take on the challenge by Eli Weaver in order to prove to myself I could do it. It wasn't until I was several days into the program that I realized I wasn't really doing it all for me, but also for Detective Rachel Donovan. I knew she would have been there to support me if she could, and the memory of her sobriety story stuck with me every time I entered a church basement for a meeting. This was the first time I'd taken on a serious go at sobriety with people who would hold me accountable for my actions. Such a promise felt heavier when it landed on others' ears, and I took that pressure to succeed with me into the pool. When the crown of my head and fingertips broke through the water's surface every day, I felt like I'd come home. Encased underwater, I swam as far as possible before surfacing for a breath in order to strengthen my lungs as well as my legs and arms. Slowly, I was coming back to myself, and I vowed to be stronger than ever in a multitude of ways.

The lead runners came into view and cheers grew louder around us along the marathon route. A park employee dressed as Goofy shot out of the crowd and high-fived some of the runners as they passed. Sanders readied his phone to record Bennett's arrival, but she hadn't come into view yet. Despite all my protests, Bennett hadn't dressed as Princess Leia. Instead, she sported a sequined purple tutu over her black running gear and a shimmery crown she'd found at a dollar store. She also donned candy-cane red-and-white-striped knee socks and a rainbow T-shirt over her running gear.

I was grateful that Detective Alison Harvey had, for the time being, vanished into the background as Bennett and I worked through the fallout of the Simmons County case. Bennett finally understood that Harvey had used her as a doorway into the BCI. While Bennett promised she would no longer communicate with Harvey, I knew that would be difficult given our line of work. I'd been learning in my meetings that I had no control over another person's behavior. Instead of focusing so much on what I didn't want Bennett to do, I was trying to focus on the positives in our relationship.

The night before, we'd stayed in one of the park hotels, and I'd spent a few hours swimming among Disney characters and Technicolor pool lanes. Bennett was already sleeping when I slipped into bed beside her. I wrapped my arm around her, spooning against her, and she gave an exhalation that was barely audible.

"There you are," she whispered to me, snuggling into my arms and not bothering to open her eyes. "Breaking in the hotel pool? I can still smell the chlorine on you."

I laughed against her neck, my long wet hair streaming over the end of the pillow.

"This is nice," she said. "Maybe we should get married."

"Or we could try living together first," I offered.

She groaned again. "Of course," she mocked me, "let's be sensible."

"Or," I posed, "we could be the lesbian version of Paul and Jane."

"Who the heck are Paul and Jane?"

"Jane was my neighbor when I was a kid," I said. "For years, she and Paul were together but lived in separate houses. He was around her place a lot, but they didn't plan to move in with one another until retirement. It went on like that for years. I've always wondered if they ever ended up in a home together."

"You don't know how it turned out?" Bennett turned to face me a moment and then laughed. "I really hope the two of them ended up together."

I agreed. "I'm just saying we could be a version of those two, however odd it might be."

"Good story, Hansen." She chuckled and squeezed my hand in hers. "I have an idea, though."

"What's that?"

She wound her fingers through mine. "Let's not make any decisions tonight."

I agreed, and we rested together in the silence.

"Ben?" I nudged her after a few minutes. "You still with me?"

Bennett's breath had fallen into the deep and slow rhythm of sleep.

❖

The crowd cheered as the second wave of runners neared the finish line. Noisemakers and air horns blasted. Bennett finished the race dead center of the first pack of runners, and I angled through the crowd to get closer to the finish line.

"One of these days, I'm going to win a marathon," Bennett had told me a few weeks prior to this race. "I'm still trying to find my stride and my strength," she'd said.

Bennett and I had been talking a lot about how an athlete must find her own rhythm, and that each has her own quirky way of getting the job done and done well. She pointed out a number of runners who had taken something that most would consider a hindrance and used it to their advantage. In her own roundabout way, I took these conversations as Bennett's way of encouraging me to get back to my own running and swimming as soon as possible. It wasn't only about sports, though, but much bigger than that—Bennett was encouraging me to get back to *life*.

"So," I'd asked Bennett, "what is your advantage disguised as a hindrance?"

She groaned. "My hips. They're too wide. I'm still working on how they could be my advantage."

"Come on, now," I teased her. "I'm quite fond of those hips."

I saw the crown perched on top of Bennett's sweaty head first, then her hips as they rushed past the finish line. She placed in the top fifty out of hundreds of runners. Once we found each other, Bennett threw her sweaty arms around my neck and gulped for air between victory screams.

When the excitement calmed down, Sanders, Bennett, and I strolled through the park on our way to the shuttle bus for Bennett. She planned to go back to the hotel to shower and rest for a few hours before she met back up with us for some Disney fun.

Bennett slipped her arm around my waist and squeezed me closer to her. "Look at you! Walking this park without your cane. I'm so proud of you."

"Well," I said, "it's not a marathon by any means, but I'm moving forward."

"Definitely," she said. "Thanks for coming to the race. It made a big difference knowing the two of you were waiting on me at the finish line."

"Are you kidding?" Sanders playfully asked. "I didn't give it a second thought. January in sunny Florida is pure paradise compared to the miserable cold in Ohio."

Bennett and I laughed with him, knowing full well how much healing his body had gone through in order to make this trip. Both Sanders and I had been through a really rough time, but we'd finally caught a glimpse of the light at the other end of the tunnel.

I sat on the hotel balcony's love seat with Bennett wrapped in my arms. It was our last night in Florida, and we waited in the darkness for the evening fireworks. Our vacation had been short and fierce. My body ached with exhaustion, and I couldn't imagine what Bennett's must have felt like after running a marathon and then walking the parks for the last two days. She'd fallen asleep after dinner and had the drowsy look of someone forcing herself to stay awake for something big.

Bennett leaned in for a kiss and then scrunched her nose. "You taste like Doritos."

"Yum." I laughed, thinking of the bag of Doritos I'd finished only an hour before. "I love that I'll be tasting that salty cheese mix on my lips for hours."

Bennett groaned, and I could almost feel her dramatic eye roll. I had to give her props, though—she hadn't badgered me about clean eating since I began the case in Simmons County.

Things had changed between us, and for the better. Maybe it was Sanders's fight with cancer, or Donovan's tragic death, or the thought that my broken femur could have been so much worse. Whatever the reason, I was grateful for the change. The last few weeks had felt more like a partnership between Bennett and me; there was a sense of equality between us that hadn't been there before.

Below us, the park lights dimmed low as they prepared for the fireworks show.

"You've gotten so strong," Bennett said. "Not just with your leg, but inside, too. I'm proud of you for taking on the ninety in ninety. It can't be easy."

"No," I said and thought about how Bennett and Sanders had kept his diagnosis from me, how they worried whether or not I was strong enough to handle the bad news. In the end, I'd been strong enough to weather that storm, and it surprised no one more than myself.

"I wonder how John Holden is holding up with the holidays behind him," I said.

Bennett gave me a confused look. "I thought you didn't like him much."

"I don't, but I still worry about him. He lost three-quarters of his family in two weeks' time. And to find out his wife had been helping Deadeye…it must be devastating."

Bennett nodded. "I don't think he suspected anything, either. I always hope for that, you know? But it generally means that the partner in the dark will get their heart broken."

Holden couldn't have imagined what was coming down the road for his family this past Thanksgiving. Arguably his wife didn't, either. I wondered how a person ever came back from losing two children to murder and a wife to prison.

This case had taught me that we are dangerously exposed and at risk at all times. We have to come to terms with that; we have to seek some peace with that uncomfortable knowledge. As Bennett pointed out, we do have some control. We can fight back. I remembered the hopeful feeling I'd had in the cabin where the words from my training had come back to me—as long as there is breath in your body, there is something you can do to save yourself. Even if we don't know what is waiting for us around the corner, we can choose to defend ourselves and fight back.

The first fireworks sprayed blue and white across the night sky. Just as the embers burned down, two more exploded in greens and yellows. Bennett and I oohed and aahed while the display picked up and multiple colors exploded into the sky. A celebration—it was the perfect way to close out our vacation.

Bennett and I sat on the balcony together long after the fireworks died down and the park's lighting returned to normal.

"I have something to show you," Bennett said, pulling her phone out of her pocket. The cool evening breeze filtered under the blanket when she moved. She flipped through a few screens and then handed me the phone.

I stared at the screen for a moment. "I don't understand. What is this?"

Bennett gave me a smile. "A house. For sale, and not that far from mine in Spring Rock."

I expanded the image on the screen. It was a beautiful house tucked inside a wooded lot with a wraparound deck that overlooked the river. I hit the home screen and handed her back the phone.

"What are you saying, Ben?"

"I'm saying that maybe it would be best for us to start over somewhere new to both of us. We both love where we live—maybe this house will pull together the best of both of those places. We can build this into a home together." Bennett settled back against my chest, burrowing under my arm. "What do you think, Hansen?"

I took a close look around me. I could smell the smoke from the fireworks wafting up in the night sky. I could feel the warmth of Bennett's skin against mine. Everything felt new and fresh, just like a brand-new beginning.

About the Author

Meredith Doench is the author of the Luce Hansen Thriller series from Bold Strokes Books. *Crossed*, the first in the series, won Silver in the 2015 IndieFab Awards (Mystery). In 2017, *Crossed* was awarded the Mary Dasher Award for fiction, an honor for an Ohio writer from the College English Association of Ohio. The second novel in the series, *Forsaken Trust*, was published in 2017 and was a Goldie Finalist for the Thriller category in 2018.

Doench's works of short fiction and nonfiction have appeared in literary journals such as *Hayden's Ferry Review*, *Women's Studies Quarterly*, *Lumina*, and *Gertrude*. She was one of the founding associate prose editors of the literary journal *Camera Obscura: Journal of Literature and Photography*.

A native Ohioan, Doench holds a PhD from Texas Tech University in English/creative writing and currently resides in Dayton, Ohio. She teaches creative writing, literature, and composition at the University of Dayton.

Website: http://www.meredithdoench.com

Books Available from Bold Strokes Books

Beautiful Dreamer by Melissa Brayden. With love on the line, can Devyn Winters find it in her heart to stay in the small town of Dreamer's Bay, the one place she swore she'd never remain? (978-1-63555-305-5)

Create a Life to Love by Erin Zak. When sixteen-year-old Beth shows up at her birth mother's door, three lives will change forever. (978-1-63555-425-0)

Deadeye by Meredith Doench. Stranded while hunting the serial predator Deadeye, Special Agent Luce Hansen fights for survival while her lover, forensic pathologist Harper Bennett, hunts for clues to Hansen's disappearance along the killer's trail. (978-1-63555-253-9)

Death Takes a Bow by David S. Pederson. Alan Keys takes part in a local stage production, but when the leading man is murdered, his partner Detective Heath Barrington is thrust into the limelight to find the killer. (978-1-63555-472-4)

Endangered by Michelle Larkin. Shapeshifters Officer Aspen Wolfe and Dr. Tora Madigan fight their growing attraction as they work together to destroy a secret government agency that exterminates their kind. (978-1-63555-377-2)

Incognito by VK Powell. The only thing Evan Spears is focused on is capturing a fleeing murder suspect until wild card Frankie Strong is added to her team and causes chaos on and off the job. (978-1-63555-389-5)

Insult to Injury by Gun Brooke. After losing everything, Gail Owen withdraws to her old farmhouse and finds a destitute young woman, Romi Shepherd, living in a secret room. (978-1-63555-323-9)

Just One Moment by Dena Blake. If you were given the chance to have the love of your life back, could you ignore everything that went wrong and start over again? (978-1-63555-387-1)

Scene of the Crime by MJ Williamz. Cullen Mathew finds herself caught between the woman she thinks she loves but can no longer trust and a beautiful detective she can't stop thinking about who will stop at nothing to find the truth. (978-1-63555-405-2)

Accidental Prophet by Bud Gundy. Days after his grandmother dies, Drew Morten learns his true identity and finds himself racing against time to save civilization from the apocalypse. (978-1-63555-452-6)

Daughter of No One by Sam Ledel. When their worlds are threatened, a princess and a village outcast must overcome their differences and embrace a budding attraction if they want to survive. (978-1-63555-427-4)

Fear of Falling by Georgia Beers. Singer Sophie James is ready to shake up her career, but her new manager, the gorgeous Dana Landon, has other ideas. (978-1-63555-443-4)

In Case You Forgot by Fredrick Smith and Chaz Lamar. Zaire and Kenny, two newly single, Black, queer, and socially aware men, start again—in love, career, and life—in the West Hollywood neighborhood of LA. (978-1-63555-493-9)

Playing with Fire by Lesley Davis. When Takira Lathan and Dante Groves meet at Takira's restaurant, love may find its way onto the menu. (978-1-63555-433-5)

Practice Makes Perfect by Carsen Taite. Meet law school friends Campbell, Abby, and Grace, law partners at Austin's premier boutique legal firm for young, hip entrepreneurs. Legal Affairs: one law firm, three best friends, three chances to fall in love. (978-1-63555-357-4)

The Last Seduction by Ronica Black. When you allow true love to elude you once and you desperately regret it, are you brave enough to grab it when it comes around again? (978-1-63555-211-9)

Wavering Convictions by Erin Dutton. After a traumatic event, Maggie has vowed to regain her strength and independence. So how can Ally be both the woman who makes her feel safe and a constant reminder of the person who took her security away? (978-1-63555-403-8)

A Bird of Sorrow by Shea Godfrey. As Darrius and her lover, Princess Jessa, gather their strength for the coming war, a mysterious spell will reveal the truth of an ancient love. (978-1-63555-009-2)

All the Worlds Between Us by Morgan Lee Miller. High school senior Quinn Hughes discovers that a broken friendship is actually a door propped open for an unexpected romance. (978-1-63555-457-1)

An Intimate Deception by CJ Birch. Flynn County Sheriff Elle Ashley has spent her adult life atoning for her wild youth, but when she finds her ex, Jessie, murdered two weeks before the small town's biggest social event, she comes face-to-face with her past and all her well-kept secrets. (978-1-63555-417-5)

Cash and the Sorority Girl by Ashley Bartlett. Cash Braddock doesn't want to deal with morality, drugs, or people. Unfortunately, she's going to have to. (978-1-63555-310-9)

Counting for Thunder by Phillip Irwin Cooper. A struggling actor returns to the Deep South to manage a family crisis, finds love, and ultimately his own voice as his mother is regaining hers for possibly the last time. (978-1-63555-450-2)

Falling by Kris Bryant. Falling in love isn't part of the plan, but will Shaylie Beck put her heart first and stick around, or tell the damaging truth? (978-1-63555-373-4)

Secrets in a Small Town by Nicole Stiling. Deputy Chief Mackenzie Blake has one mission: find the person harassing Savannah Castillo and her daughter before they cause real harm. (978-1-63555-436-6)

Stormy Seas by Ali Vali. The high-octane follow-up to the best-selling action-romance, *Blue Skies*. (978-1-63555-299-7)

The Road to Madison by Elle Spencer. Can two women who fell in love as girls overcome the hurt caused by the father who tore them apart? (978-1-63555-421-2)

Dangerous Curves by Larkin Rose. When love waits at the finish line, dangerous curves are a risk worth taking. (978-1-63555-353-6)

Love to the Rescue by Radclyffe. Can two people who share a past really be strangers? (978-1-62639-973-0)

Love's Portrait by Anna Larner. When museum curator Molly Goode and benefactor Georgina Wright uncover a portrait's secret, public and private truths are exposed, and their deepening love hangs in the balance. (978-1-63555-057-3)

Model Behavior by MJ Williamz. Can one woman's instability shatter a new couple's dreams of happiness? (978-1-63555-379-6)

Pretending in Paradise by M. Ullrich. When travelwisdom.com assigns PR specialist Caroline Beckett and travel blogger Emma Morgan to cover a hot new couples retreat, they're forced to fake a relationship to secure a reservation. (978-1-63555-399-4)

Recipe for Love by Aurora Rey. Hannah Little doesn't have much use for fancy chefs or fancy restaurants, but when New York City chef Drew Davis comes to town, their attraction just might be a recipe for love. (978-1-63555-367-3)

Survivor's Guilt and Other Stories by Greg Herren. Award-winning author Greg Herren's short stories are finally pulled together into a single collection, including the Macavity Award nominated title story and the first-ever Chanse MacLeod short story. (978-1-63555-413-7)

The House by Eden Darry. After a vicious assault, Sadie, Fin, and their family retreat to a house they think is the perfect place to start over, until they realize not all is as it seems. (978-1-63555-395-6)

Uninvited by Jane C. Esther. When Aerin McLeary's body becomes host for an alien intent on invading Earth, she must work with researcher Olivia Ando to uncover the truth and save humankind. (978-1-63555-282-9)

Comrade Cowgirl by Yolanda Wallace. When cattle rancher Laramie Bowman accepts a lucrative job offer far from home, will her heart end up getting lost in translation? (978-1-63555-375-8)

Double Vision by Ellie Hart. When her cell phone rings, Giselle Cutler answers it—and finds herself speaking to a dead woman. (978-1-63555-385-7)

Inheritors of Chaos by Barbara Ann Wright. As factions splinter and reunite, will anyone survive the final showdown between gods and mortals on an alien world? (978-1-63555-294-2)

Love on Lavender Lane by Karis Walsh. Accompanied by the buzz of honeybees and the scent of lavender, Paige and Kassidy must find a way to compromise on their approach to business if they want to save Lavender Lane Farm—and find a way to make room for love along the way. (978-1-63555-286-7)

Spinning Tales by Brey Willows. When the fairy tale begins to unravel and villains are on the loose, will Maggie and Kody be able to spin a new tale? (978-1-63555-314-7)

The Do-Over by Georgia Beers. Bella Hunt has made a good life for herself and put the past behind her. But when the bane of her high school existence shows up for Bella's class on conflict resolution, the last thing they expect is to fall in love. (978-1-63555-393-2)

What Happens When by Samantha Boyette. For Molly Kennan, senior year is already an epic disaster, and falling for mysterious waitress Zia is about to make life a whole lot worse. (978-1-63555-408-3)

Wooing the Farmer by Jenny Frame. When fiercely independent modern socialite Penelope Huntingdon-Stewart and traditional country farmer Sam McQuade meet, trusting their hearts is harder than it looks. (978-1-63555-381-9)